THE
LAST EXIT

THE
LAST EXIT

LeROY FUEHRER

TATE PUBLISHING
AND ENTERPRISES, LLC

Published by Tate Publishing & Enterprises, LLC
127 E. Trade Center Terrace | Mustang, Oklahoma 73064 USA
1.888.361.9473 | www.tatepublishing.com

Tate Publishing is committed to excellence in the publishing industry. The company reflects the philosophy established by the founders, based on Psalm 68:11,
"The Lord gave the word and great was the company of those who published it."

Book design copyright © 2015 by Tate Publishing, LLC. All rights reserved.
Cover design by Rtor Maghuyop
Interior design by Jake Muelle

Published in the United States of America
ISBN: 978-1-68028-044-9
1. Fiction / Thrillers / Crime
2. Fiction / Mystery & Detective / General
15.06.18

THE LAST EXIT

Dedicated to:

This story is now in print because of the support of many friends and family. Many thanks go to my sister Delores and her family in WA State-My sister Jane and her husband Ken in Bloomington, Minn.-My son Kevin and his lady, Rachel, in South Dakota-My son Timothy in Calif.-To Lady Di and her family in AZ and SD.-To Don and Katie for all the help in the social media area as well

I also want to give many thanks to my friends at Tate Publishing for all the help they have given me.

To the law enforcement officers across this great country I give total thanks for a job well done.

Above all I need to dedicate this story to Mrs. L. Kindelspire-A beloved English Teacher at Leola HS.

She kept it interesting, made sure you understood it and that you did it right- Rest in Peace Mrs. K.

Chapter 1

The storm was blasting the windshield of the Chevy Suburban with unrelenting fury as the vehicle slowly crept along the crude motor trail near the base of the Bradshaw Mountains. The blowing dust absorbed most of the power from the headlights, and as a result, Vicki found that her visibility was almost down to zero in many places. The resulting dim view of the road caused the front tires to come dangerously close to the edge of the road, and there was a steep slope waiting to claim the unfortunate driver and the vehicle if a wrong move was made. The driver leaned forward until her breasts flattened against the spokes of the steering wheel, but even that extension of her vision didn't help her see the road when another heavy blanket of sand and dust blasted the area she was trying to drive through. Her hands were trembling as she continued to slow down until the wheels were barely turning; and, although unwanted, she began reliving the set of circumstances that had forced her out onto this lonesome road at two o'clock in the morning.

It was after midnight and Vicki had been driving west on her way home from work where she was a hostess, as well as assistant manager, at one of the better restaurants in the downtown Phoenix area. The pretty five-foot-two brunette was well liked and usually had to turn down several offers by the time the end of her shift came about, but this was one of those times she wished she'd taken up one of the offers she'd received.

She lived by herself in an isolated section near South Mountain Park. It was a quiet but growing neighborhood that hadn't yet been conquered by the urban sprawl, which, in her opinion, was decimating the beauty of the desert. She wasn't far from home when the small VW bug had almost crashed into her vehicle. She'd been alert enough to slam on the brakes as the wildly speeding car approached the intersection from her right. As soon as she saw the vehicle approaching the intersection, there was no doubt in her mind that the driver had no intention of stopping for the red light.

As it turned out, the driver in the little yellow bug was in such a hurry he didn't even try to use his brakes as he attempted to take the corner at full speed. The man's pale face appeared in her headlights as he shot by, and she thought the face appeared extremely frightened as he was looking over his shoulder instead of watching the road and working just a little harder to make the corner safely. Her eyes grew wide as she saw the man starting to work the steering wheel much too late. She heard the tires starting to squeal as they fought for traction, but the speed was too great for the amount of rubber touching the road, and the car quickly started to drift sideways. Vicki's mouth hung open in total surprise and apprehension as the scenario seemed to unfold in front of her in slow motion.

The out-of-control vehicle slid sideways until it came in contact with the curb on the far side of the road, and then the wheels on the right side simply folded under and the driver's side of the car started to lift off the ground. Vicki brought her hand up to her mouth as she watched the vehicle beginning to make its roll in the air. She sat unmoving, but her heart was hammering as the bug completed a full roll in the air and then began throwing dirt and auto parts into the air as it continued rolling on the ground.

She watched the little yellow bug as it slowly completed its last quarter roll and ended up on its top. The sudden silence now brought Vicki out of her trance, and she quickly reached for her door handle. Her door was almost open when she saw movement coming from the wrecked vehicle. The man who had been driving was struggling to slip out of the driver's side window and, from Vicki's point of view, didn't appear to be too concerned with the condition of the car as he stood shakily by the rear wheel and stared in the direction he'd come from.

The man suddenly straightened, turned away from the car, and began sprinting away from her position and into the darkness of the vacant lot. Considering the accident and how he'd emerged from the car, the man moved with a speed that surprised her. Her door was still open but even over the beeping of the door alarm and the country music on the radio, she had no trouble catching the loud sound of a screaming engine and then the sound of tires screeching as the approaching car closed in on the intersection.

The driver of the big Lincoln had the VW in his sight, and apparently, that was all he was looking for because he drifted through the intersection with all four tires smoking and squealing. The door to the big limousine was open even before the car come to a rocking halt inside the cloud of blue tire smoke.

The whites of her eyes began to show more noticeably, and the knuckles in her hands turned white as she gripped the steering wheel with her right hand and the door handle with her left. She watched the well-dressed man getting out of the silver painted car, but her attention was focused on the gun he was waving around with his right hand.

It was obvious that the man was either very upset or angry because in his rush he never even looked in the direction of the tan Chevrolet van that was setting in the road just short of the intersecting streets. She watched as the man came to a sliding stop beside the wrecked car and then bent down to look inside.

When the man straightened beside the wrecked car, Vicki clearly heard the man's irritation and impatience, which showed up in the form of swearing. The man started to look all around, and his head was just starting to move in her direction when some sound or movement off to his right quickly pulled his attention back to the south. Seconds later, the man was running in the same direction the driver of the VW had gone. The two men looked so similar that if it hadn't been for the clothes the men were wearing, she'd have trouble picking out which man went to which car. If she had been forced to relate all the different characteristics she'd already seen in these men, there would only be two real differences in the runners she would have been able to come up with and those were rather quite simple and very obvious. The first difference was that the driver of the VW had run in fright while this man was running in anger. The second difference was that the driver of the limo was running with a gun in his hand and he appeared to have every intention of using it.

Vicki had no delusions about what was transpiring and while she didn't really want to get involved and put her own life in jeopardy, she knew she had to get the police involved before someone was killed or injured because of her inaction. She closed her door softly to keep from bringing the man's attention to her, but even through the metal and glass of the car door she heard the popping sounds of a gun. She was sure the man with the gun had just found the first driver, and she also knew she had to get out of there in a hurry before the man with the gun returned.

Vicki pulled the gearshift down and sharply turned the steering wheel to the right. She was sure a fire station was located about two miles down the road, and she was also sure they could get the police involved a lot faster than she could. Besides, she didn't want to lead the man in the Lincoln to her home.

She began to make a gentle right and slowly began to accelerate in what she hoped was going to be a silent getaway from this man. What she saw, when she looked in the direction the two men had run, was a sight that made her heart hammer even harder than it had done earlier. She caught a brief sight of the man running in her direction, and he was waving frantically as he passed the wrecked remains of the yellow VW. Vicki found herself being pressed deeper into the seat as she pushed the accelerator tight against the floorboards. There was no mistaking the man's intentions as the popping sounds occurred again. Although it had never happened to her before Vicki knew exactly what was causing the thudding sounds against the rear of her car. The hits against the back of her car were as loud as anything she'd ever heard; and even the scream that rose out of her throat, the squealing of the tires, and the roar of the motor wasn't enough to drown out those menacing sounds.

Her throat went dry in an instant when the remote-controlled mirror on the driver's side suddenly disappeared in a shower of shattered glass as the bullet continued on through the thin metal that had housed the mirror.

Panic struck at her as she looked in the center mirror and saw the man racing for his car. She knew her worst fears had just come into being because she had just witnessed what she was sure was a murder, and now the killer was going to make an attempt to eliminate his only witness to the crime. She knew her mind was not playing tricks on her. There was no doubt in her mind about what he was attempting. He was coming after her with the sole purpose of eliminating her.

As she raced down that dark lonely street, her eyes seldom left the center mirror for more than an instant as she tried to will the other car to slow down and turn around. The Lincoln continued to pick up speed as it followed in her wake, and she knew it would take a lot more willpower and persuasion than she had in her power to make him go away. Her heart jumped into her throat when she finally realized that she had passed the fire station before she had even given any thought of where it was. She realized she had just passed her best chance to get the police involved before the man caught up with her and something extremely unpleasant happened to her. She tried to pull her mind out of the panic mode because she knew exactly what would happen if she continued on without thinking clearly.

The ramp to the freeway was rushing to meet her, and in a fraction of a second, she made a quick decision to head for a more populated part of the town. She pushed on the brake pedal, and almost instantly, the heavy vehicle began to drift as the brakes locked.

By the time she released some of the pressure on the brake pedal, the Chevy was already sideways in the road; and when the tire smoke cleared, she found she had gone across the road and was now facing the direction she'd come. With the complete lack of road traffic at this time of night, it didn't make any difference that she was parked on the wrong side of the road; but the position she was now in gave her a perfect view of the headlights that were rapidly approaching.

Vicki took her foot off the brake and jammed the gas pedal down to the floorboard as she twisted the steering wheel. The big motor roared as she started to turn, and the hot tires squealed on the pavement as the rubber fought for grip. The car fishtailed several times as it pushed its nose down the ramp and onto the freeway, but she wasn't about to back off any because the limo was only yards behind her now.

The big rain tires of the suburban began to howl as the machine picked up speed. When she looked into the mirror again, she felt a little satisfaction when she saw that the big Lincoln was no longer closing in on her. When she looked down at the speedometer, she almost went into shock when she saw that the needle was setting on the impossibly high number of 110.

The heavy vehicle moved smoothly up and down on its springs as the tires rolled over the concrete road and found the dips and swells that went unnoticed at slower speeds. She rolled through the freeway transition that took her from eastbound on I-10 to northbound on I-17. Although the barrier came dangerously close to the passenger side of the car, she didn't lift her foot off the gas pedal even though the steady squealing sound of protesting tires caused goose bumps to raise on her arms and neck. When she started down the long ramp that would take her onto the freeway heading in the direction of Flagstaff, she looked in the mirror once again and saw that the driver of the pursuing car hadn't slowed down either. As Vicki headed north, she roared past the seemingly endless off-ramps as she sped along on the freeway. The infrequent cars she passed seemed to pay her no mind as the pair of speeding cars flew down the concrete road. She quickly became more dismayed because she had been hoping to see red lights coming up behind them. She had been praying that a highway patrol car would take notice of them because of the speed they were moving, and she was also praying that the sight of those flashing lights would be enough to scare off the pursuing car.

As she looked into the mirror, she saw the distance between the two cars was more or less remaining the same; and as the overhead freeway lights snapped by them, she got a strobe-like effect of his face. The look she saw on his face turned her blood to ice. The added trouble with the situation now was that because he was so close, and also because she had gotten so far from the regularly patrolled streets, she was afraid to slow down. She knew that with every streetlight she passed, she was now drawing nearer to the darkness that signified the edge of town; but now she was afraid to hit the brakes because she was sure the Lincoln would overtake her before she was able to find a place of safety.

As her car sailed past the Happy Valley turnoff, she felt her heart dropping another notch and she began to feel the desperation and despair even more. There were only a few lights scattered across the landscape now as she looked about.

She felt a strong pang of hope vibrate through her chest when she looked in her mirror once more and saw the headlights of another vehicle coming into view. She watched wide-eyed as the new set of lights slowly closed the distance between itself and the Lincoln that was following her. She found herself praying once more that she would see red lights beginning to flash as that car got nearer to the pursuing limo, but instead she watched the car lights moving into the left lane. It didn't take long before she knew the cars were side by side, and still there wasn't any sign there would be flashing lights. She had to wrench at the wheel to straighten the car out because she had gotten so absorbed with what was happening behind her that she had wandered across the centerline and her wheels were starting to straddle the white line on the left edge of the road. She managed to straighten the car out after the rear of the big Chevy did some sharp fishtailing. Vicki could feel the sweat forming on her upper lip even though she felt chilled through and through.

When she looked into the mirror once more, she saw the other car had moved away from her pursuer and was catching up with her in a hurry. With the help of the lights from the trailing Lincoln, she was also able to tell that the car catching up with her wasn't a police car; that knowledge caused her heart to drop a little deeper in her chest. The approaching vehicle moved out of the viewing range of the center mirror. She looked over where the mirror had been so she could see where the other car was. She felt a chill shooting down her spine once more when she looked down and was reminded how close that bullet had come. As the smaller car began to pull alongside her, Vicki was becoming aware of how hard she was gripping the steering wheel because the muscles in her arms were beginning to tire from the unaccustomed strain. She was suddenly having thoughts that maybe this was someone who had been called by the man in the Lincoln. As that thought hit her, she found that her breathing rhythm had once more reverted to the mode where it was coming short and fast.

The newcomer had backed off on the throttle until they were rolling along the freeway only feet apart but going at the same speed. Vicki took her eyes off the blurred concrete for a quick look at the car that was pacing her, but all she could see was a little of the paint on the fenders around the headlights. After almost fifteen seconds of tearing down the freeway side by side at 110 miles an hour, the driver of the other car must have gotten tired of the game. Over the engine noise and the growling tires of her own vehicle, she heard the engine in the other car respond; and seconds later she saw the laughing face of the teenager as he pulled his midsixties Mustang away from the big Chevy. For her, it was a matter of life and death; but for the boy who was driving that little red Mustang, it was simply a matter of showing the drivers in those two big and expensive cars that he had a lot more under his hood than they did and that they couldn't hold a candle to his fire-breathing dragon.

As soon as she saw that the car passing her wasn't a partner to the pursuing Lincoln, she began pressing her palm repeatedly on the horn and flashing her lights from bright to dim and back again; but the taillights of the red Mustang continued to grow smaller as it rapidly pulled away from her. The smaller car was far ahead of her when she caught the sight of his brake lights. For a few seconds, she felt a tinge of hope coming back to her. But the car only slowed down long enough to make the corner, and by the time she reached the Carefree turnoff, the red car was already almost a mile east of the freeway and going strong again as it headed in the direction of the towns of Carefree and Cave Creek.

Once more, Vicki took a chance and took her eyes off the road as she looked into the mirror above the dash. Her heart climbed into her throat when she saw the big car gaining on her. She was sure she didn't have a chance to get away from this guy if she tried to slow down for the off-ramp because her hands were shaking so hard that she was finding it hard just keeping the car rolling in what could only vaguely be called a straight line.

Tears of fright and frustration blurred her vision as she flew by the turnoff because she realized how slim her chances of getting out of this situation alive and in one piece were becoming.

When the lights of Black Canyon City came into view as she topped the rise, she again began having hopes of seeing a DPS patrol car either parked beside the road or seeing one coming up behind them. That hope dimmed along with the last sighting of the lights of the town in her mirror as she crossed over the ridge on the north side of the town.

The rest stop several miles north of Black Canyon City held almost a dozen trucks and five or six cars, but none of them were showing the light bar on the top that she'd been hoping for. The fact there wasn't a police car in the rest stop didn't really matter because once again she knew she was going too fast to make the turn at the end of the off-ramp, even if there had been a police car parked in the huge parking lot. She knew that if she was going to have a chance of seeing a police car in a rest stop it would have to be at Sunset Point. That was still another twenty five miles north of where she now was.

The car reacted violently as the heavy vehicle pushed its way around a sharp turn on the freeway, and it was then she realized how windy it had gotten. She hadn't given the wind any thought because until now she'd just put the tugging and pulling, which had caused near lane changes, down to her lack of fast driving experience. Her brothers had always driven fast and had always gotten excited when they talked to her about their experiences, but it was something she had never gotten any enjoyment out of. Until now even the legal speed limit on the freeway had always been just a little too fast for her.

She looked down at the speedometer and saw that it was straining to hold 102 as the heavy vehicle slowly gained elevation while it followed the road upward along the side of the mountain. As she looked down at the speedometer, she also saw that the temperature gauge was going upward as well and now it was setting uncomfortably high in the gauge. She knew the other car had been inching up on her, but now her hurried glances in the mirror showed the big limo was now closing the gap between the two speeding vehicles just a little faster than it had been.

The headlights of the second car got so close to her own vehicle that she lost sight of them until the silver limo pulled out to pass her. As soon as the second car was forced to nose its own way through the wind, its forward momentum also slowed. For almost a mile, the nose of the silver car came dangerously close to the center of her car; but it was having trouble passing her front door because, muscle wise, the two speeding cars were too evenly matched.

The two cars were so closely matched in power that so far they had been running pretty evenly until the engine on the Chevy began showing her what the temperature gauge had been telling her for the past ten minutes. When the engine bogged down several times on that long uphill run, it lost just enough power and speed that the limo was able to pull alongside the big Chevy. As soon as the big silver limo pulled alongside the Chevy, she saw the passenger window beginning to open as the man held his finger down on the window button. When it was fully open, her heart stopped for a long moment because when she looked over she saw the pistol being raised and aimed in her direction.

She did the only thing she could think of and that was to jam her foot down on the brake pedal. Before the man was able to fire the gun, the Chevy was already far behind him because he still had his foot pressing on the gas pedal while the front end of the Chevrolet was being pulled down with the force of her braking.

As the speedometer dropped, she got a quick glimpse of an off-ramp sign. She'd gone by this road many times but had never been interested enough to explore what the town of Bumblebee was all about. Right now it wasn't interest in the town that caused her to aim the nose of her rig down the ramp, but instead it was her belief that she was going to be able to gain a lot of distance on the limo if she was able to get back on the freeway and head back the way she'd come.

The only problem that arose to prevent this from happening was the way the wagon was fishtailing. She was still moving faster than she should have been in order to make the corner, and her speed caused the rear end of the Chevy to swerve out of control and hit the north concrete abutment. It rebounded so hard that when she slid past the southbound on-ramp, which she so desperately wanted, it was the tail of her suburban that was facing the way she wanted to go instead of the nose of the rig. By the time she'd gotten the car straightened out, she was already on her way down the narrow two-lane paved road that led in the direction of the small town of Bumblebee.

It didn't take long for her to find out how hard the wind was blowing or how much dust was accompanying the howling wind when she left the protection of the raised highway. Up on the freeway there had been the added benefit of the roadway elevation that she didn't have here, and it really began making itself felt as she started down the winding road. She almost missed the first corner because she was expecting a straight road and almost didn't see the turn because of a heavy curtain of dust as it blew through the area.

The big tires on the Chevy let loose with a long, low growl on the corner as the heavy van leaned heavily and fought the turn. She struggled hard to keep the big vehicle between the white lines that marked the edges of the narrow road, but then she saw a sign on the edge of the road that sent a surge of panic flowing through her. There weren't very many words on the sign, but it told her volumes. The sign that was whipping back and forth in the wind simply said "Primitive road, pavement ends ahead," and it was almost obscured by the blowing dust.

The sharp corners of the winding road were also shrouded by the dust. This lack of clear vision caused her to come dangerously close to losing control of the van several times. She would have had problems driving this road under normal circumstances, but now her tears of fear and frustration compounded her control problems.

The closest she'd ever come to violence was about a year ago, and that happened when she'd slammed the door on the man she'd been living with. He had simply walked into the apartment one day after work and quite blatantly asked what she thought about another girl moving in with them. She didn't even bother answering his question and had cut their affair off at the roots. She was the happiest when she looked at little puppies and pretty dolls. Her peaceful life had not prepared her for what she was now facing.

The dust-blurred sign, which announced the town of Bumblebee, flashed by as did the vague appearance of darkened buildings on either side of the road. It only lasted a short moment before it disappeared along with much of her hopes of making it out of this situation alive and in one piece.

Vicki fought to keep the rear tires on the road after the sudden appearance of another corner caught her unaware once more. When she managed to bring the car under control again, she found she was now facing the wind and dust head on. She quickly realized that with the last turn she'd made, the mountain beside her was now blocking the radio station she'd had on when this ordeal had begun. The static between moments of music was becoming a very irritating factor. She quickly reached over and turned the radio off. She felt her skin crawling when she got the full sound of the wind and dust that was blasting the car she was driving. It had been a long, dry summer; and now, although the temperatures had moderated enough so it was comfortable during the daytime, the long months with no rain had allowed the ground to become so dry it didn't take much in the way of wind to make it move.

She shook her head in order to focus her attention on the present problem of the road instead of what had happened to force her into this predicament. She realized that by not paying attention to where she was going she could do just as much damage to herself by going over a cliff as the gun-carrying man who was following her could do. The thought of slowing down scared her even more, but she forced herself to drop her speed to a crawl because of the poor visibility as well as the fear of what would happen to her if she happened to go off the roadway out here in the middle of nowhere. She hadn't had a glimpse of the headlights of the Lincoln since shortly before she came to the town of Bumblebee, and that occurred when a relatively calm period allowed her to see the dim and distant glow of his headlights. But she knew he was still back there. There was no doubt in her mind the man would continue after her until he had completed his mission. She kept hoping that some side road would appear so she could strike out in another direction, but nothing of the sort materialized. Fresh tears of despair moistened her eyes when the thought hit her again that his present mission was to simply kill her and it was looking like there just wasn't much she could do to prevent it.

The wind began hitting the broad side of the Chevy as it moved into the open and away from the protection of the steep wall of stone she'd been alongside. It was normal reaction that caused her to turn the wheel slightly in the direction of the oncoming wind, but she wasn't ready for the sudden drop when the front wheels crossed the edge of the roadbed as the road turned sharply to the right. Before she could react with her brakes, the front wheels were already past the stopping point, and then, with all four wheels sliding, the heavy van disappeared over the edge. She didn't hear the crunching sounds as rocks met the bottom of her vehicle, which was nosing down the slope, because her screams were filling the inside of the van.

Chapter 2

L t. Jim Gray frowned as he looked down at his superior while the big, and overweight, man leaned back in his soft chair and contemplated his obnoxious underling. Jim wasn't interested so much in doing things by the book as he was doing what was needed to get the job done. Being ordered to put his drug case on the back burner when he knew he was getting close to something very big was very irritating to him. However, going by past experience, he knew that when Captain Harris got that look in his eye, he, of all people, would not get the man to change his mind. Several of the street patrolmen had unsuccessfully tried to give him the nickname of a character that Clint Eastwood had once portrayed in his younger acting years, but he had quickly put his foot down on that. He hadn't hesitated to use a little force to go along with his verbal objections. Jim knew he could be hard to get along with at times, but mostly it was because he couldn't tolerate slackers when there was something important that needed to be done. It wasn't what he accomplished or didn't accomplish that had gotten him into trouble so many times with his superiors in the past, but instead, it was his way of doing things. He believed that it was the results that counted and not the method he used to get those results.

Lt. Gray was just under six feet and weighed close to two hundred pounds, with very little of that being fat. His light brown hair was clipped short because he didn't like messing with it in the morning. He hated wearing any kind of headwear, and as a result, his face had a deep tan and everyone knew it wasn't from lying out by the pool.

When he questioned a suspect and sort of leaned on him, it wasn't his fault if the man blurted out a few facts that were pertinent to the case he was working on and maybe just happened to be what he was looking for. Jim also wasn't above letting the right kind of information slip out on a man he was looking for in order to make that man come looking for him for protection. He was one of the first to admit he'd had several cases thrown out because of his method of getting the goods on his target, but he also knew he had a much better and more important arrest record than the average officer on the force. It was his conviction record versus his arrests that was in question much of the time.

Jim could see the fire in the captain's eyes as the man pushed his way out of the soft chair he'd come to spend so much time in. When he stood, he dwarfed the lieutenant with his six-foot-eight frame that had come close to carrying 350 pounds. As the man put his knuckles on the desk top and leaned in Jim's direction, there was a strong suggestion of garlic on his breath. Jim was sure that odor was intended to cover the odor of the booze he regularly kept in one of his desk drawers. It was strong, but it didn't quite do the job.

As Captain Harris took a deep breath, he saw the lieutenant easing away from the desk, and the captain knew it was his breath that was causing the movement. He maintained the look of steel as he leaned just a little farther and was successful in his attempt to keep himself from grinning. He was very proud of his effect on the working force under his control. Whether it was due to his breath or his size, he felt a surge of power whenever he viewed any form of submission from his underlings. Seeing the outlaw lieutenant backing up and giving him more room was, to him, a definite show of submission, and he was determined to keep the man in that mode.

There was a deep growl in his voice as he said, "Gray, I know you like to do things your own way, but we've bumped heads once too often and it's all been because of your attitude. I'm tired of the way you try to bull your way around so I'm just going to tell you this, and it better be the last time that, in this department anyway, your method of doing things your own way to get things done is now over. From now on, you'll do things by the book. From now on, you'll follow my orders to the letter. I want you to understand that I'm only going to say this once, and I want you to keep that in mind for all times in the future. The investigation you've been working on has gotten us nowhere, and it is causing this department a lot more in time and money than we can afford to throw away. We can't afford to spend all this money on manpower that is accomplishing absolutely nothing."

Harris saw the lieutenant was going to make a rebuttal, but his quickly upraised hand stopped anything Gray had to say as he continued. "From now on, I'm going to be keeping you on a tight rein, and to insure your cooperation I'm going to partner you up with someone who will make you toe the line or you'll answer to me."

Harris straightened his frame so he could look down at his subordinate before he continued. "Last night there were several reports of shots being fired not far from the freeway in the south part of our town." He reached down and picked up a manila envelope, which he tossed across the desk in Gray's direction before he continued speaking. "Jennifer will be riding along with you from now on. She is to be involved in everything you stick your nose into, and this is something that I have no intention of arguing about." The captain punched the top of the desk with his fist at each word in order to emphasize his intent. "You are off the William's drug case. You have a shooting to investigate. You now have a partner by the name of Jennifer Sullivan. End of discussion. Pick up Jennifer on your way out. Get out!"

Jim glared at the big man, but he bit his tongue and kept his mouth shut because he knew his boss was just itching to pull his badge. They had never been friends, but for the past three months, their relationship had gone from rough to extremely rocky. He reached down and snatched the envelope off the captain's desk. He hated to leave with the appearance that he was backing down, but he also knew he didn't dare push the big man's buttons much more today. Jim had no trouble backing down, seeing the big man was just a little too eager to have a confrontation.

Jim angrily stormed out of the captain's office and slammed the door behind him as he headed for his own cubicle. There were a number of officers who didn't bother to hide their grins as he stomped by in the direction of his desk, but most of the people who had heard the rumbling of Harris and the hasty exit of Gray simply avoided his eyes. He tossed the envelope onto his desk as he dropped into his seat, and then he sat and fumed. He'd seen the chubby little Jennifer, but he didn't know anything much about her except that it had been rumored she'd spent a considerable amount of time in the captain's office during the past month since she'd transferred in. He'd heard that the girl had been running a lot of the man's errands. He'd even heard some rumors about the two of them making a circuit of a number of the local motels, but that was something he couldn't have cared less about. What he was mainly concerned about was that with her along all the time, he'd be very limited with the amount time he could concentrate on his primary investigation, which he had no plans of dropping. He knew he'd have to ration the amount of time he'd be able to spend in that area, but he certainly wasn't quitting his investigation. He was extremely confident that from now on the captain would have an up-to-the minute report of all his activities at all times. He also realized it was too early to try to figure out a way to get around this new obstacle, but he let a few scenarios drift back and forth in his mind. This was just another obstacle that he'd have to find a way around. As far as he was concerned, there was always another way of doing things. This was just another corner that he'd have to shave down.

After a half hour of fuming, consuming five antacid tablets, and not finding any solution to his latest problem, he took a deep breath and opened the manila envelope. He read over all the telephone reports they'd received about the shooting, and then he read the police report that had been filed by the responding officer. He sat and looked at it for a long time as he tried to figure out what he was supposed to investigate on this paper-thin problem. All he had were the reports of some shots being fired and that some faint tire skid marks had been found near where the shots had been fired. Therefore, he had no witnesses to grill, no weapons, no victims, and no vehicles. Other than the reports here on paper he didn't have anything to go on at all.

Jim came close to filing the entire contents of the envelope into the trash can, but he stopped himself at the last second. He opened a fresh pack of antacids and popped two more into his mouth.

Very reluctantly he picked up the reports, and for a long moment, he glared at them. With a deep sigh, he stuffed them unceremoniously back into the manila folder and just as reluctantly headed for the area usually occupied by Jennifer, which was the water cooler.

He saw Jennifer was within ten feet of the cooler. She was talking to another young female officer, who had just transferred in from one of the outlying precincts. He could see the reservation in her eyes when he got near the women. As soon as she saw him coming, she stopped talking and stepped to the side so he could pass if he wanted to without having to step around her. The pair of young women watched him as he maneuvered around several desks and then stopped in front of them. Despite the fact that he didn't want her as a partner, he couldn't help but notice that she had a pretty face, and he liked the way her blond hair was coiled around the back of her head. But now, at close quarters, what he noticed most of all was that her arms, legs, and face didn't match her thick waist. Jim mentally shook his head and quickly took his eyes off her frame as he turned his attention to the problem at hand.

When he stopped in front of them, he had every intention of being civil; but when he started talking, his words came out short and clipped. He could see the aggravation and defiance in her eyes as he curtly told Jennifer he was heading for the car and that if she wanted to go along she'd have to hustle. He had unintentionally made it very clear that he didn't want her along. He had nothing against her, and even though he didn't want her along, he hadn't had any intention of being that rude to someone he hadn't even spoken to until now. It wasn't starting the partnership off on too good of a note.

He started to open his mouth to explain the situation to her and to apologize for taking out his frustration on her. When he turned his head and looked directly at her, he was able to see the angry glare in her eyes; he quickly changed his mind and simply shut his mouth. His first thought was to simply let her boil. Leaving her standing by the water cooler, he simply turned and started for the front door.

Jennifer had to go to the other side of the building to get her purse from the top of her desk, but she was right behind him as he stepped off the curb near his assigned car. Anger was clearly defined on her face as she slipped into the car. He shoved the key into the ignition, but he didn't make any move to start the car; instead, he stared at the steering wheel for a long time. Finally he turned his head and started to speak, but just as he opened his mouth to explain his position, he found her beginning to talk at the same instant.

Both of them began talking at the same time, and for a long moment, they both talked hard and fast as each of them tried to get the upper hand on the "conversation." Finally Jim put his fingertips up to her mouth. For a moment, he thought she was going to shorten most of his fingers, but when he pulled his hand back he still had all of his fingers and it was now quiet in the car.

Jim leaned back against the door and said, "Since I've got the rank here, I'm going to have my say first. Period!" He hesitated for a moment and then he continued. "When Harris told me I was being pulled from the case I was on, which I considered important, I wasn't too happy. When he put me on this trivial investigation about this reported shooting and also told me I now had a partner, well, I will tell you I got very pissed off. It's been seven years since I've been saddled with a partner. I like working alone; I work good alone, and that's the way I want to keep it. I especially don't need a partner that's going to have a direct line to the captain and will be updating him on everything I do." He held up his hand to stall her obvious urge to begin talking. "I just want you to know that I had no intention of taking my, ah…hostility and my, ah…anger out on you. I don't think you want to be here with me any more than I want you. I'm sure you know you have gotten quite a reputation for doing anything the captain asks and that is another reason I didn't want you along. I know everything I do will be reported to Harris in record time. But nevertheless, that still doesn't excuse my curtness. For that I want to apologize. I had no right to talk to you in that manner."

Tears were glistening in her eyes as she said, "I hope you really understand that I don't want anything to do with you. I can think of several hundred officers I'd rather be working with. You've also got a reputation, but yours is for being rude as well as being completely uncaring for any rules or regulations. Everyone knows that you'd rather kick a door in and take your chances with the suspect on getting off in court because of your actions instead of simply waiting for a search warrant." She squirmed in her seat for a moment, and when she continued speaking, her voice sounded soft and hurt as she added, "You really don't care how deep you cut, do you?" She saw his eyes flicker away from hers for an instant, but they came back and locked on her eyes when she said, "I worked hard in school to get the highest grades I could because I want to make it in this field, and I intend to do it on my own. I know some of the lowlife people working here have made some remarks about the way I've been working alongside the captain, but there's been absolutely nothing between us that wasn't in a professional nature. Just let me tell you this much, mister, I've never done anything that I'd be ashamed to tell my mother or father."

Jim saw that her jaw muscles were working as she leaned back into the seat and stared at the brick building in front of them. He didn't miss the tear that trickled down her cheek or the anger in her eyes either. He sat quietly for a long moment while he thought, and then in a soft voice, he said, "Let's go through this just like we were conducting an investigation. I'm going to ask you a few questions, and I want you to understand that I'm not accusing you of anything. I just want to get to the information that's relevant. I think I just picked up on something that's going on here that I didn't realize before."

Jim unconsciously stared at her feet, which were snuggled in regulation black shoes, and was momentarily intrigued by their small size. He looked up and said, "You do realize that you've been saddled with the reputation that you're sleeping with the captain on a regular basis, don't you?"

Her face was instantly transformed into an angry mask, but before she could tear into him, he quickly put his hand up and said, "I'm not accusing."

Jennifer dropped her hands on her lap and stared at them for a long time before she looked up and said, "Yes, I've heard those stupid accusations. I just want you to know that there is absolutely no truth in them." She stopped any farther protests when she saw a big grin appearing on his face and demanded, "Would you explain to me what you find so funny?"

Jim's grin slowly faded as he held up his hand and answered her. "I'll answer that in a moment, but first I'd like to get some more answers to a few more questions. All right?" He waited for her nod, and then he asked, "You're not going to deny that he takes you home every Tuesday and Thursday, are you?"

Her eyelids narrowed, and she came close to hissing as she said, "I don't have a car, and Captain Harris has been nice enough to offer me a ride on those days so I wouldn't have to mess around with the bus. I have to make two transfers in order to just get within walking distance of my apartment. That means sitting out in the heat for a long time before I'm able to get home. He said it's on his way anyway so what's wrong with that?"

Jim nodded his head but instead of answering her question again, he asked, "I think its common knowledge to the people who work with you that you live in the area of Sixty-Seventh Avenue and Camelback. Right?" He watched as she opened her mouth to speak. But instead, she simply gave a curt nod. He looked down at the dash for a moment before he asked, "Did you know Captain Harris lives on the other side of town? The major crossroads nearest his residence happens to be on Shea and the far side of Scottsdale Road. When he takes you home, he has to go southwest of here when in reality he lives northeast of this precinct. Roughly figuring, I'd say that would add about fifteen to eighteen miles to his route home, wouldn't you say?"

She didn't answer but instead just stared at him with a look of disbelief on her face. He added a little more information as he said, "Every time he gives you a ride home, on those Tuesdays and Thursdays, it's impossible to get in touch with him on the phone at his home. Until around seven o'clock, his wife will tell anyone who tries to get in touch with him on the phone that he isn't home yet." Jim chuckled for a moment and then he said, "I don't know if his wife is on to the real reason he's having her do that, but nevertheless, it's being done every time he gives you a ride home. It probably makes him feel like everyone considers him a real stud if he can get people to believe that he's able to get a gal like you twice a week." Jim released a thin smile for a short moment, and then, before she could pull herself together and respond, he said, "I thought it was a little odd when it happened but...well, several weeks ago I wanted to get some more help on the drug case I was working on, and I went to his home. I was arguing with him in his living room when the phone rang. Right away he put his hand up for silence, and then I heard his wife saying he wasn't home yet from work. As soon as the phone was hung up, we started in on each other again, but there wasn't a chance of missing that grin on his face when she answered the phone that way. That happened around six on a Tuesday afternoon."

Her eyes were flashing in anger as she hotly responded, "I want you to know that I am not, nor will I ever be, a...a...a sperm receptacle for that man. Nothing has ever happened between us, and that's the way it's going to stay." She suddenly reached for the door handle, but she stopped moving when she felt the firm grip of Jim's hand on her shoulder.

He dropped his hand onto the seat as soon as he was sure she wasn't going to bolt out of the car. He took a deep breath and then he looked into her eyes and was grinning as he said, "I never heard of a woman being referred to that way, but anyway, why don't you wait a while before you tear into Captain Harris. If you go into his office the way you're feeling now, you'll most likely be looking for a job when you come out."

Jim finally realized how hot it was in the car. He reached down to the steering wheel post, turned the key, and immediately set the AC on its highest setting. For a long time, he felt only a blast of hot air hitting him. As he pulled into traffic, he looked over at her for a long moment before he said, "Why don't we do this my way, sweetheart? Let's do some investigating on this shooting thing first before we try to solve the little problem with that lover of yours."

He was laughing with gusto as she told him that he really was a horse's butt like everyone said.

Chapter 3

There was a wall of silence between Jim and Jennifer as they spent the next two hours canvassing the neighborhood where the complaints of gunshots had come from. They found that anyone who wanted to venture a guess on where the sounds of the shots had come from pointed to the same direction. All the people made sure Jim and his new female partner were aware of the fact they were getting the same information that had been given to the uniformed investigating officer who had responded to their calls earlier that morning.

They had taken a quick look at the intersection in question as they breezed by on the way to talk to the people who had confessed to hearing the shots. But now, as they again approached the rubber skid-marked area in question, they began to look much closer. Jim pulled to the side of the road and gave the location a quick look-over. Before he got out, he reached for the flasher and placed it on the top of his unmarked Ford.

They stood in silence for several minutes as they stared at the faint evidence of what appeared to be a simple traffic accident. Jennifer broke the silence first when she said, "There's nothing here to warrant an investigation. It looks like someone just came close to having an accident a while back."

Jim didn't answer her for several minutes as he stared at the faint rubber tracks. He turned around and looked south, but now he had a puzzled look on his face. He gave a quick look in her direction before he said, "To begin with, I was inclined to come to the same conclusion. But I'm not so sure right now."

Jennifer stood and watched as the lieutenant slowly walked through the sand and brush that covered the southeast corner of the intersection. Her brow furrowed when she saw him bending over to scratch and dig at the ground several times. But her interest wasn't intent enough to get her shoes and dress dirty from the dusty ground, which also held more than its share of dress-snagging weeds.

There was a thoughtful look on his face as he slowly returned to the sidewalk. She watched his actions as he went from staring at the faint rubber marks on the pavement and then turning to look back at the empty shrub-covered lots on the north side of the road. She watched him for several minutes before she couldn't stand the silence and suspense any longer. "What in the world are you looking at?" she asked. "I don't see anything out of the norm here that you can't put down to someone coming close to having an accident."

Jim slowly took his attention away from the marks on the road long enough to move beside her. He stood close to her and then he extended his arm to full length as he pointed and said, "Sweetheart, I was thinking the same thing at first, but now I don't think that's the case. If you look real close, you can see the tire marks of a small car. It looks like the driver was trying to make a turn while holding too much speed. The driver tries to turn, and right there you can see where he loses it and it begins to move sideways in this direction. Now, if you look real close, you'll see the larger skid marks go over the top of the smaller ones, but they stop while the smaller set of skid marks continue on." His mind was trying to unravel some more strings she had yet to see as he stared along his arm at the scene he was pointing at.

"I can see where the tracks merge, but that doesn't mean anything. Besides that, the tracks look like they're weeks old." She added, "And don't call me sweetheart."

He turned around, faced the empty lot, and continued his thoughtful narration. "There are gouges in the hard ground back there that were recently caused by something heavy and hard. Those gouges were filled in real nicely, but the ground at those spots is dust-soft, not brick-hard like the rest of the ground. It almost looks like someone went to a lot of trouble to erase any sign of trouble in this intersection."

Jim turned to look at Jennifer as he said, "I'm going to throw it out the way I read this. I'm going to verbally reenact what I think happened here, and I want you to let me know if you see any flaws.

Without waiting for an answer from her, Jim said, "I see a small car, probably something like the Ford Escort or something like that. I'm going to make a guess it was speeding and tried to make this corner, but it was going too fast. It hit the curb and flipped. It landed in the brush back there right about the time a second car arrived. The second car is a much bigger one, but this one gets stopped just on the south side of the intersection, within ten feet of the curb." He turned around and looked south again as he continued. "The driver from the bigger car runs up to the small wrecked car, and then we have the shots that were heard and reported. The man puts the pedal to the metal and hightails it out of here, and on the way, he calls a couple of his friends. With the help of a tow truck and some brooms or whatever, they clean up the scene before the police get here." He looked over at Jennifer and asked, "Well, how am I doing so far?"

"Not really too good but go on and finish. I'll make my remarks when you're finished."

Jim only shook his head as he stared at the marks on the road and said, "Sweetheart, I'm afraid that's about all I've got right now. I'm pretty sure that what I said happened actually happened, but I don't have any idea as to why or what occurred before or after that."

Jennifer looked down at the skid marks. "All right, tell me why it looks like those skid marks were made weeks ago." Her eyes snapped in his direction as his words dawned on her. She quickly added, "And don't call me sweetheart."

Jim pointed to the center of the eastbound lane. "Do you see how much cleaner the pavement is as soon as you get within six inches on either side of the skid marks? I'm guessing someone did a lot of broom-pushing to get those marks wiped out so they looked that way. It would have been a lot of work, but I think they did just that. I think then they gave the entire area a real light coating of dirt and sand. Whoever did all that probably figured that after several hours of traffic, it would look quite normal. From the looks of the scene here, it looks like they came pretty close to accomplishing just that."

She slowly nodded her acceptance of his version of how he saw it, but then she asked, "Now what about all those shots that were fired? The reports of the number of shots the people heard varied from four to fifteen. You'd think it would only take one shot, or at the most two, if the driver of the first car was involved in some kind of an accident because chances are he'd be a little beat-up and pretty easy pickin's." She shrugged her shoulders and then took a deep breath. "I pretty much agree with almost everything you've said so far. It all sounds quite feasible, but the number of shots that were fired just doesn't make sense."

The thirty-five-year-old lieutenant slowly shook his head. "I'm afraid I don't have an answer for that, sweetheart. I just don't."

Jennifer was quiet for a moment before she pointed and said, "Do you think those tracks over there had anything to do what happened last night?"

Jim looked to see where she was pointing, and then he stared at the westbound lane where he could see tire marks that showed a rapid acceleration out of the intersection and heading north. A number of scenarios immediately began forming in his mind as he moved to step off the curb so he could inspect the tracks from a closer vantage point.

Jennifer grabbed the belt of her new partner and jerked him back just as the semi's air horn blast split the air. Jim almost fell to the ground from the force of her pull combined with the air flow from the speeding truck that blew by them in a cloud of sand and dust. He regained his balance, and then he threw a series of verbal volleys in the direction of the distant, and speeding, eighteen-wheeler. For good measure, he added a one-fingered salute.

Jim brushed at the dirt on his face and shirt before he started across the road once more. He stood and stared at the black marks for a long time before he turned and faced Jennifer. "You know, we just might have discovered why so many shots were fired. I think there was a witness to whatever happened here and that person tried to get away as fast as they could. That's why this vehicle left the scene with tires smoking and why the other car responded in a similar fashion." He stood quietly and stared at the ground, but his mind was racing as he attempted to fit all these irregular pieces into something he could recognize.

Jennifer's soft lips formed a pout as she tried to follow his line of thinking. But now she was having trouble making anything believable out of this whole mess. She slowly shook her head. "No disrespect intended, but I think you're grabbing a lot of irrelevant facts and trying to make something here that doesn't exist. How do you tie in this set of tracks, which are in the middle of the street, with those over there on the south end of the intersection? You've got two lanes going west and two lanes going east. You've also got a wide center turning lane, so that puts these tracks a long way from whatever happened over there." She shook her head once more and added, "I could go along with the scenario you drew up earlier, but this part just doesn't make any sense."

Jim continued staring at the tracks as he raised his hand and stopped Jennifer's verbal show of her disbelief. Without raising his eyes from the tracks on the road, he said, "Let's just run through the complete scenario from start to finish as we can see it now."

He stepped onto the yellow stripes that separated the different directions of travel at the intersection, and then he faced south as he continued speaking. "A small car comes from the north. It tries to make the corner but fails. The small car rolls and ends up in the brush on the south side of the road over there. Another car, a larger one, comes into the intersection with all four wheels trying to bring it to a stop." Jim now raised his hand and held up a couple of fingers as he turned and looked at Jennifer. "Remember that first house we checked? The old man said it was just a few minutes before one, and he had taken his dog outside to let it do its thing before he went to bed. He said he'd heard two shots to start with, and then a half of a minute to a minute later, he heard a lot more shooting. All right now. Let's assume the man in the larger car was in pursuit of the driver of the small car for some reason, and after the first car went out of control, the second driver goes up to the wrecked car and there the first two shots were fired. The man heads back for his own car when he sees that he's had an audience. The driver of the third car sees that a problem is about to envelope him, and he decides to leave suddenly. That's when the second man fires the remainder of the shots that had been heard."

Jim pointed down at the tracks in front of him. "The wide heavy tracks from the third car show me that it was also a heavy one just like the second car, but it was probably more of a working vehicle judging from the kind of tires. These tracks look like something you'd find on a four-wheel drive that's used on rough roads. You can see where the pursuing car, which has regular highway tires, burned his tracks right over the top of these tracks that have the coarser tread." He looked up from the pavement and faced north as his mind raced.

The young female officer glanced from the tracks to the road that headed north and then back to her partner's face. It was clear that she wasn't completely convinced, but she was trying to see his line of thinking. Her eyes lingered on his face for a moment as she took in his clean, shaven jaw as well as the intense look in his eyes. She wet her lips unconsciously right before she looked to the north. After several seconds, she broke the silence. "Well, I guess we know they headed north. Now what? There aren't going to be any tracks to follow after we leave this intersection, so what do you suggest now?"

With her interruption shattering the scenario he had been dwelling on, Jim made his mind leave the action as he had been envisioning it and forced his mind to come back to the present. It took a long moment before her question soaked through his scrambled thoughts and he was able to consider making an answer.

He never let his eyes settle on any one spot for more than a second or two as he said, "I guess the only thing we can do is head north from here and see if we can find someone who saw any-thing, or if they left any rubber marks when they turned off to go in another direction. But the first thing I want you to do is get my camera out of the car and take as many pictures as you think are needed of the tire marks on the road as well as the ground where the alleged accident occurred. When you're done with that, we'll do some driving. The way both cars left this intersection, there has to be something to tell us which way they went. Sooner or later, we should find something, or someone, that'll tell us what kind of vehicles we're looking for."

Jennifer started to cross the street to get the camera from the unmarked Ford, but she stopped and looked back when she heard him chuckling. She pulled her neck in and began to squint when she heard him laughing as he suggested that maybe they could do it the easy way and just put an APB out for two heavy vehi-cles. When she resumed her journey to his car, she was seriously wondering if he was lacking in sanity or if it was just his sense of humor that was completely out of whack.

On their drive northward, Jim stopped at several convenience stores along the way, but no one on the early morning shift had reported seeing anything. He got Jennifer busy writing down the workers names so that when time permitted, they could contact them for questioning later on.

The Ford was just picking up speed from the last convenience store stop when Jennifer began turning her head as they passed a large building. She got a quick look at several men washing a big yellow truck out in front of it. She sat quietly for a long moment, but then she looked over at Jim. "You know, as nice as it was last night, maybe those firefighters back there were sitting outside when those two vehicles we're supposedly looking for headed north.

He quickly swung his head around and looked back at the receding building in the rearview mirror. When he turned forward again, he was nodding his head. "That's a very good thought, sweetheart. Like they say, nothing ventured, nothing gained. Or another saying that goes something like not leaving any stone unturned, et cetera, et cetera."

Jennifer grabbed the door armrest as Jim gave the steering wheel a quick twist. Over the accelerating sound of the engine, she barely heard the blaring horn that came from the pickup that had been forced to slow down to the speed limit when Jim turned in front of it. She looked back and saw the driver of the pickup had not slowed down as much as he should have, and now the blue-and-white Blazer was only several feet away from their rear bumper. When she looked over at Jim, she saw he was also viewing the scene behind him through the use of the inside rearview mirror. She had begun getting a little nervous that a confrontation would quickly escalate, but his grin quickly overshadowed her fears. She watched as he reached for the flasher that was lying on the seat between them. She observed his slow, controlled movements as he hit the window button and then reached out to set the magnetized flasher on top of the roof on his side. Her eyes quickly shifted to the rear window, and she almost laughed out loud when she saw the front end of the small Chevy quickly dipping lower as the suddenly fearful driver quickly applied his brakes.

Jim began to laugh out loud when he pulled into the turning lane, and the small pickup slowly passed them. The young man was wearing the normal working clothes of the everyday worker, but Jennifer only noticed the tattoo on the man's arm that advocated "white power."

The S-10 slowly moved past the decelerating Ford in the turning lane, and Jennifer didn't hesitate to slowly shake her finger in his direction. The driver tried to pretend he hadn't done anything wrong or that he didn't see her admonishing action as he looked straight ahead just like nothing had happened. But the look on his face told another story. Jim didn't say anything about the man's actions as he watched for an opening in the traffic so he could turn in at the fire station. But Jennifer was quick to call out "butthead" just as the blue-and-white pickup passed beside them.

At the fire station, they quickly learned that the shift change had occurred at eight o'clock that morning and also that it had been a quiet shift for the crew. Jim's hopes of getting some pertinent information began to rise as the fireman told him the crew had not gotten a single call all night. Jim got all the information he needed so he could contact the off-duty firemen at a later time. Five minutes after stopping in front of the fire station, they were pulling back into the northbound traffic.

When they reached the freeway access intersection, Jennifer suddenly sat straighter in her seat and quickly pointed, but Jim had already seen the tire tracks on the pavement. There was no questioning the urgency that had been on the minds of each driver as the leading car tried to get away and the trailing one tried to prevent it.

Jim made a right-hand turn as if to pull onto the freeway, but as soon as he made the corner, he pulled onto the gravel shoulder and stopped. With the flasher doing its job on the top of the Ford, the partners walked back to the intersection. Jim was staring at the tracks of the car that had spun out of control when he suddenly heard clicking sounds. He turned and looked in Jennifer's direction. She was taking pictures as fast as the camera could move the film into position. He found his own attention glued to her as she snapped picture after picture.

Her attention was so completely wrapped up with taking the pictures that she didn't notice how openly he was watching her actions. As he watched her, he still couldn't understand how that thick waist was attached to the same body that the slim arms and shapely legs were connected to. He watched as she brought the camera up to her pretty face for another series of pictures of the tracks on the road.

When the light changed, Jennifer quickly stepped to the center of the road and snapped some more close-ups. When she looked back at Jim, she quickly saw he was staring at her. For a brief instant, she felt like he was standing by the bathroom door in her apartment and watching her as she got ready for a bath while wearing only her bra and panties.

She felt her face getting red as the thought crossed her mind, but when she started back to the side of the road, his eyes remained locked where she had been. She realized that it had been her imagination that had been running loose. She took a deep breath, and her face lost some of its redness when she decided it really had been just her imagination. As she looked at her partner, the thought hit her that it could easily have been an unconscious desire that had made her think those thoughts. She shook her head to dispel that absurd thought. She moved beside her new partner and waited for him to break out of his thoughtful spell so she could learn what he was reading into this part of the puzzle.

Jim tried to make it appear that she had pulled him from a deep, thoughtful trance when she tugged on the sleeve of his short-sleeved shirt. He blinked several times as if to bring himself back to the present. He had no intention of letting her know that he had been indeed watching her quite intently, and he had been enjoying the view.

He shook his head, but what she took as an attempt to bring himself back to the present was in fact an attempt to push her, as a woman, out of his mind. He had too many things to concentrate on and too much work to get done to waste his time on a pretty face and a shapely butt. He just could not allow himself to get involved with any female no matter how pretty she was. He had a promotion to work on, but more important than anything else, he had a drug case he needed to concentrate on. Jim was very sure that if he solved the drug case, he would be able to cut the amount of drugs coming into the area to at least half. It wouldn't eliminate the drug problem, but it would certainly slow down the flow and give a few more kids the chance to grow up in a slightly better environment. There wasn't even a shadow of doubt in his mind that crime and drugs ran hand in hand. He knew that if nothing was done to stop the cycle of crimes and drug use, it was something that would continue to escalate as they fed off each other until it was completely out of control.

He looked down at his blond partner for a long moment before he said, "Run back to the car and get the camera. I want to get some pictures of this intersection as well."

Any thoughts that he had been watching her quickly vanished as she listened to his request. She looked up at his face with surprise. "I've already taken a lot of pictures of this intersection. Where have you been?"

Jim allowed himself to show what he hoped came off as an embarrassed grin. "I guess I've been doing some deep thinking." He hesitated for a moment before he added, "I'm ready to head on if you're done with what needs to be done here."

When they got back into the Ford, they sat and watched the traffic moving on the freeway for several minutes before Jennifer finally broke the silence. She looked away from the heavy traffic moving past them on the freeway and stared at his thoughtful face for a long moment before she said, "Well, now what? Do we go down the freeway until we see some marks where they exited the freeway? Heavens, we could end up in Apache Junction, Tucson, or even Flagstaff before we see anything, and even then we'd have no way of being sure we were still on the right track."

Jim didn't take his eyes off the heavy flow of cars and trucks that went roaring past the eastbound on-ramp. "Well, I'm not so sure where to go now, sweetheart. We could check every off-ramp intersection, but like you mentioned, with I-10 crossing I-17 just a couple of miles away, we'd have more off-ramps to check than you could shake a stick at. On top of that, there's still the fact that if they slowed down for an off-ramp and made their corner without leaving a good trail of tire marks to follow, we could go right on by and never know it."

Jim reached down to the ignition. Seconds later, the big engine rumbled as it waited for him to make his move with the gearshift lever. Jim frowned for a long moment before he said, "About all we can do right now is try to find somebody who saw something. We've got a list of names now, so we'll have to do enough interviewing until we can determine who was driving what and why they were driving the way they were. Until we've got something we can sink our teeth into, there isn't a whole lot more we can do."

His mind had drifted back to the subject at hand and was no longer on the amount of thigh that was visible on the seat near him. Despite his objection at being pulled away from the drug investigation, he was beginning to see where a problem had arisen. Now, instead of seeing a shapely leg encased in nylon hose, it was fully on the problem at hand. The biggest problem at this point was that he felt he was at a road block that was devoid of any kind of detour sign that would give some indication of which way to go.

Jim pulled the gear selector lever down to drive. As they merged into the rapidly moving traffic, he looked over at her for a quick moment. "Sweetheart, when we get back to the office. I want you to check with the highway patrol and with the police departments of any of the cities that border the freeway system near here. We need to know if anyone heard or saw anything that pertains to what appears to have happened in this neck of the woods. I'm going to make some calls to the crew of the fire station and to the workers from the convenience stores and set up some meeting times to find out if anyone saw anything that might help us."

Jennifer took advantage of his silence while he maneuvered into the transition lane so he could go north bound on I-17. "I'm going to get Selina, the new officer I was talking to this morning, to help me. She used to work at the Glendale office, and she'd know who to call there. But the first thing I'm going to do is give Captain Harris a piece of my mind. Nobody is going to do what he's been trying accomplish and get away with it." A look of anger was back on her face as she added, "I've enjoyed not having to mess with all the bus rides, but when I get through with him, he'll be sorry he ever met me." She turned her head to watch the traffic, but suddenly she looked back at Jim. "And don't call me sweetheart!"

Jim hid the amusement he was feeling. His face was devoid of any kind of feeling as he said, "If you confront him on that sub-ject, you're probably going to be the one that's going to be sorry. He'll most likely have you transferred with a very unfavorable report following you into your next job, and you know what that will do to any hopes of promotions you might have in mind." He hesitated for a short moment, and then he added, "What he'll probably do on top of that is hint around to everyone in the office that he caught you messing around with some of the officers or maybe that you might be bedding down with me now."

Jim slowed down for the off-ramp at Thunderbird Avenue and then pulled into the left-turn lane. As he waited for the light to change, he added, "Besides that, what's your lover going to do if he knows you're angry with him? You just might find you've got competition when he takes the time to take a good look at that new officer."

Jennifer looked over at him in anger. "He's not my lover!" She turned to look forward once more, but Jim didn't miss hearing her adding, "Butthead."

Jim couldn't hide the grin he was feeling at her show of anger. "Whatever you say, Sweetheart."

She tried to maintain an angry look on her face so she could conceal the way she was feeling, but there just wasn't any way she could hide the glint of amusement in her eyes as she turned to glare at him.

Chapter 4

When they entered the three-story brick building that housed their precinct headquarters, Jim made sure he steered the young blond officer safely past the captain's office. He knew the fireworks would occur eventually, but he wanted to avoid any premature confrontation. Lt. Gray wanted to use the freedom he still had at his beck and call to do a lot more digging into the drug case. He knew that once she started raising a fuss over the captain's alleged conduct with her, he would be feeling the fallout just as much as she was going to. Only when Jennifer was thoroughly involved with her assigned job of making phone calls did he head for his own cubicle to begin making his own calls.

He was just hanging up the phone from getting his first real lead when the intercom buzzed. When he answered the phone he heard the captain's voice growling in the background as his secretary spoke to him. The captain's secretary told him, in no uncertain terms, to go directly and immediately to the commander's office. He was to go there posthaste, ASAP, or even faster if he could manage it.

Jim leaned back in his chair as he tried to figure out what he'd done wrong this time. The commander had been much more tolerant of his style of investigation than Captain Harris had been lately, but apparently, something in particular had really created a knot in somebody's shorts this time around. He sat back and did some deep thinking for the next five minutes, but he couldn't think of anything he'd done so unusual that would warrant such an urgent call from the commander himself. Finally, with a deep breath of resignation, he pushed himself out of the chair and headed for the opening of his cubicle.

Jim was several strides away from his desk when he heard his phone ringing. He took another two steps before he stopped and listened to another ring. He sighed once more as he turned around and reentered his office.

"Gray here." He said, expecting to hear either the captain or his secretary berating him for his slow response to the captain's order to report to the commander's office. What he got on the other end of the line instead was a strange voice with a Hispanic accent.

The speaker sounded somewhat sleepy as he said, "Yeah, my wife said you called me earlier when I was sleeping. My name is Ramon Pena, and I was on duty at the fire station last night. What did you want to know?"

Jim sat down on the edge of his desk and mentally crossed his fingers for luck. "We had an incident last night, and I was hoping you might have seen something. The crew that took over for you guys said the night had been pretty quiet. I was hoping you might have seen something out of the ordinary somewhere around one o'clock. Maybe something like a couple of wildly racing cars or some distant shooting or something like that?"

There was a pause, and then the man hesitated between words. "If I did see something, does that mean I have to...well, I mean, do you think...do I have to...like, go to court to...testify?"

There wasn't any chance of missing the frown on Jim's face as he moved around the desk and dropped into his chair. He took a deep breath to make sure he kept his irritation in check because he knew how the common individual felt about getting involved with the police and the unending paperwork that went hand in hand with it.

"No, at this time I can't see where you would have to do any testifying. This investigation is primarily to find out what happened a couple miles south of your workplace. We aren't even sure anything illegal happened, and it isn't speeders we're interested in. I'm sure you guys see quite a few drag racers and speeders zipping by your station because of its remote area. We're not interested in the average speeder, but if you noticed anything unusual, I'd like to hear about it. We're trying to find out what happened last night and who was involved. That's all."

It didn't take long before Jim heard a deep sigh from the other end of the line, and then Ramon said, "Well, yeah, it was pretty quiet last night. After dinner, we sat around and watched TV for a while. But like the usual, there wasn't anything on, so we started playing cards. I wasn't having very much luck with the cards, so I went outside. The temperature was getting real nice and comfortable at that time, so I just sat down and stared at the stars. You know, when I went to Arizona State, I spent a semester studying the solar system. Did you know that—"The man's voice stopped for a long moment after he heard Jim softly clearing his throat.

The man's voice was softer when he started his narration once more. "Sorry about that. My wife says I have a tendency to wander at times. Well, I was sitting outside the station from about twelve fifteen until just a little after two when I started getting sleepy. It was somewhere around one o'clock when I saw a little yellow Volkswagen going south. That guy really had the motor in that little bug wound up. It didn't take long before one of those big cars, I think it was a Lincoln or something like that, came flying up the road. It really looked like this guy was trying to catch the yellow bug. Well anyway, it wasn't long after they went by that the Lincoln came back. Only now it looked like he was chasing a different vehicle."

Jim had bolted forward in his chair when Ramon had mentioned the yellow VW heading south with a Lincoln on its tail, and he began writing on the back of one of his memos that he'd never answered. After Ramon mentioned the Lincoln coming back in the other direction, Jim stopped Ramon's narration and asked, "Did you get a good look at the Lincoln? Could you see what color it was or maybe even what the driver looked like?"

Ramon paused a moment and then he said, "The Lincoln had an older, boxy shape. It wasn't like some of those new ones with nothing but rounded corners and no real shape. This one looked square and well built and not like an upside-down bathtub. It's one I wouldn't mind seeing parked in my front driveway every morning. The color of it was something like silver or maybe a light gray. It went by the streetlight so fast I didn't really get a good look at it either time. And as for the driver? All I can say for sure is that this man wasn't black and that s as far as I can go. Oh yeah, he did have black hair.

"What really struck me funny about the driver of the yellow bug was how scared he looked. He was looking over his shoulder like a ghost was after him when he went past the station, and I got a good look at him. Black or dark brown hair, clean-shaven, and scared, but nothing more that I can think of. He was just sort of an average-looking kind of guy."

The young lieutenant had a strong urge to ask why the man hadn't called the police when that had happened. He forced himself to be silent and almost had to bite his tongue instead. He allowed the man to continue but took a deep breath to calm his feelings. And then he said, "Go on. What else did you see?"

There was a long hesitation before the man started speaking again. "Well, he came back about a few minutes later, but this time he was chasing after a big tan Chevy going in the other direction. Looked to me like there was a woman behind the wheel, but I couldn't really tell because as soon as I saw the Lincoln coming back in the other direction, I was watching it instead."

Jim looked up when he saw movement at the door of his cubicle. He spotted the angry face of the captain, but he quickly turned his attention back to the telephone and said, "You're sure the Chevy was tan? Also you said it was a big Chevy. What do you mean by that?"

"It was a light tan Chevrolet Suburban, probably about three or four years old. Really made a lot of tire noise, like it had mud and snow tires on it. A female was driving it. That's about all I can tell you."

Jim ignored the hand gyrations of his boss as he asked, "Did you happen to hear anything right before you saw the Lincoln the second time?"

There was a long hesitation this time before the man made any attempt to answer. After another deep sigh on the far end of the phone, Jim heard the man saying, "All right! I heard some shooting. I'd guess there were probably about seven or eight shots." There was another momentary lull before the man added, "I heard two shots, and then about a minute later, there were about five or six more. I just figured that some drunks or gangs were messing around, that's all."

Gray sat for a moment and listened to the silence on the phone while he watched the stern face of his supervisor. Finally, the young lieutenant broke the silence and said, "I'd like for you to do something for me. Take a sheet of paper and write down absolutely everything you remember that happened last night, and I'll pick it up at your house later today. All I can say right now is that it's very important. Thanks for returning my call."

Jim hung up the phone and then he stared at the notes he had written down. He was brought out of his revere when the captain loudly cleared his throat. He looked up and stared at the man's face for several seconds before he released another deep sigh. It was with deep misgivings that he pushed himself out of his chair once more. He would have made a bet that he knew what was going to hit the fan in only a minute or so. Again!

When he left his cubicle, he was followed by Captain Harris. The man dogged his heels until he walked into the commander's office. Jim saw the man was talking on the phone, so he walked to the window and leaned against the wall as he looked at the artificial jungle outside and below the glass in front of him. It had been the commander himself who had pushed for the large tree-covered patio under his window. As he stared outside, Jim's mind returned to the telephone conversation he'd just had. His mind was so deeply engrossed in the shooting incident he didn't even realize the phone in this much larger office had been hung up and that the commander was now talking to him.

Commander Hamilton finally got his attention by balling up a sheet of paper and throwing the wad at him. Jim's previous conversation disappeared, and his mind suddenly went blank when the paper bounced off his temple.

Jim had a bewildered look on his face for several seconds until he finally collected his thoughts and got his train back on the track once more. When he looked at his two superiors, he did notice the complete lack of humor on their faces as they glared at him. He took a deep breath and quietly made his way to the chair that was centered in front of the desk directly opposite the lean, tall man with gray hair. He knew he was in for an interrogation and just hoped that there would be a complete absence of chains and electrical contraptions designed for their amusement.

For several minutes, Commander Hamilton simply sat back in his chair and glared at Jim. The man didn't even seem to blink an eye as he stared at his underling without saying a word. Jim had a humble look on his face, but his fingers were beginning to drum on the arms of his chair. They didn't know how hard he was fighting to maintain a cool demeanor. Although he was really fighting against it, his temper was short enough right now that he was about to start into the commander. He was almost ready to start chopping at the forest and just let the chips fall where they would. He wasn't very happy with the way things had turned out—being pulled off the case as well as ending up with a partner—so his temper was just a little on the short side. Just as Jim opened his mouth to start his own version of a verbal butt-kicking, the commander also started to speak.

The commander was used to having his orders followed to the letter, and now Hamilton raised his hand and said in a forceful tone, "Whoa! I'm the one who's going to do the talking and you're going to do the listening. Got that?" Hamilton watched Jim closely until the man slowly closed his mouth and resigned himself to whatever was in store. Hamilton slowly nodded his head and then he got to his feet and moved around the desk where he parked a lean thigh on the edge. "Lieutenant, I just got off the phone from talking to the states attorney. He's got three complaints on his desk, and they all concern you." The soft voice of the commander continued to get harder and louder until the man was almost shouting. "Where do you get off using that kind of aggressive action when you make a simple arrest? Right now, it looks like the force is looking at a lawsuit in the multi-million dollar amount just because of your aggressive and obsessive behavior. And all because you had some half-baked idea that Tom Williams is living the soft life because he's dealing in drugs. I think you're so far off base that you're missing the whole ball game. Never in my whole life have I ever seen such a complete disregard for rules and regulations."

The commander paused for a moment to take several deep breaths before he started once more. "You've caused the department to spend so much time and money on that nonexistent case that we've had to curtail several other investigations that were starting to bear fruit. Just so there's no mistaking what I'm telling you, I'm going to spell it all out for you. You didn't seem too impressed with the information that was given to you by your captain. So let me state it in very clear terms so you won't misunderstand what I'm saying. You, Lieutenant James Gray, are now off any phase of that Williams drug investigation, as you call it. Now is there anything you don't understand about that?" The last part of the one-sided conversation was done in a shout. The commander's face was beet-red when he finally sat down in the huge office chair.

When Hamilton was seated, he quickly poured iced water into a glass and made an attempt to cool his overheated and overworked throat. Just as soon as Jim thought the head office tirade was coming to a close, he saw Harris moving up beside him.

Harris bent over and faced Gray eye to eye. There wasn't any smile on his lips either when he said, "I've told you over and over to use a little more tact and a lot more sense when you go out into the field. You really did it this time. We just received word from the states attorney's office that the arrests you made on Henderson, Wales, and Meyer have all been thrown out because of 'contaminated evidence,' as they called it. According to the information I just got from one of the assistant state attorneys a few minutes ago, the court is going to throw out every bit of evidence we've been able to put together on the men we suspect of being the real drug dealers. Because of you, we don't have anything left to go on now. The way you mishandled the case spoiled all our leads, which we had been hoping to use to put a stop to this drug business. You have single-handedly eliminated any chances we had of stopping the drug dealers that have been harming and killing so many kids in this town. On top of that, you twisted all the evidence we had just so it would lead to your Williams case instead of in the right direction. Gray, you're a pain in the…neck." Harris turned and walked over to the window and looked out at the lush greenery.

Gray shifted his eyes from the back of Harris to the baleful face of Hamilton as the man stared at him. There wasn't any warmth in the commander's eyes as he contemplated the man he regarded as his rogue officer. The view appeared so comical that Gray had the urge to laugh at the looks he was getting, but he knew that would be the proverbial straw. He leaned forward and put his elbows on his knees as he moved the focus of his eyes down to the toes of his cowboy boots in an effort to keep from laughing out loud.

It didn't take very much time before his thoughts trailed away from the verbal reprimands he was getting and were once more on the VW, the Lincoln, and the big Chevrolet. He tried to apply several variations to the scenarios he'd already been entertaining, but he wasn't very happy with any of them. He felt very confident of the fact that he was looking at something very important. But until he knew why the Lincoln had been involved in that two-way chase, he would be clutching at straws regardless of whichever scenario he grew to believe was the correct one.

He leaned back in the chair as he began to entertain another thought, but his eyes suddenly crossed paths with the commander's. His mind quickly cleared as he heard the man saying, "If you can't handle that, then I'll assign someone else to do it. And instead of working in the role of detective, you'll simply find yourself working under the hoods of the motor pool cars. I'm fed up with the ineptness you've demonstrated on the job as well as your inability to follow orders." His face was red once more as he stared at Jim's impassive face. The thin, red-faced, and angry man hesitated for a long moment before he shouted, "Do you think you can handle that?"

Jim put a thoughtful look on his face as he slowly stood up and said, "Yes, sir. I'm very confident that I can uphold my end of it." He was quiet for a moment before he added, "And I want to thank you for your concern on the matter." He hoped the old man wouldn't ask any questions because Jim had no idea what the commander had been talking about before he'd agreed to handle his end.

Jim stepped up to the desk and bent slightly as he reached across the cluttered desktop. He saw the commander staring at the proffered hand in disbelief for a long time before finally raising his thin hand and clasping the muscular one belonging to the man he'd just chewed out. The young officer released the thin, frail old man's damp hand, made a military about-face, and started for the door. He didn't look at his captain's face, but he easily saw the man was clearly surprised by the show Jim had just put on.

Gray was halfway back to his own desk when he heard Harris calling his name. Jim took a deep breath as he stopped and turned around. He was somewhat surprised at the look he saw on the heavy face. Instead of seeing a look of anger on the face of Captain Harris, he saw a very thoughtful look. Jim also didn't miss the way his eyes wandered around the huge office before they settled on his face.

Harris stopped in front of Gray, and when he spoke, it was without moving his lips. His eyes resumed wandering around the office as he said in a very soft voice, "Get your jacket and follow me. We've got to talk."

Jim's surprise showed up in his voice when he said, "Jacket? It's almost a hundred degrees out there." He was going to say more, but the captain's abrupt order of "Just do it!" made him stop with his mouth open but with nothing to say. He watched as the man brushed by him brusquely as he headed for the door. Jim stood and watched his supervisor in stunned silence until the man was almost at the front door before he finally moved to retrieve his jacket.

Chapter 5

He finally found his old windbreaker in a deep corner of the bottom file drawer. He had to shake it several times before a lot of dust and some of the wrinkles began to smooth out. The result still showed that it had been in a drawer for the past six months. When Jim stepped outside, he found the captain busily retying his shoes at the bottom of the steps. As Jim approached him, the man straightened with a deep intake of air that told him that it had been a huge chore to bend over the way he had been doing.

Jim started to step off the sidewalk in the direction where Harris usually parked his car, but a hand on his elbow stopped him. He saw the look on the man's face as he started to walk along the sidewalk. For once, Jim was at a loss of words. He had never seen that look on his captain's face in the entire time he'd known the man.

They walked without talking. Even while they waited for the light to change so they could cross the street legally, there was still silence. When they got to the middle of the next block, Harris finally spoke. He got a wide-eyed questioning look from Jim when the he said, "Bend over and tie your shoes."

Harris had to repeat his request a second time as Jim looked down at his cowboy boots. Before the young officer could say that he didn't even have shoelaces, Captain Harris added, "Just do it. While you're down there tying your shoes, I want you to sneak a look back and see if there's anyone following us. If there is anyone following us, then this little meeting of ours is off, and I want you to just keep on following the sidewalk. I'm going to make a left here into the alley, and I'll try to find another way.

Jim's forehead was furrowed in puzzlement as he slowly bent over to "tie" his boots. When he finished with the first one, he changed positions so he'd have a better view of his back trail. While his head appearing to be facing the chore he was supposedly working on, his eyes were busily scanning the foot and motor traffic around them. He slowly straightened and then he said, "Everything looks normal. I didn't see anything out of order."

Harris slowly resumed his walk, but when they approached the opening that led into the alley, he began to turn into it. Because he was walking on the street side of the sidewalk, his turn into the alley literally pushed Jim in the same direction but ahead of him. Seconds later, they were out of sight of anyone on the street unless they just happened to be passing the alley.

Jim didn't like the situation it appeared he was being squeezed into. He was becoming just a little apprehensive with both the location as well as the captain's actions. He slowly eased his jacket until it was over his left arm. This left his right hand free to grab the gun that was facing forward on his left hip. He knew the captain hadn't missed the move, but the man didn't say a word as he continued walking. They appeared to be heading for a parked street sweeper on the right side of the alley in the center of the block.

Jim's muscles were tensed and ready for action when his walking partner stepped behind the street sweeper. A delivery truck was parked behind the sweeper, and it effectively blocked almost all avenues of sight from anyone who might inadvertently pass by. His eyes were constantly roving as he looked for any sign of possible ambush. Those eyes were not only scanning up and down the alley, but he was also trying to check out every window within sight. He didn't know what the captain was up to, but considering his actions as well as their relationship in the past, he wasn't going to take any chances. He still wasn't sure what the captain held in his hand under the raincoat that was draped over his arm.

His attention became fully immersed in the heavy man when he heard his captain say, "We don't have much time." He turned his full attention on the lieutenant as he said, "I had to do it this way because I'm convinced my office is bugged. I believe my car is also, and I'd also make a big bet that they got into my house and planted some bugs there as well. I've got to be very careful about what I do or say, or I could find myself looking at the roots of daisies and all the other kinds of flowers they have in cemeteries, if you get my meaning."

The captain moved nearer to the edge of the street sweeper for a moment as he glanced up and down the littered backstreet again. The look on his face didn't alter even after he saw that the street was empty of both foot and wheeled traffic. Everything appeared to be quiet and normal, but Captain Harris knew how serious the situation was, and he also knew exactly what would happen if anyone happened to witness what he intended to do. There was no doubt in his mind that it would be curtains for both of them if he happened to make even one small mistake.

The captain pulled his jacket higher onto his arm until his hand was exposed. The muscles in the young officer's body lost some of its tenseness as the man shoved a roll of papers in his lieutenant's direction. Harris took the time to do some quick looking around as he said, "I have to be very careful. I wasn't even that sure about you for a long time because there are some very dirty people around us." He saw his officer was going to start asking questions, and he quickly put up his hand to hold off the questions until he was finished. His face almost appeared gray in color as he started again by saying, "Just shut up and listen because I don't know how much time we'll have to talk. I believe you're on the right track with Williams. He's as dirty as they come, but our biggest problem is that he's not in it alone. I think the police commissioner is in on it as well as our own

Commander Hamilton. I haven't gotten anything directly linking Hamilton with Williams up to this point, but right now I think he's in it up to his neck. I've got some information, but it isn't something I can prove right at this point."

Jim started to open the roll of paper sheets in his hand, but the captain reached out and stopped him.

"You'll have time to do that later when you're away from the office. Be careful who you talk to or even where you do the talking. I don't even want you to assume that your own apartment is bug-free. They may have bugged your car as well. And I'm not talking about spiders or cockroaches. I just want you to know that you're getting into dangerous territory with anything involved with Williams. That's why I tried to get you away from it until I had a chance to let you know how deep the water is." The captain took a deep breath as he stopped talking long enough to scan the alley once more before he continued. "You know that car accident that Tony Sanchez got killed in several weeks ago? Well, I don't think it was an accident. The commander made sure one of the rookie officers did the report on that accident. It came off on paper as an accident because the kid had no idea what to look for. Hamilton was very pleased with the way that report was filed. I think Sanchez was getting too close to something, and they figured something had to be done." Harris stared at his feet for a second before he looked up and added, "I don't know if Hamilton is in this or not, or if he's just buckling under the pressure he's getting from higher up. But I can't take any chances because one wrong move will get both of us killed if he is mixed up in this."

While his captain talked, Jim tried to find some way to arrange his jacket so it wouldn't be so obvious that he was carrying papers that could possibly be very damaging to Williams and his cronies, even though he was very engrossed in what the man was saying. Jim had a sudden thought, and he quickly found that the way the papers had been rolled up, it allowed the incriminating evidence to neatly curl around his shin as he slipped the papers into his boot. He hung his wind breaker across his left shoulder and used that motion to scan the alley himself.

Captain Harris watched Gray's actions and was relieved that the young man showed that he believed the situation was as he'd described it and that he didn't think his supervisor was really losing his marbles instead. When Harris saw Jim checking out the alley, he said, "From now on, anything we discuss on Williams will have to be done secretly. I don't want you to even mention anything about the case to anyone unless you're absolutely, positively sure beyond any shadow of doubt that they're clean." He hesitated for a long moment for effect before he said, "You've got to be dead sure, or you'll just be dead. And that goes for me as well."

Jim shook his foot to get the papers settled a little better before he said, "What about my new partner? Jennifer is pretty stewed at you and some of the rumors that have been making their rounds."

The start of a grin touched his lips, but Harris cut it off abruptly. "Yeah, well, I had to make Hamilton think he had something on me so I sort of let the word spread that she and I were, well, had something going." A wistful smile touched his lips again as he added, "It sure would be nice though if it were true, wouldn't it? She's quite a gal." He gave his head a quick shake to get back on track. "No, there shouldn't be any problem with any leaks getting out with her working beside you. I'm quite sure she's clean, but I'm going to leave the subject of trust between the two of you strictly up to you. You'll have to be the judge of that." The big man looked up and down the alley once again. "We're going to have to break this up before someone sees us standing here like a couple of guilty shoplifting teenagers." He started to turn in order to leave, but he stopped and looked over his shoulder as he added, "Be careful. I don't want to see another report like I did on Sanchez." He gave a quick wave at Jim's boot before adding, "His 'accident' report is in there too."

Before Harris could leave, Jim said, "If you're heading back to the office, you'd better let me get Jennifer away from there first. By now, she's finished the chores I gave her, and with all the free time she's had to think about it, she's probable ready to tear into you." He looked at the captain for a long moment. "I'm going to have to think of something to tell her so she won't blow the lid off." Jim was grinning as he added, "I suppose we could try to get her to stay at your place on Tuesdays and Thursdays so your story would hold up."

Harris grinned back and released a soft sigh. "That sure would be nice. She's one sweet-looking dish. Don't expect my wife would be too happy about the arrangement though."

Jim watched as the captain's grin faded as he turned to walk away. The man was big, but he carried his weight quite well as he rounded the corner and disappeared around the side of the delivery truck. He didn't move from the spot where he'd been standing as he ran the unexpected events through his mind. No matter how many times he ran it through his now-anxious mind, he was still having trouble believing it. If he'd been a betting man, he would have made a huge bet that Captain Harris would have been the one to watch, but now he was finding out that he had a firm ally in the man. Then again, he thought, does he really have that kind of ally in his boss? His brow furrowed once more as the thought hit him that maybe this whole thing was a setup to make sure Harris would be the first one to receive any new information he might uncover. He shook his head and moved away from the sweeper. He saw Harris had just reached the street and was turning the corner as headed for the longer route back to the office. He moved beside the street sweeper and tried to appear nonchalant as he started back. He didn't notice the light blue import that was parked in the street at the end of the alley. He saw nothing unusual with the car or the way the lean man with black hair observed his captain as the man headed back to his office. Harris had no idea that he was being watched as he headed back to his office. Jim also didn't see that the man was quite interested him as well as he began moving back down the alley in the direction they'd come from.

The street was in heavy use as he headed for the end of the block, in order to cross safely, his cell phone suddenly sent tingles down his leg as it vibrated. It took a moment before he realized what was happening because his mind was running in circles because of the kind of information he'd just gotten from the captain.

His caller wasn't interested in any long winded conversations over the phone but he was certainly willing to meet with Jim in order to give him a quick update on the project he'd been given only days earlier. Many rumors had been going around about some of the crimes he suspected Williams had been involved in. In order to get a little more information out of the confusion and to make some sense out of this mess he had contacted one of his snitches. The man's main concern was 'bring money'.

Clarence gave the appearance of being a senior citizen when in reality he was only in the later stages of the forties. A lifetime of drugs and booze had aged the man but his redeeming feature was his ability to get information where many others had failed.

The man was standing between several buildings that housed a small tire store on one side and a not-so-busy pizza place on the other side. He was nervously pacing as he waited and as the detective pulled up to the curb there was an obvious look of stress on his face as well as a brief show of relief.

Jim found it a little off when the man refused to come out into the open as he stepped out of his unmarked car but he accepted it considering the nature of the man as well as the type of information he was attempting to sell.

After scanning the street as well as the fronts of the buildings for any ominous, suspicious or threatening presence, and coming up negative, Jim stepped into the narrow corridor. While Jim had been taking time to check his surroundings Clarence had retreated farther into the narrow opening. Jim gave little thought to it as he left the sidewalk and quickly advanced on the man.

Clarence was more nervous than he normally had been on earlier meetings but, with his mind still working on the problems he'd recently discovered, Jim ignored these suspicious actions. Now face to face with his snitch Jim quickly asked the same questions he'd asked while on the phone earlier. More than once the man stumbled over his words but was making no sense until, in frustration, Jim finally held up his hand to stop that rambling.

"What's going on here? You stated over the phone that you had some good information for me if the money I had offered earlier was still there. Well, I'm here and I have the cash, like I promised, but the troubles seems to be coming from your end. Let's get to it. What have you got for me?"

Clarence took a step back, which placed him tightly against the wall of the tire shop. Jim had seen how nervous the man had been but now it almost appeared that he was having a panic attack. He was now sweating freely and his right hand was pressing tightly against his chest. Jim now also noticed that he was staring in the direction of the back alley.

Jim followed his gaze and saw two men walking in their direction. The walls were a bit over four feet apart and it was clear that these two men would need much more room if they were to attempt to walk side by side.

Before he even had time to become uneasy with the arrival of the two men a scuffling sound of shoes on the front end of the passageway brought his head around. The light was behind them making it difficult to identify any of the members of the trio coming in his direction from the sidewalk side of the small alleyway.

The men arrived simultaneously and they all stopped just out of reach. It only took Jim several seconds to realize who these visitors were, and what they apparently wanted. He finally got a good look at the last arrival and saw that it was none other than the man he wanted to desperately to put behind bars.

Nothing was said for a long moment as both sides studied their counterparts. Jim was the first one to speak as he acknowledged the leader of the men surrounding him. "Well, I can see that you are finally out in the open, Williams. I'm surprised to see you out in broad daylight like this. Here I thought vampires usually slept during the day time."

The frown on the man's face didn't change as the he grated out, "Can that crap, will you? You've got a big mouth that we just might have to do something about and I think that today is a good day for that. You've been pushing me around for quite a while and I don't like it. As a matter of fact I'm tired of it."

He tried to give the impression of being deep in thought for several seconds before he added, "You've really become a pain and it looks like I just might have to do something about it right now. This is such a nice location, so if we.....well, if we just happened to see you shaking down poor Clarence here, well, we'd have no choice. You know, it would be our responsibility, as upstanding citizens to take care of him, wouldn't it?"

Williams turned to the man standing against the wall, who was visibly shaken as he tried to look small in hopes of being missed when the action started. With his finger pointing at the frightened man he made it a point to slowly lower his thumb, as if he were holding a gun. "Clarence, if you know what's good for you then you know this never happened and you were never here. Now beat it and make sure you keep your mouth shut if you know what's good for you. How long you live will depend on how well you keep quiet."

The scared snitch shot out of that open space and seconds later the sounds of his feet going down the back alley was all that was heard. With the first sign of the man's departure Jim moved to place his back against the wall. His heart was hammering because right at this moment he could see no way out of this situation with less than a severe beating, although he was sure that they intended to go far beyond that.

Upon arrival he'd put his jacket on as he'd gotten out of the car and right now his hand was under his jacket right at the belt line. The grip of his pistol was no longer being held down with the leather strap and his fingers had already begun easing the pistol out of the holster.

He was reluctant to pull his gun because he knew the others would also be pulling triggers on him. It was clear that every one of the five men was enjoying this confrontation, although most of the joy was clearly written on the face of Williams.

With his gun still resting on the edge of the holster, but firmly in his hand, he decided to wait until it was clear what they intended to do. He was very confident about what they had in mind but he wasn't all that much of a hurry to speed things up. He'd always known that there was always that chance of getting killed while on duty but right now if this was going to be the end for him then he wanted to make sure that he took Williams along with him. Right at this moment he was still standing behind his bodyguards, leaving him no chance to take out the man before being filled with lead from those guards. He needed to take that kingpin along with him if his time had arrived now.

"You're sure quiet now. Not like you were in court a couple of weeks ago when you were testifying against me. There you couldn't shut up long enough to take a breath."

The men fronting Williams moved slightly aside as their boss pressed forward enough to make sure his intended victim was able to see him clearly. The scowl on his face seemed to radiate hate as he presented enough of his body that Jim was given a small amount of hope that he'd find enough of that body when he started firing his pistol. He stared back as the man contemplated a series of actions he might want to be able to take on this man who had hunted him for so long.

"When we searched your apartment earlier this week I was hoping that you'd at least have a dog, or maybe a cat. That would have made it more interesting when we made you watch as we started to whittle away on the mutt. I'd like to see your reaction if you just had to sit there and squirm while watching as pieces began dropping off."

Jim could see that the man's face was getting shiny and he'd begun breathing faster when he began describing his method of torture. He'd strongly suspected that Williams had been responsible for a number of killings, even if he wasn't the known shooter, but now he was showing how the thought of blood and pain were exciting him. Since the man had blown into town he had been behind the heavy influx of drugs, the increase in prostitution and possibly was even into the matter of sex slavery that he'd heard about lately. Now more than ever, in Jim's mind, he knew it was imperative that Williams needed to be taken out of the picture.

"Come on now, Jimmy Boy. Talk to me. Too bad you aren't real friendly with some broad so we could pick her up and let you watch us taking care of her as well. We could give that gal a lot more activity in one night than you could in a couple of months. When we got tired then we could start on her with a dull knife. All this time you could sit there and watch the entire show. Do you think that would get your attention? Come on speak to me. What do you think?"

Jim tried to keep his face blank because he knew that Williams was simply trying to anger him, although there was not a doubt that this character was very capable of doing the things he had just referred to. With a slow shake of his head he answered the man, "What do I think? I think you are sick. You need to turn yourself in and get some medical help. Right between the ears."

Jim knew things were about to happen and although he was hesitant about starting a gunfight he also knew he wasn't going to get a better chance to take out Williams before his own end came about. Getting out of this situation alive was not something he was contemplating any longer but that narrow spread between the bodyguards at least was giving him a chance of getting Williams first.

His gun was still under his jacket but now in his hand so all he needed was to twist his wrist enough so it would put the muzzle in line with Williams's body. He almost had to smile when he gave thought to the damage his jacket would sustain because when he pulled the trigger and sent several bullets out through he was going to find a lot of lead going through his jacket in the other direction. His finger was tightening on the trigger because he knew they were about done having their fun and it was about to hit the fan.

His finger was showing white around the trigger in anticipation when suddenly one of his bodyguards, who had come from the back alley, pointed past Jim and exclaimed, "Hey Boss. Look there."

Jim felt an exhilaration that almost made him finish the pull on the trigger. Sitting in full view at the front of the passageway was a regulation black and white. Two officers were watching what was happening and the officer in the passenger seat clearly had his fingers wrapped around the barrel of the .12 Ga shotgun that was secured to the dash. The facial expressions on these two officers gave a strong indication of what they were going to allow to happen.

Jim immediately saw the reaction on Williams face because they both knew if a shooting started right here and now, which openly involved officers in their official duty, that there was going to be a lot more pressure on them, then if just one detective was mysteriously found dead in an alley.

The man was really scowling now as he attempted to think his way out of this predicament but he clearly wasn't having much success. After almost a minute of glaring at Jim the man finally growled his order to leave by the back alley. It was clear that he didn't want to pass anywhere near the police car. As he pushed past Jim he stopped and poked his finger into Jim's chest and made sure his intention was clear. "You and I aren't finished with this yet. I'm going to turn the dogs loose on you. You've been running around too long but that is about to end. Make sure your will is made out because you are finished." He gave one last push with his finger before he rushed to get into the middle of his group of bodyguards as they pushed to leave the area.

Jim watched as the man caught up with, and passed, two of his guards then proceeded out of sight. Jim viewed the men leaving with the knowledge that he'd never come as close to death as he just had. He eased his pistol back into his holster and easily noted the tremor in his hand. He wanted to get out of the heated confined space he'd been tricked into but first he needed to take a number of deep breaths before he trusted his feet to do as he requested. He's often heard the phrase 'saved by the skin of your teeth' but now it held a lot more meaning to him because he really knew how it felt.

The officers were still sitting as they had been but now the intense look that had been there was no longer there. The driver was even smiling when Jim stepped up to the car door. He leaned down so he could converse with the men as he began to express his gratitude for their timely arrival. "I don't know how you managed to show up just when you did but I do want you to know that you just saved my life by showing up when you did. I don't know how to thank you properly but just know that my appreciation is there in full force."

The driver leaned forward as he addressed the detective, "I'm Officer Tanning and my partner is Officer Mayes. We were ordered to kind of keep an eye on you by Captain Harris after he saw you leaving the parking lot. When you took off instead of coming into the building he gave us a call and said there might be a problem. Looks like he knew what he was talking about. It sure didn't look any too friendly in there."

Jim had no problem nodding his head in agreement with that statement. He tossed in another round of thanks before he headed for his car. This had been a very close call and he was well aware that the next time Williams had a chance at him it was going to be done with a lot more planning and thought. This confrontation had failed because Williams had some big need to brag and threaten but the next time was going to end up differently, if Williams had anything to say about it.

Chapter 6

Jennifer was just coming out of the captain's office when Jim entered the building. There was no mistaking the angry look on her face as she looked around for the object of her consternation. Jim quickly moved in her direction, but just as he got within ten feet of her, he saw her looking past him. As her eyes widened, he saw her anger begin to show itself even more. He took a quick look behind him and saw Harris just coming around the corner from the commanders office.

Before she could say a word to anyone or get anyone's attention, Jim grabbed her arm firmly and steered her away from the confrontation that had been brewing in her mind. She tried to pull her arm away from his grip but very quickly found that she wasn't going to get away from him that way. The angry look on her face became mixed with surprise as he put himself in the way, used his body to block Harris's view of her, and forcibly began to push her into an unused cubicle. Jennifer was so stunned by his actions that her reaction was to drop her jaw and simply do as he ordered.

Fire was dancing in her eyes, but she heeded his urging to stem the flow of words that were at the tip of her tongue. The angry look on her face changed as it took on a mild look of curiosity. Jim looked over the five-foot walls to make sure they wouldn't be overheard.

Even though he was sure they were alone and wouldn't be heard more than five feet away, he made sure his voice was soft as he said, "I just got some surprising news. Until I have time to brief you on some of it, I want you to treat the captain just like you always have. His safety, as well as yours and mine, depends on what gets said from now on. Try to act normally so you don't get anyone's attention focused on him." He saw her mouth opening and he knew she was going to object, so he quickly touched his forefinger to her soft lips. His face lowered until he was looking straight into her eyes. "Listen, sweetheart. This is very important. Please trust me on this. I'll explain all of it later. Something has come up that has sort of blown things apart. This is not the time or place to start a riot. All right?"

As soon as he removed his finger from her lips, her tongue was sliding along where the pad of his finger had been pressing lightly. She saw immediately that he had seen that unconscious action of her tongue, and now it angered her that he was just looking at her with that all-knowing look on his face. Her face began to turn red as she struggled to find something to say. The only thing she could think of to say was "I told you not to call me sweetheart." She watched him turning to leave before she added, "Butthead." She almost returned the grin he showed her before he turned the corner on his way back to his cubicle. She touched her lips once more with the tip of her tongue, and then a soft smile began to show as she looked out of the cubicle and saw his broad back moving away from her. Her smile grew a little wider as she, just a tiny bit louder, repeated, "Butthead!"

Jim was itching to look at the papers wrapped around his leg inside his boot as he sat at his desk, but he didn't make a move toward the papers. He knew he was getting a little paranoid, but until he knew who and what he was working with, he didn't mind the feeling. He knew it would keep him alert until he got things straightened out in his mind.

The phone call from fireman Ramon Pena was once more on his mind, and he didn't notice Jennifer standing in the doorway of his cubicle until she moved in and put her hand on his shoulder. He looked up suddenly and saw the anger was gone now from her face. Only a look of curiosity that was mixed with a touch of anxiety or apprehension was all that remained.

Jennifer looked at him for a short spell before she bent lower and whispered, "Just what's going on? I just talked to Captain Harris. He called me into his office, but all he said was that he wasn't going to be able to give me a ride home tonight. He seemed so different, but as soon as I opened my mouth to ask him a question, he said he was busy and for me to beat it. What in the world is going on here?"

Jim frowned as he pointed to the cubicle walls and leaned in her direction as he whispered back, "Can't talk now. The walls may have ears." He glanced down at his watch and then he said in a normal tone, "Three forty-five. Well, I want to make a stop at the home of a witness before quitting time. I want to pick up some papers from a fireman called Ramon. If you're ready to go home, you can ride along. On the way back, I'll drop you off at your place. Maybe I can get some questions answered on the way." He looked at the notes on his desk for a moment before he looked up at her again. "I'll meet you at the car in about ten minutes." He looked quizzically at her for a moment before he softly whispered, "You didn't say anything to Harris concerning that certain subject, did you, sweetheart?"

Jennifer quickly answered in a soft voice. "I didn't have a chance to ask him anything before he told me to beat it. No, I didn't spill any of the beans. I just wish I knew what was going on here." She started to turn away but stopped as though she had remembered to say something. She opened her mouth, but instead of saying anything, she just stood and looked down at him because it had been very clear where his eyes had been focused when she'd turned away from him. She saw his big grin coming, and then she shook her head and said, "Butthead." She didn't miss seeing his grin widen before she walked away in the direction of her own area. She was also aware of the muscles tugging at the corners of her own mouth as she walked right past Salina on her way to get her purse and lock her desk.

Salina turned and watched Jennifer as she walked by. She wondered what could have been so intriguing and humorous that it would have brought that look to her face.

Jennifer was itching to start asking questions when she got into the Ford, but before she could say anything at all, she saw a short printed note in Jim's hand. When he handed it to her, she saw that it simply read 'Car bugged??? Don't say anything important.' She stared at the note in dumbfounded confusion as he pulled out into traffic. When she looked over at him in anticipation of seeing that usual grin of his, which would show her that he was joking, she saw the sober and thoughtful side of him instead.

She tagged along with him when he walked up to the Penas' house, but there was only time for one quick question before Ramon answered the door. All she learned was that, yes, he was serious about that note. She tried to get another question answered on the way back to the car, but his attention was riveted on the sheets of paper he'd gotten from the man.

Jim didn't have much to say on the way to her apartment. When he pulled into one of the few parking places available, he took a notepad from the glove box. She leaned closer as she watched him printing neatly. She was stunned at first, but then she didn't hesitate to nod her head when she read "Your place not bugged!!! Talk there???"

Jennifer climbed the steps ahead of him, and he couldn't help but marvel at her legs and backside. The problem came when his eyes wandered higher to her waist and upper hips, and the sight caused him to frown and to mentally shake his head. He had an intense desire to ask about the unusual thickness of her waist, but instead, he bit his tongue and simply watched her calves and the movement coming from under the back of her skirt as she climbed the steps.

When he stood beside her on the landing as she fished for her keys, he saw that she was wearing a smile of amusement. But she quickly made it clear that she wasn't going to let him in on her little secret. As he watched the little extra sway of her hips when she entered her home, he wondered if it didn't have something to do with the added show on the way up the steps. He'd watched her walking many times before and had never seen that much action before. He took a deep breath and let it out with a loud whoosh before he followed her into the living room of her apartment.

She moved to the refrigerator, and several moments later, she was handing Jim a drink. Her smile appeared genuine as she said, "I only have vodka and orange juice. Hope you like it. I'm going to get out of these work clothes. You can have a seat there and get ready for a lot of questions because I've got them lined up and waiting." She started to enter the bedroom, but she stopped and stared thoughtfully at him for a long moment before she slowly moved through the doorway and carefully closed the door behind her.

When she reappeared ten minutes later, Jim almost dropped the remainder of his drink. His drink had really gotten his attention when he took his first sip because although it had been orange juice and vodka, he quickly found that the amount of orange juice she had added had just been sufficient to add some color. He forgot about the drink completely when he saw her coming out of the bedroom.

When he saw her standing there in the matching skirt and blouse, he was completely stunned because there wasn't a hint of the thick waist he'd been seeing since she'd started working in his division. Instead of the thick waist, he saw a slim, beautifully curved waist that was in perfect proportion to the rest of her. It made her well-formed breasts appear even more desirable, which he hadn't thought possible. When he watched her walking back to the refrigerator, it printed an image on his mind he knew would be very hard to erase.

Only when she started speaking did he finally realize that she was watching him. He closed his mouth and tried to stop looking, but the change was so dramatic that he was having a great deal of trouble taking his eyes off her figure.

She was laughing when she said, "All right, now let's get our minds back on the problem. You've got a lot of questions to answer. Remember?"

Jim took a deep breath. "You want me to get my mind back on the problems at hand, huh? Yes, ma'am. But never has mortal man ever been given such a monumental task as such as you have attempted to impose upon me." He took another deep breath before he added, "But first of all, let's get a very important subject taken care of first. What's with the thick padding for a waist? My word! What a body! And you're hiding it?"

Her smile faded. "All right. Do you remember when I told you that I worked hard in school because I intended to make it good in this field? Well, I intend to be a success, but I also intend to make sure that it's because of what I know and do, not because someone likes my figure or my face." She looked as though she was getting ready for a fight when she added, "Can you accept that?"

He finally forced himself to meet her eyes. "Yes, sweetheart. I sure can, and I admire you for taking that stance. It's got to be hard to do what you've done. Yes, I can accept that."

Jim saw the urge to fight leaving her eyes as she stood in front of him. She reached for the glass in his hand, but he said, "Just do a refill with the orange juice. I think I'll need a clear mind when I start going through the papers I brought along."

She took a quick look at his hands. "What papers? You weren't carrying anything in your hands when you came up here." There was laughter in her eyes as she hesitated for a moment. "The only thing I saw you carrying in your hands was your bottom jaw.

Jim was forced to grin as he recalled his view coming up the steps. He knew she had hit the nail on the head. He was still grinning as he reached for his boot top. "Well, all I can say in my defense is that there was some beautiful movement going on in front of me." Jennifer's grin abruptly left her face as she watched him pulling the sheaf of papers out of his boot. Despite all the questions she intended to fire at her new partner, she simply stood quietly with her mouth hanging open.

Jim didn't say anything more until he was sitting at her kitchen table and shuffling through the papers and trying to get the curl out of them. Several of the first sheets he glanced at were concerned only with the accidental death of Sanchez, as it was reported by the rookie, and he placed them to one side. While he started reading the next sheet, Jennifer wasted no time in sitting down across from him at the table. She quickly picked up the papers he'd placed off to the side and began reading through the accident report.

As she read farther into the report, the effects of her puzzlement began to show on her forehead in the form of deep lines. She glanced at him after getting halfway through the report in her hands, but he was obviously quite engrossed in the report he was holding in his own hands.

Not a word was exchanged between them for the next hour while they read through, and digested, the entire sheath of papers. Finally, Jim leaned back in his chair and stared at all the information lying on the table between them.

Jennifer looked at him with furrowed brows. "Where did all of this stuff come from? Some of this is really classified stuff. Nobody should have access to material like this. How'd you end up with stuff like this?"

Jim clasped his hands behind his head as he attempted to decide where to start passing on all the information he had decided to share with her. He closed his eyes. "I had a long talk with your lover this afternoon. He's turned out to be something completely different than I'd ever expected."

Jennifer's brow furrowed even more as she tried to figure out what Jim was talking about. Suddenly, she made the connection, and she made a hissing sound that would have scared a cat.

When he opened his eyes, he saw Jennifer's eyes were only slits as she glared at him. He forced a grin back as he closed his eyes once more and started to formulate his next presentation for her behalf.

Before Jim had a chance to begin the thinking he needed to do, Jennifer's icy voice broke into his concentration. Her eyes were still slits as she glared at him and said, "Listen, butthead. He isn't now, never has been, nor will he ever be, my lover. Got that?"

Jim was trying to show that he was contrite about calling Harris her lover, but he also knew he was far from succeeding at the task. When he looked up at Jennifer, he easily saw that she was having her own problem hiding her own grin. It was clear that she was getting just as much enjoyment over their mutual harassment as he was.

The grin slowly faded from his face as he said, "I talked to Harris today, and what I learned has really changed who I'm going to have to concentrate on, as far as exposing." He hesitated for a moment and then he added, "Unless this is some kind of elaborate scheme, and I'm being set up by Harris." Jim sat and stared at the papers littering the top of her table before he continued by telling her everything that occurred between the captain and himself at that "back alley meeting." When he finished, he looked at the woman who was sitting very subdued and quiet across from him. He looked into her eyes for a long moment before he added, 'It's getting to look pretty ugly here. I want you to think long and hard if you want to continue working with me on this case. Harris is sure that Sanchez was murdered because he was getting too close to someone or something. If you decide to continue beside me in this case, I think it's only fair to warn you that this case could be hazardous to your health. Like permanently."

He hadn't intended to tell her about the incident with Williams earlier in the day, but on second thought, he wanted to impress on her how dangerous the situation was. She appeared shocked when he gave her a quick rundown on what had happened. For a long moment, she simply stared in his direction with her eyes open wide. He knew he had achieved his objective.

The young, curvaceous, and blond-haired Sullivan showed she was taking his warning seriously. But she was still quick to tell him she intended to stick by him on this case. She demonstrated her eagerness to help by quickly placing the Sanchez accident report in front of him and saying, "There has to be something more to this accident. It shows that Sanchez was reading over several reports as he was walking in the direction of his car when he was hit. It shows that he was walking north when a south-bound car swerved to miss a jaywalker. According to the reporting officer, there were no skid marks because it happened so fast there wasn't any time to hit the brakes." She looked up at Jim with her eyes wide as she said, "That's rubbish. Even though I don't have a car right now, I've owned several in the past. And I think if I was afraid of hitting a pedestrian, the first thing I'd do would be to turn so I would miss hitting that person, and a second later I'd be jamming on the brakes. From the looks of this picture, this guy plowed into Sanchez's parked car, just as he was getting into it, at more than the legal speed limit with no hint of any kind of brake use. It even says here that the driver of the second car wasn't even charged or ticketed because it had been an unavoidable accident. The officer did report that they never found the jaywalker or even anyone who had seen one."

Jim said, "That's probably the reason Harris said he didn't think it was an accident either. He's made me wonder about quite a few people that I hadn't given second thought to before now, and for a while, he even made me think twice about trusting you." He ignored her raised eyebrows as he continued. "Right now, I'm even questioning Harris because until I can find out for sure where everyone and everything fits, I know my life depends on what I do and who I trust." He looked around the room for a long moment before he looked into her brown eyes. "If you could put a number on it, I suppose I'd have to say that I trust you about 99 percent, and I hope you have the same reservations with the people you know because that will make you just a little more cautious about anything you say or who you decide to trust." He never took his eyes off hers during his little speech, and they maintained eye contact as he added, "This is serious, sweetheart. We're talking about life or death here. This isn't a case where you can say 'Oops, I won't do that again' because you won't be around long enough to even make that kind of mistake a second time."

He looked at her intently for several seconds. "Well, if you don't understand the seriousness of this by now, and I think you do, then it won't make any difference because we'll both be targets for some big guns before long." Jim hesitated for a moment. "I think we'll be targets before long anyway. But at least now we have the edge on what they're trying to pull, so we just might be able to prolong it just a little. At least on the results they want." He leaned against the back of the chair and took a deep breath. "Now that's enough with the speechmaking. Now, if you're still sure that you want to stick with it, let's get busy and see if we can solve some of these puzzles."

Jim took a sheet of paper from the pile and turned it over. He was thinking out loud as he began to write. "First of all, we have a report of shots and evidence of violence down south. We now have got two witnesses as well as a fair description of three cars. Number one is the small car. That one was a yellow VW. Number two is the car that chased car number one as well as number three. That number two car was a silver or light gray Lincoln. Number three is the car I believe was a witness to a possible execution and was chased north at least as far as the freeway intersection. That one was a late model tan Chevrolet Suburban."

He moved his pen lower on the sheet. "We've got the so-called accident that killed Sanchez. We've got the strong possibility of our own department being bugged." He suddenly raised his head and looked into the pretty face of his new partner. "Oh yeah, I almost forgot. Just after my little meeting with the commander, I got a call from one of the clerks at the first convenience store that we checked out. She said she was taking a cigarette break in front of the store when the cars blew by heading north. She gave the same description of the two cars speeding north that Pena did. So now on top of all that, you've just got to add that little meeting I had with Williams today."

For a long moment, Jim stared at the notes he'd written before he began once again. "I had Wales and Meyer connected to a shooting, which the police have now listed as 'gang related.' The witness I talked to had seen enough to pick them out of a mug shot book, but now they say the man is 'no longer available.' And they're also saying the evidence I'd collected was now contaminated and is no longer admissible." He stopped and looked up at her for several seconds. "All of this sorta makes you wonder, doesn't it?"

Jennifer didn't answer in words, but the look on her face told him that she agreed. She leaned back in her chair as she stretched her arms over her head and tried to relieve the strain on her back. That movement from her immediately made him loose all track of what he'd been thinking.

Jennifer caught the look on his face, but she was able to stifle the laughter that tried to shake itself loose from deep within her.

Jim took a deep breath and tried to shake some thoughts out of his head. He pushed himself to his feet and looked down at his partner. "I've got to hit the road. I want to make a couple of calls yet, and if I don't do it pretty soon, it'll get to be too late."

Jennifer surprised him when she said, "You can make your calls from here if you want to. And if you don't mind the couch, you can stay here as well."

He looked over at her couch for several seconds. "If I stayed here, do you think I'd be satisfied with sleeping on the couch? No, I think I'd better slide on out of here while my mind is still functioning. That way, I won't be disappointed, and you won't be angry with me. Besides, it's going to be a long day tomorrow."

He stopped by the door, and as he looked back, he said, "Lock the door when I leave, and I'll see you at work tomorrow, sweetheart."

Jennifer twisted the security lock after he left, and then she leaned her head back against the door. She released a soft sigh before she uttered a disappointed "Butthead."

Chapter 7

It was almost noon when Jennifer stepped into Jim's cubicle and found him staring angrily at a pile of crumpled sheets that littered the floor near his wastebasket. She watched as his frown deepened for a moment and then almost disappeared, only to return seconds later with more intensity. He was leaning forward in his chair with his elbows on his knees and was holding several sheets of paper loosely in his hand. The angry look never left his face even when he looked up and saw Jennifer standing in the opening. He sat back in his chair, but as his back touched the fabric of the backrest, the paper slipped out of his hand and spiraled to the floor. He glanced down at it, but he didn't make any effort to pick it up.

The papers were lying right by one of the wheels of his chair. To keep it from being run over, just in case it was something important, Jennifer bent over and retrieved it. Without looking at it, she extended her arm and offered it to Jim.

The angry look returned to his face when he saw the paper once more, and he turned his back on her as he pulled his desk drawer open.

Her eyes grew wide when he showed his back so brusquely because even after only one day of being his partner, she'd had the strong feeling that she could do enough to straighten him out that they would make a good team. She'd also had some very personal and warm thoughts concerning the two of them after he'd left her apartment last night, but now his action not only surprised her but also pained her. She could feel the tears beginning to form, but as she placed the papers on his desk, she got a quick glimpse of the subject of the letter. Her pain was completely forgotten, and her tears were quickly wiped away; they too were forgotten. She stared at the big black bold heading, but the only word she was able to focus clearly on was the word "Suspended."

As the word "suspended" rolled off her tongue, he turned around and faced her. He stared into her eyes for a short moment. "That's right. Looks like I pulled one string too often and just a little too hard." He saw Jennifer was going to offer her thoughts on the subject, but before she could say a word, he reached up and touched his fingers to her lips. Then with one hand, he pointed at the wall while the other one pointed at his ear. She quickly acknowledged his meaning, and when he nodded his head in the direction of the door, Jennifer didn't hesitate to lead the way.

"What in the world is going on, Jim?" She was quick to ask as they moved away from the doorway of the police station. Her face showed that she was still having trouble believing what she'd read.

Jim motioned for her to head in the direction of his unmarked car, but when they got near the parking lot, they saw a sign on the car's windshield that made it very clear that the car had been impounded. He stood in the middle of the parking lot, and he tried to contain his temper while he stared at the car that was out of his reach now. Several plainclothes officers walked by them and softly snickered when they recognized him. Apparently, they already knew what had happened in the commander's office several hours earlier. Their faces quickly lost their grins when Jim whirled around and faced them.

He didn't bother turning back to face Jennifer when he said, "Well, Harris wanted me to come to his office several hours ago, and I guess now is as good a time as any. I need that car for a couple more days yet."

His face was hard and lined with anger as he entered the police facility once more. Jennifer was on his heels as she tried to find out what had caused his suspension. She was also trying to get him calmed down enough so he wouldn't find fifteen officers sitting on him to restrain him.

When Jim stormed through the door that led into his boss's office, he found Captain Harris staring back at him. Jennifer saw that if a prize had been offered for the angriest appearance, then they'd have been satisfied to share that prize. Jim stood in front of the desk and glared down at the big, seated man while he sat and glared back.

Jennifer stood wide-eyed off to the side and behind the man who had only been her partner for a little over twenty-four hours. She was afraid that these two men were about to come to blows and tried to tell both of them to calm down. She tried to make a case for both of them by saying that everything could be worked out if they talked things over, but she immediately found both men glaring at her. She dropped her eyes and slowly took a deep breath as she moved one more step to the rear.

When Harris began talking, his voice was short, clipped, and heavy with anger. "I want your badge, gun, and car keys right now." He stared at his former officer for over a minute before the man started to move. As the called-for items were slammed onto the desk top, the man continued to say, "Gray, you stuck your nose into the wrong place for the last time." He reached up and touched his ear with his left hand. "I wasn't joking about what I told you yesterday." The man continued to bellow out his reprimand as he took the confiscated items off the desk and placed them in the bottom drawer of his desk. When he straightened out, he was holding a shoe box and he held it out for Jim. As the man took the small box, he said, "I don't know how long this suspension will last. It may just be for a week or two, or then again it just may be permanent. All I'm going to say now is, don't call me, I'll call you." He stood and stretched his back for a moment before he made a simple shooing motion with his hand.

Jennifer's eyes grew even wider when Jim simply turned around and started for the door. She had been expecting that smelly stuff to hit the fan, but he hadn't said a word throughout the entire tirade. She saw that Jim had stopped and was waiting for her to exit first. When she didn't move, he reached for her arm and helped her out of the captain's office. She had intended to make her own thoughts known to this big, pompous jerk, but now she was finding herself propelled down the hall and away from the man's office.

Her anger from being manhandled in such a manner was beginning to boil over, and as she turned her head to stop his actions, she found his fingers pressing against her lips. She quickly realized that he was in fact in control of what he was doing and that the action of keeping her silent was, in all possibilities, for the good of both of them. Now fully confused, she felt her anger quickly dissipating and being replaced with confusion as they stepped through the doorway of the building and felt the furnace blast of the Arizona summer heat. She matched him pace for pace, but her steps slowed down when she saw him heading directly for his former assigned car. She stopped walking when she saw him taking the impound sign off the Ford and staring at the covered parking where the higher officials were assigned shaded parking. She saw the clear look on his face of what he'd like to do with the sign, but instead, she saw him opening the door and tossing the sign in the back. She opened the passenger door and joined him in the vehicle. She knew she was violating the rules now as he much as was by just being inside this car, and it made her more than just a little nervous.

Her nervousness was forgotten when she watched him opening the shoe box because she quickly saw that under the papers, most of which were blank, were his gun, badge, and car keys. She stared at the shoe box with her mouth hanging open until she finally realized Jim was speaking to her.

Jim reached into the box, which he'd placed on the seat between them, and quickly placed his gun back into his belt holster. He took the sticky note off his badge and dropped it into the box. The last metallic item he took out was his car keys. He looked over at Jennifer and saw the amazed look on her face as he retrieved his precious items. He hesitated for a moment before he said, "You didn't see a single thing that happened here, and from now on, you have no idea where I might be. Have you got that?"

Jennifer was quick to point to her ears and then at the dashboard of the car. Jim grounded her fears when he said, "I asked Harris to run a surveillance check on the car. It came out clean."

He reached into the box and rummaged through the papers until he found the sheet he wanted. He held it up for her to see. "This is proof that our illustrious commander put through an awful lot of phone calls to none other than Tom Williams himself. It's a mighty thin piece of evidence, but when you add up a lot of small pieces we've found lying around, they can make a very big case." He saw Jennifer had picked up the sticky note that had been stuck to his badge. He saw she was trying to figure out what the printed lettering, "Tnk X2," was supposed to represent, and he quickly said, "Captain Harris was telling me to think twice before I let anyone know that I still had this badge and that I was still working on the case he assigned me to originally. We had a very late-night meeting at his home last night. I had to make sure the stakeouts were well settled in their cars before I went in under their noses."

He didn't stop talking when Jennifer loudly repeated, "Stakeouts?" Instead, he just nodded his head and said, "What I need for you to do is go back in there and see what else you can dig up. Harris and I both think this shooting that you and I started investigating yesterday is linked to Williams, and we're starting to make them just a little nervous. I'm absolutely positive that's why I've been placed on 'unpaid leave until farther notice.'"

Jennifer said, "All my life I've wanted to become a police officer. I wanted to make a difference for the people out there, and now I find that it's just as dirty inside police headquarters as it is out on the street." She shook her head slowly as she stared at her knees.

Jim slowly reached over and touched her arm. "Just remember, sweetheart, that you don't hear anything about the thousands of good officers who are out there doing their job in the best way they can. It only takes one rotten apple to spoil what the good officers have been building all along." He watched her wiping a spot of water from her brow as she frowned at what he'd said. It was then that he realized they'd been sitting inside the car with the doors closed while the sun was unmercifully beating down on the metal skin of the Ford. He slipped the key into the ignition, and seconds later, the air conditioner was pushing the last of the warm air out of the air ducts. Even the movement of the warm air felt good on his face now that his mind had been alerted to the heat inside the car.

He looked around the parking lot for a moment. "Harris is going to try to get some more evidence on Hamilton today. I want you to pick up all the information that Harris is able to get today, and then I'll meet you at that little bar I told you about on Bell Road. I don't think anyone will bother with you yet because right now you look like an innocent bystander in this little feud between the officials who rule and me." He looked seriously at her for a long moment before he added a few more items to the list of things he wanted her to do. When he started again, he emphasized the first word so she would realize the risk she was taking. "*But* I want you to make sure no one knows about what you are planning to do and that you aren't being followed. Sweetheart, I don't think I have to tell you that lives are at risk here. My life is at risk. Captain Harris's life is at risk as well as your own." He looked in the direction of the police building. "Right now, I think you'd better get back in there before they link you with the opposition and start watching you as well."

Jennifer quietly stepped out of the car and then watched as the Ford moved into the street and disappeared into traffic. She turned around and started for the cool interior of the police building. When she looked up at the glass-encased building, she saw the big form of her captain standing there and her smooth way of walking suddenly faltered. He was standing by the window with his hands on his hips, and his eyes were focused directly on her.

When Jim stepped into the cool confines of Riddle's Bell Bar, he wasn't very happy. All he'd managed to accomplish during the afternoon was to photocopy all the evidence he'd been able to accumulate and send it to a lawyer friend who he was sure wasn't remotely involved with Williams or any of his shady buddies. He wasn't exactly pleased with his progress that afternoon, but at least he knew that if something "happened" to him, the evidence against Williams would still be available. He made his way to an isolated table stuck into a corner by the rear wall and dropped onto the lumpy bench seat.

Jim was on his second beer when Jennifer stepped into the dimly lit building and tried to find him through the near darkness. He quickly stood and waved his arm until she spotted him.

She was almost breathless as she slid her shapely bottom across the cracked plastic seat. She didn't bother looking around to see who was watching her as she reached inside her purse and pushed several papers across at him because she was confident that he'd already satisfied himself about the other customers who were inside the bar. She didn't bother with small talk like "Boy, it's hot out there today," but instead, she quickly said, "Captain Harris handed me these papers and let me know that you were to get them ASAP. I didn't even take the time to look at them." She gave her order to the barmaid, and she felt her hackles rise when the young and shapely blonde very rarely took her eyes off

Jennifer's suspended partner as she stood by the table and waited for the order. Jennifer felt her blood pressure rising as the barmaid stood with her hip pressing against his shoulder. She was just about ready to throw real daggers instead of just staring at the woman.

Jim was just finishing his hamburger and was washing it down with his third bottle of beer when several men stepped into the bar. They looked around and quickly spotted Jim and Jennifer sitting along the back wall.

When the men stopped at their table, there weren't any greetings offered. Instead, they heard the lead man saying, "I want to ask you a few questions, but I also want you to know that anything you say can be used against you and that you can have a lawyer present if you want one. You know how the rest of it goes." There wasn't any friendliness in the man's eyes or his voice, nor was there any reluctance shown as he continued to say, "Where were you about an hour ago?"

The men had interrupted the barmaid as she was checking on their drinks, and the two men were quick to show their displeasure when the shapely blonde interrupted them and said, "This guy's been sitting here since just before four o'clock. I know that for a fact because he opened the door for me when I was coming in for my shift. That was at three forty-five, and he ain't left his chair other than for goin' to the can."

Jim slowly slipped out of his seat. When he stood up, Jennifer saw he was looking down at their lead man. He didn't waste any time trying to find out why they were looking for him. His first question was "What's going on? Who sent you after me?"

The second plainclothes officer looked at his partner for a long moment before he finally received a curt nod. He turned to the supposedly suspended officer and said, "Well, you're going to find out sooner or later anyway, so I guess it won't hurt anything to tell you." He sent a quick glance in Jennifer's direction as if he wished she wasn't present at the time, but then he added,

"Someone driving a car that looked an awful lot like yours was involved in a hit-and-run just a little after four. The witnesses reported seeing a driver who looked a lot like you. They also said there was a female rider along who matched the description of your partner here."

Jim didn't bother with the second man. Instead, he focused his attention on the man in charge. "Like this young lady said, I've been here for a couple of hours already so you go and tell Harris I had nothing to do with any hit-and-run activity."

The men stared at Jim for a long moment before the lead man said, "Well, that's going to be hard to do. Captain Harris was the one who got hit. He's dead." He looked down at the barmaid standing behind Jim. "You're lucky you've got this witness to back up your story." He looked up at Jim. "Just make sure none of you try to leave town. We're going to have a lot more questions for you. All of you."

As the men moved away from the table, Jim slumped down into the seat and stared at the scarred tabletop. Jennifer found she was so much in shock by what she'd heard she didn't even realize how the barmaid was helping her back into her seat across from Jim's. The pretty blonde quietly looked at both of them before she departed to continue on her rounds.

It took several minutes before Jim was able to speak. "It looks like we're getting pretty close to the rotten apple. Sanchez first. Then Harris. I'm positive they're going to come after me next. The first thing they'll probably do is try to put enough pressure on that gal so she'll change her story. Or maybe even make her leave town for places unknown, if they allow her to live. If they can't get me through the legal channels, they'll go after me like they did Harris." He looked up at Jennifer and said, "From now on, you'll have to stay clear of me and make it look like you don't even want anything to do with me." He saw she was going to raise an objection, but he quickly added, "Right now you're the only contact I have in that office. You're going to have to keep your eyes and ears open for anything that will help us nail these…" Jim stopped talking because he found he was too angry and upset to continue. When he had learned of the captain's reasons for being so gruff and loud, he had formed a fresh opinion of the man. He had come to respect the big man a great deal in the last twenty-four hours.

Jim stared at Jennifer for several minutes in total silence before he finally turned in his seat and beckoned for the barmaid. As the blonde stopped by the table, he said, "First of all, why did you tell them I'd been here that long? They're going to be back to question you, and they're not going to be very polite."

The young female ignored Jennifer as she leaned over the edge of the table in Jim's direction, allowing her loose top to hang away from her assets. "I think I'm a good judge of character. Besides that, I like you. If you need someplace to stay for a while until things cool down, I think I could come up with an address." She was smiling softly as she looked into Jim's eyes. "Those clowns don't scare me. You can be sure that my story won't change."

Jennifer found herself getting a little warm under the collar as she watched the barmaid making moves on the man she'd have liked to have made those same moves on for herself. She opened her mouth to tell the barmaid to buzz off, but before she could say anything, she heard Jim telling the woman to call a cab. She didn't miss the little pat he placed on the barmaid's butt as she moved away from the table or the smile he received in return.

"Just what do you think you're doing?" She demanded as soon as the blonde was out of hearing range.

Jim grinned. "Just trying to make sure she doesn't change her story too quick." His face turned serious. "I'm going to have to move fast because from now on, I'm not going to get much room to turn around or much time to do it. You're going to have to find a phone you can call from that won't have a bug attached." He scribbled a phone number on his napkin and slid it across the table. He let her read it several times, and then he tore it up and dropped it into the ashtray and touched a match to the small pile. "I don't have much time because they're going to be after me. So the faster you can get me the word, the longer I'll live. Well, maybe anyhow."

The blonde barmaid moved through the sparse crowd and stopped by their table. She only looked at Jennifer long enough to tell her that the cab was waiting for her outside. She turned her smile on full force as she faced Jim while Jennifer bit her tongue and collected her things.

"Do you want a lift home?" Jennifer asked as she ignored the fact that he still had the keys to the Ford in his possession. Her face took on a darker hue as she heard him saying that someone would probably be waiting for him if he went home. He said they'd probably make it look like he surprised a burglar, there was a fight, and he was on the wrong end of the gun when it "accidentally" discharged. She felt the temperature rising and she couldn't keep her anger out of her voice as she said, "So I suppose you're going to take her up on her invitation for a place to stay. Isn't that right?"

She didn't wait for an answer as she turned away from the table. The jukebox was blaring out another early fifties rock and roll song, but as she started for the door, it wasn't hard to hear her voice as she said over her shoulder, "Butthead."

Chapter 8

Jim finished pulling his boots on, and then he looked over his shoulder at the sleeping form under the covers. The activity-filled night that he had spent with the lovely barmaid had been very satisfying as far as the sexual encounters had been concerned. It was in the aftermath of the active night where he found himself very disappointed and very unsatisfied. He left a brief note in which he told her that it would be better for her if he wasn't around for a while and also a lot safer. He told her what the prosecution lawyers would do to her testimony if they ever learned that he had spent the night with her. As he placed the note on her kitchen table, the face of Jennifer popped into his mind again and that gave him even more reasons for misgiving. He knew she had wanted him to stay over on the night when he'd been at her apartment, but he had put her off because he hadn't wanted to put her life in jeopardy. He also hated to admit that this small gal simply scared him beyond reason. What would she say now if she found out he'd actually slept with the girl he'd only met last night?

Jim shook his head as he slipped out of the apartment and softly closed the door. The sun wasn't up yet, but he was sure several of the men he wanted to talk to wouldn't be heading for bed for several more hours. For those men, the night was their time to make money and score points.

He parked his car almost a block away to make sure he didn't give any warning to the men he wanted to visit. When he turned the knob, he found the door hadn't even been locked, and he quickly took advantage of that fact. When he closed the door, the sun was just beginning to show over the mountains far off to the east. The house was silent, but there was a very identifiable odor lingering in the big rooms. As he quietly opened an interior door and stepped into the attached garage, he saw two men talking quietly as they sat around a card table. The biggest man was black, and he was dividing his attention between listening to rap and to the whining of his white partner. Jim watched for several minutes as the black man picked out the right-size chunks and pushed them closer to his partner who put the chunks of drug into small ziplock bags. The men almost turned the table over in their fright when former Lt. Jim Gray began the process of informing the men of their rights.

The men started to reach for their guns. However, because they had shifted the locations of their guns on the table in their fright, they were looking down the barrel of Jim's .38 Special long before they had the guns in any semblance of use. The gun being pointed in their direction plus the look on his face quickly caused the two men to put their guns back down on the card table.

He knew he had to make a decision because he faced the biggest threat of personal harm from the big black man, but he faced the loss of an easy talker if the white man slipped out of his grasp. Jim solved his problem when he tossed his handcuffs to the white man and ordered the man to secure himself to the water heater setting in the corner.

Jim's gun was back in the holster, but his hand was resting on it as he motioned the big man into the house. He threw back one last look before he closed the door to the garage and focused his attention on the big black man.

He stood quietly and stared at the man he'd ordered to sit in the kitchen chair. Jim slowly nodded his head and then he said, "Tony 'Ghetto' Waltman. I knew I'd find you sooner or later. If I remember correctly, I think you're looking at thirty years if you get caught messing around with drugs again. What's your poor invalid mother going to do when she sees her boy getting sent up again? I suppose it's going to be the state-run poorhouse for her. What do you think?" He waited for an answer as he watched the man squirming on the seat of the kitchen chair.

There wasn't a trace of fear in the man's voice as he said, "Hey, man. You ain't got nothin' on me. I was just walkin' by this place, and that whitey said he needed a light for his cigar. You got nothin' on me, lootenent. You just leave me be, and I won't be sic'n them lawyers after you for hoorassment. You dig, man?"

Jim pulled out the chair directly across from Ghetto, and then he parked his thigh on the backrest of the chair as his boot made a depression in the soft plastic seat. There was a soft smile on his face as he looked at the self-assured black man. He quickly saw that his smile was causing the man to lose some of his cockiness. He made it appear that he was relaxed and very sure of himself, but he also made sure his right hand remained resting on the butt of his Special.

"I'm going to give you a little information so you will know what kind of information I want in return. Several weeks ago, a guy by the name of Sanchez was killed. They called it an accident, but it was murder. Yesterday afternoon, a guy by the name of Harris was killed. They called it hit-and-run, but it was murder. I want the men who did the killing. I'm not interested in your penny-ante drug business. You give me some information to go on, and I'll forget all about who I found here or what was going on."

Jim waited for several minutes, but apparently, Ghetto had decided he would have no problem getting out of anything the law would attempt to throw at him. Jim finally broke the silence. "All right, if that's the way you want it." He put his foot back on the floor and raised himself to full height. "But now, let's get serious about this. What do you think would happen if I were to hit some of your competitors' operations and made sure to drop your name as being the informant who I got the information from? Or maybe I could let Mister Tom Williams know that you're the one who's been giving me the information all along that I've needed to hang him out to dry. What do you think your lawyer friends would do to help you in circumstances like that?"

There was no mistaking the attention he'd gotten from the black man when he altered his attack. Jim decided to trust his instincts, and he pulled a notepad from his pocket and threw it on the table in front of the now-sweating big man. He gently laid the pen on the pad before he backed away from the table and said, "I'm going back into the garage to question your partner. You're going to be in here alone. If you decide to run...well, I won't be in here to stop you. I do want you to believe me when I say that what Williams and his crew will do to you for being an inform-ant would make life in prison seem like a honeymoon vacation. I think you know that what I'm saying is pure fact. When you're in here alone and are tempted to run and hide, just remember that I'm not after you. I want the men who killed those officers. No one will ever know where I got that information unless you spread that news yourself. If you try to run without giving me the information I need, then you'd better get used to looking over your shoulders because someone will be coming after you sooner or later."

It was cool in the garage, but the man was sweating as he stood beside the water heater. Jim sat down in one of the chairs and casually inspected the guns that had been left on the table. He slowly looked up at the scared man and said, "Your partner finally made up his mind, and now he's busy making a list for me. The two of you don't have much choice because if you don't talk to me, you'll have to talk to someone else. Might be the lawyers or it might be some of the men Williams has hanging around him all the time. I heard Williams can be pretty crude when it comes to getting the information he wants."

The nervous white drug manufacturer squirmed and whined for several minutes until Jim shrugged his shoulder and headed for the door. "Seems like a shame to die for something you don't know anything about. I'll leave the key to the cuffs on the table, and your friend can turn you loose. That is, unless he hasn't been writing down all the names and addresses I want. If he hasn't done what I wanted done, it just might take a while before someone comes along and sets you free. Might even be someone from the drug enforcement office, but it'll most likely be someone from the Williams crew." He took several more steps toward the door before he turned around and asked, "Is there anyone special you want informed about your death? Any special kind of flowers you want sent to your funeral?"

The man tugged at the handcuffs that connected him to the water heater as he cried, "Hey, man. You're in trouble yourself. You can't go around doing things like this."

Jim slowly walked back to the man and said, "If you don't want to talk to me because you think I'm in trouble, then I suggest that you just stop and think about how much trouble you'll be in if you don't talk to me. Someone killed several good officers already, and if I don't get the information I need to haul them before a judge, I'll see to it that someone pays the price for not talking. It's your choice." He took another pad and pen out of his pocket and placed them on the work bench that was butting up next to the heater. He turned and walked to the door without a single look back even though the man was whining about how much his lovely wife and loving family needed him. Jim picked up the keys and left the garage without looking back.

The big black man was gone when Jim entered the kitchen, but since he'd been expecting the man to be gone, he wasn't particularly perturbed by the man's absence. He found the pen and pad lying where they had been, but now where the first page had been blank, there were a series of names, dates, and places filling the first page of the pad. Most of the information he saw written on the sheet he'd already gotten from other sources, but two names on the list were new to him and so was the fact that a new factory for the drugs had been set up. The black man had written that he didn't know the exact address of the drug house, but he'd drawn a crude map and had given a fairly good description of the house as well noting the major cross streets near it. Next to the description of the house the man had printed the initials "TW." Jim looked at the initials, and immediately, he saw the name of Tom Williams blaring out at him. Jim was very aware that he could be wrong about the name that went with those initials, but right now he'd be willing to place a huge bet on his hunch. Jim was sure he'd have no trouble finding the place. All he had to do was watch the foot traffic around the houses for a few days or else simply watch until he knew what kind of "groceries" they were having delivered.

Jim waited for about ten minutes before he went back into the garage. He'd wanted to give the man enough time to think, sweat, and write. When he picked up the pad, he found much of the same information the big man had written on his pad, but this man had been able to furnish him with the complete address of the place that the black man had been describing and had left the initials TW beside.

Jim reached into his pocket for the key and unlocked the cuffs. When the cuffs slipped off the man's wrist, Jim saw the man hurrying directly for the card table where the guns were lying. Before the man got within five feet of the table, he came to a sliding halt when he heard the hammer of Jim's .38 Special being cocked. Jim watched the startled face turning gray when he saw the gun aimed at his head.

"What are you doing?" He blurted and then he added in a whining voice, "I was just gonna get my gun. Paid over $300 for it. I need it to protect my family."

Gray slowly shook his head and said, "You must be high on that crap you've been making. Do you really think I'd let you get your hands on a gun in this kind of a situation? All I'm going to tell you is that if you touch either of those guns, it'll be the last thing you ever do. Now you have the choice of either getting out of here as fast as you can or else make a grab for one of those guns." The man showed his indecision as he stood and alternated his eyes from Gray to the guns. The man's head was swiveling back and forth as he tried to make up his mind. The man's knees almost gave out on him when Jim hollered, "Now! Make your decision."

The whining little man gave his gun one quick last look before he bolted past Jim. Seconds later, the suspended plainclothes detective heard the rear door slam, and then he listened to the rapid crunching of gravel as the man raced along the side of the house. He listened to the roar of a big engine and then the squeal of tires as the man began looking for a safer place.

As he picked up the guns, he made sure he collected the silencer that was lying beside the automatic. He also made sure he hadn't left anything lying around that would lead the police to himself. When he stepped back into the kitchen, he took a used napkin from the table and used it to keep from getting fingerprints on the phone. After he reported the location of the streetside lab, he hung up the phone on the insistent operator. The young woman was very determined to get his name and to keep him on the phone, but she failed with flying colors.

Jim didn't waste any time getting out of there because he was very aware that a car could have been very close to this location when the call went out; he could be looking at mere seconds in which to remove himself from the scene. When he stepped out the front door, he tried blend in with the surrounding area. He needed for things to look as normal as possible to keep from drawing attention to himself and to stay alive. Seconds after he dropped the towel-covered guns beside him on the seat, he heard the sound of squealing tires moving in on his location.

The tires on his own car were working hard to grip the street surface without leaving twin streaks of rubber as Jim pushed down on the throttle. He knew he was in trouble when he got a glimpse of a speeding police car through the gaps between houses. He quickly saw the police car was heading for the same intersection he was, and there was no doubt in his mind that unless he did something fast they'd arrive there at the same time.

Jim made a split-second decision as he hit the brakes and swerved to the left side of the street. As the police car careened around the corner, the young male driver was given the view of a car pulling out of a driveway as the driver began heading for work. The officer didn't question why the sun visor was pulled down and was hiding most of the man's face when the sun wasn't a factor. The young officer didn't give Jim a second glance as he accelerated past.

As Jim quickly left the scene, he was puzzled by the quick response of the police. He didn't think they'd have been that alert so they could respond to his call this quickly. Well, he had other things to contemplate.

During the next two hours he used up several gallons of gas on rolling surveillance as he moved from one address back to the next and back again. When the layout of the drug houses was totally familiar to him, he abandoned that part of his plan and moved on to the next phase.

Jennifer answered the phone before it finished blaring its first ring. Her voice had a cheerful and musical note to it until she found out who she was talking to. When she realized Jim was on the far end of the line, she quickly adopted a strict, angry, and suspicious tone of voice. She ignored his hurried questions while she repeatedly asked where he'd been because she'd been calling his place all morning and all she'd gotten was his voice mail. He wasn't able to stem her curiosity to her satisfaction because he couldn't simply tell her that her phone could also be tapped, but after enough sidestepping, he finally got her to agree to meet him at a diner nearby during her lunch break.

Jim knew he still had almost an hour to go before she would be there, but he entered the diner and found an empty booth by a window. He got out his pad and started doing some deep thinking. He finished his burger and was only on his second cup of coffee when Jennifer slid in across from him. He'd been expecting an angry and suspicious woman, but the pretty blonde sitting across from him now was anything but.

She was cool, calm, and collected but was not overly friendly as she quickly filled him in on the events that had happened after Harris had been hit. The matter of a complete moron getting the promotion to the temporary position of captain was something that didn't surprise Jim at all. When she gave Jim that information, she appeared to be somewhat disappointed when his facial expression didn't alter at all.

However, she saw Jim's expression alter dramatically when she reached into her purse and handed him a handful of papers. She let him read briefly in silence as she placed her order and then she said, "I was able to get into the captain's office early this morning, and I spent a lot of time at the copy machine. I told a couple of people on the early shift that I'd been told to pick up my review yesterday but I'd forgotten to. They really couldn't have cared less that I had something in there or even that he wasn't going to be returning at all." She looked down at her long fingernails and murmured, "It's sad, isn't it? You spend your whole life working hard and doing things you believe in and twenty-four hours after you're gone you're already a piece of forgotten history."

Jennifer took a deep breath, and then she leaned back against the backrest. "You're going to have to be very careful from now on because they've put out a description of your car, and on top of that, now you're wanted for car theft as well."

Jim looked up from the papers in his hand. "With these papers you've given me, you've given me a good handhold on what I need to nail Williams. Thanks for the warning about the car as well." He looked up at her pretty face as she stood to leave. He took a deep breath and tried to smile. "Sweetheart, I owe you one."

Her voice was cool and calm as she said, "Yes, you do. I hope you think of that tonight when you crawl into her bed again." She raised her hand to stop him from speaking, and then she looked out the window for a long moment before she looked at him. "And don't call me sweetheart." This time her eyes didn't have a twinkle in them as she started to walk away. Just as she brushed by on her way to the door, he heard a cold voice saying, "Butthead."

Chapter 9

Jim parked the Ford in the alley behind the body shop and made his way around the building. After he checked for any form of surveillance, he headed toward the office door. Several years ago he'd "misplaced" some evidence that would have put the owner behind bars for a long stretch, and now he was hoping he'd be able to get a little favor back in return. He found the man sanding on the rear fender of a beautiful yellow Corvette. The man didn't look up when he heard Jim saying, "It sure is a shame to see you sanding something that looks that pretty."

"You got to rough it up a little so you can remove all the imperfections and so the finish coat of paint will stick." He made several more passes with the sanding block before he stepped back and looked at his handiwork. When his head turned and saw who was standing behind him, the man's face quickly lit up. "Hey, Jim boy. How's the world treating you?" He tossed the sandpaper block on the floor and wiped his hands on his coveralls before he stuck his hand out in greeting. "Come on inside. Got coffee on, and there's a couple of sweet rolls left in there."

He started for his office, but when he reached the door, he realized Jim was still standing where he had been. Slowly the man turned around and came back. He looked into Jim's eyes for a moment before he said, "You're in trouble, ain't ya?"

"Yes, Frank, I sure am. I hate to impose on you, but I need a set of wheels." Jim took a deep breath to start giving him some of the details, but before he was able to resume talking, he found Frank already speaking.

"You ain't imposing." The man said, "I did some stupid things a couple of years ago, but you kept me from spending a lot of time behind bars because of that stupidity, and I'll never forget that. I've gotten married since then, and I'm a daddy now. Got another one on the way." He stood in front of Jim. "I'm a happy man now, and I've got you to thank for most of that. You just tell me what you need, and I'll see to gettin' it done."

Jim quickly gave him a brief rundown on his predicament and then he said, "What I need is a set of wheels that won't stand out like a sore thumb, but I need something that's got power, just in case."

Frank led the way as they walked back out into the alley. He stood and looked at the car for a long moment before he said, "Tell you what I can do. You just leave that car with me for a couple of days. I'll bring it into the shop, put a new color on it, and put on some clean plates. I've got a wrecked car beside the shop that just happens to have the plates you need. Once you get your problem straightened out, I can paint it the old color again if that's what you want and stick your old plates back on. No one will ever know the difference. What do you think?"

Jim stood and thought for a long moment although he knew he'd be much better off if he took Frank up on his offer. He hated to do it that way because of the chance that Frank could get into trouble. He also knew the car he was in possession of right now had everything he needed, which included the police radio. He finally said, "I hope you know how much this will help me out. I'll pay for your work in cash so you don't have any paper trail leading back to you."

Frank snorted. "If you so much as pull a dollar bill out of your pocket, I'm going to consider it an insult. Not only that, I'll probably file a complaint with the police department on you. You got that? Now go and grab the stuff you need outta the car. I'll have this car unrecognizable by the police in a couple of hours." He looked up and down the street for a moment and then he said, "I got a compact in the shop I usually use as a loaner or for running after parts and paint. Use that in the meantime. Give me a call in about two days to finish this job and give the paint some good drying time." He grinned. "With the heat we got here, it won't take long."

Jim stepped aside as Frank got into the Ford and closed the driver's door. He saw how willing this man was even though it would be tough on him if he happened to get caught at it. It felt good to know that someone remembered or even cared that he had tried to be fair to some individuals who he figured had gotten a raw deal. He gave the same remark to Frank that he'd given to Jennifer, only this time the response was different. When he said, "I owe you one," he heard Frank telling him that he still owed Jim more than he could ever repay.

Frank was already busy on the body of the Ford when Jim drove the blue Dodge Neon out of the shop. The riot shotgun, his 30-06 with the scope, and his vest were lying in the trunk of the small car, but he had his backup pistol under the front seat of this car. He'd had the small .32 under the seat of the Ford for three years and had never touched it other than for a cleaning. The papers he had gotten from Jennifer were in a paper sack beside him on the seat. He was starting to feel a little better.

Time was dragging for Jim now that he'd finished the chores he considered most important. On a hunch, he called Jennifer's number at work. Her voice turned cool and businesslike when he identified himself as a "friend" of Captain Harris. She'd recognized his voice immediately, and he could almost feel the ice in her voice. Her voice slowly lost some of its coolness when he started telling her which questions to ask of the officers who were investigating the captain's death. He didn't want to be on the phone too long just in case they were trying to trace his call, but he wanted to be sure the investigation was being conducted properly and that the right questions were being asked. Harris hadn't been a friend of his, but he had been murdered because the man was working on the same case that he himself was. And in the past few days, he'd developed a great deal of respect for the man. It went against the grain to think that a piece of scum like Williams would do something like that and actually feel sure he could get away with it.

Jennifer was interrupted twice, and he was more or less put on hold longer than he cared for. He wanted to get this phone call over although it was being made from a grocery store. Even though he'd be able to mingle easily with the people inside the store, there was still the chance he would be spotted by the police if the call had been traced.

The second time Jennifer came back to the phone, she started talking like she'd been distracted and wasn't concentrating on what he was telling her. He was midway through a sentence when she interrupted him. "I just had a report dropped on my desk, and I think you'll want to hear about this. The night before last, a kid in a Mustang was picked up in Carefree for speeding. It says he was placed in the jail cell because he resisted arrest and argued so much with the officer. The arresting officer said he really had a handful with the young man because according to him he shouldn't have gotten the ticket." She paused for a moment before she added, "Now listen to this. He said he shouldn't have gotten the ticket because several minutes earlier he's the one who got passed by a couple of cars. He said they blew by him like he was standing still. One was a tan Chevrolet Suburban, and the second one was a silver Lincoln."

Jim had been a little miffed when he was interrupted in that fashion, but he quickly forgot about it as he listened to what she had to say. For several seconds, the phone line was quiet except for the normal static, but then he got his mind working again and asked, "And this kid is still behind bars there?"

When he received an affirmative answer, he quickly said he was going to head up there and talk to the kid himself. Before he could hang up, he heard Jennifer telling him she wanted to go along. She said those words so powerfully that he knew it wasn't a request. He was tempted to tell her that it was out of her jurisdiction, but then he knew she'd tell him the same thing. She'd tell him that not only was it out of his jurisdiction, there was also the minor fact that Harris had been ordered to pull his badge. There was no doubt in his mind that Jennifer would remind him that, according to the police in the station house, he was really only a civilian. A wanted civilian with an arrest warrant out on him.

Those were really only minor matters because what was really bothering him was that he didn't want to rehash the argument they'd had earlier about him, the bar maid Amber, and Jennifer. For a reason he couldn't explain, or didn't even quite understand, he was very reluctant to do anything else that would cause Jennifer any kind of grief.

When he pulled into the police parking lot, he saw Jennifer was already standing by the door and waiting for him. He kept his face averted as several uniformed and plainclothes officers entered and exited the building through the same doorway Jennifer had used. She barely had time to close the door on the small car before he released the brake, engaged the clutch, and motored out of the parking lot.

He didn't know if it was Jennifer or the poorly working air conditioner in the small car, but he was uncomfortably warm as they eased their way onto the northbound freeway. Jennifer was chattering like nothing had ever happened, but the more talking she did, the more uncomfortable he was becoming.

Jim's discomfort was apparently very obvious because Jennifer finally reached over and turned down the radio. "Look, Jim. I was way out of line both last night at the bar and again today at the diner. I have no hold on you nor do I have any right to ask you to change your way of life. What you do is strictly your own business, and from now on, I'm going to keep my nose out of it. I'm sorry about some of those things I said to you. I was out of line." She sat back against the seat and looked out at the desert scenery as they drove north.

Jim was silent for several miles, but when he answered it was like she had just finished talking. "The only problem with that is you were right about what you said. I guess I'm earning my title as a butthead, right?"

The surprise in her eyes slowly turned to a twinkle as she turned to look at him. Seconds later, he heard the musical sound of her laughter.

Jennifer tried to keep the chatter going while they drove, but long before they got to the towns of Carefree and Cave Creek, it had gotten quiet in the small car. Jim sat quietly and stared at the road ahead of them, but his mind was actually on the blonde sitting beside him. There were a million things he wanted to say and ask, but he couldn't force a single word out.

When they arrived at the Carefree station, the desk officer quickly let them know the kid had been released several hours earlier. The woman didn't want to give them the boy's address, but Jennifer quickly took over. Minutes after she flashed her badge at the woman, they were on the way to the home where the fast driver lived with his parents.

The father of the boy was still hot under the collar and came close to ordering the officers off his property when he found out who they were. It was clear the kid had convinced his father that the law was in the wrong and that he'd spent time behind bars just because he hadn't shown the officer the respect the man had demanded. Jim had let Jennifer go to the door ahead of him because he was sure the man wouldn't try anything with the female officer. It didn't take Jim long to find out different when the man tried to move her away from the house physically. Jim quickly stepped out of the car and placed himself between the angry man and Jennifer. The pushing stopped, but the show of bravado continued until Jennifer finally offered the man a choice between a quiet talk with the boy or getting the Carefree Police to reinstate the incarceration order. Neither of the officers had any idea if that could even be done, but it was obvious that the father didn't want to be the cause of his son going back to jail. He quickly backed off although it was a very reluctant move.

When the young man came out of the house, Jim gave the father a strong suggestion to remain near the house while he questioned the lad in the driveway. There was a very glum look on the man's face, but he didn't make a single objection.

The three of them gathered around in front of the Neon. Jim, in an attempt to ease the boy's fears, said, "Just relax, Alan. We're trying to get some information on the cars that passed you. I've just got a few questions to ask. Where were you when you encountered those vehicles? How fast were they going? How close were the cars to each other? Those are the kind of things we want to know. We believe one of the drivers is guilty of some major crimes. Just take your time, son, and tell us what happened."

Alan immediately began a long tirade in which he continually berated the local police until Jim finally slapped the hood of the car and scared the boy into silence.

Jim looked down at the boy's surprised face, and with an angry voice, he said, "Look, kid, we're willing to go to bat for you on this matter, but we want the truth. To begin with, I'm very sure that you weren't the one who got passed. If that Mustang is equipped the way I was told it was, then it should have flown by those heavier vehicles with no problem. I'm sure that Mustang doesn't have anything smaller than the standard 283 under the hood." He took a deep breath as he leaned closer to the boy. "I can't see you letting a couple of cars like that pass without you making a strong effort to show them up. If you can convince me that you're telling the truth, I'm willing to try to get those speeding and resisting arrest citations rescinded, but I want you to understand this much right now. One more...ah...misrepresentation of the truth, and you're on your own to take your chances with the court. Now why don't we start all over from the beginning?"

When Alan started talking, Jennifer stepped closer to the lad and held her small tape recorder close to his face so she wouldn't miss a word. The lad became so engrossed in the tape recorder and in separating the truth from his long-winded line of fiction he'd given earlier that he didn't see his father taking up a station right behind him.

Alan took a deep breath, and then he said, "That Mustang has a 351 with a four barrel on it. I've got a four speed with a special rear end I got from a mechanic friend of mine. That old girl will really fly. Me and my friend switched rear ends a couple of weeks ago, and then we took it out on a test run. I didn't even give it all the gas on that run because we were going too fast already. My friend clocked us at over one hundred and thirty, and I had about an inch of throttle left yet. Bet I could have hit one fifty."

Jim nodded his head. "That's about what I figured. Now let's go back a little, and you can describe the cars, drivers, and what they were doing." Before Alan could begin talking once more, Jim raised his hand and added, "Just want to let you know that this tape recorder will not be used against you. It's strictly for our own use. I want to make sure we keep all the facts straight after Officer Sullivan and I leave here."

Alan nodded his head, but even with that statement, that his words wouldn't be used against him, he was still having trouble giving the two officers the information they wanted. He was finding that it was very difficult for him to talk about his speeding in front of the police when he'd already given a statement to the local police, where he'd gotten very emphatic, that he'd been wronged and shouldn't have gotten the ticket. He felt the recorder tapping his shoulder as Jennifer tried to break the long thinking spell, and then he started, "I was coming back from a friend's house, and as late as it was, I didn't think there would be any cops out on the road. So I opened it up. Dad wanted me back home by midnight, and it was already after one so I kicked it. Not far from the edge of Phoenix, I caught up with those two cars I told the police about. When I pulled up beside them, I had to slow down to one ten. I had to laugh when I stepped on the gas and left them in the dust like I did. I turned at the Carefree turnoff and headed home. That's about all that happened."

Jim nodded his head. "Can you describe the cars you passed?"

Alan didn't have to stop to think when he said, "The car in front was a tan Chevy Suburban, and the second was a Lincoln Town Car."

Jim quickly said, "How about the drivers? Can you describe them? Is there anything else you can tell us that might help? There just might have been some nasty business going on that night, and anything you can tell us just might help save a life."

Alan slowly shook his head. "Well, I couldn't even see the driver of the Lincoln because of the dark windows on his car, but the female in the front car showed up real clear. She had the rearview mirror set the way you normally would so the headlights on the Lincoln really lit up her face." He laughed briefly, and then he added, "She was the whitest white woman I ever saw. It looked like she never came out until the sun went down."

Jim looked at Alan with a thoughtful look on his face. "Could her whiteness have been caused by fright? Maybe she was afraid for her life."

Alan looked at Jim, and it was clear that he was entertaining that thought for the first time. He looked down at his shoes for a moment. "I guess that could be." He took a deep breath. "As soon as I went around the gal, she began hitting the dimmer switch. The lights must have gone from dim to bright at least twenty times before she quit." He was quiet for a moment, and his face lost some of its color before he looked up at Jim. "Do you think she was trying to tell me that she needed help?"

Jim shrugged his shoulders and softly said, "I really can't say for sure, but right now that certainly would be my guess. I want to thank you for your help. We'll stop at the police station before we leave town. I'll see what I can do about that ticket." He lowered his head a little and then he added, "I think you'd better slow that thing down a little before someone gets in front of you and gets killed because you couldn't stop." He nodded to Jennifer and then started for the Neon.

He'd only taken two steps when he heard the lad saying, "You aren't going to tell my father what really happened, are you?"

The lad's face had lost a little of its color when he learned about the possible danger the young woman might have been in. When he heard his father's voice coming from right behind him, where he'd been standing and listening, the rest of the color drained from the lad's face in a hurry.

As Jim and his partner walked away from the father and son, they heard the father saying, "You lied to me when you said you hadn't done anything wrong. You told me that they were picking on you because you got into a fight with one of the officer's sons. You caused me to lock horns with those officers, and now I find out that you've been lying. Just what in the…"

The man's voice continued to get louder, but the closing of doors on the Neon blocked the sound. As the tires began to lift dust from the gravel driveway, they saw the man holding out his hand. They also saw the lad digging into his pockets with his right hand. They were sure there would be no more speeding tickets for young Alan for quite some time.

If the officers knew about Jim's suspension from the police force, they either didn't care or else they didn't let it show. Jim and the pretty blonde officer had to argue for fifteen minutes before the arresting officer agreed to drop the charge of resisting arrest as well as tearing up the speeding ticket. The deciding factor had been Jim's description of the parting scene they'd gotten where the father had been demanding the keys to the souped-up car.

They replayed the tape several times on the way back to Phoenix. Each time they came to the place where the lad described the flashing lights on the Chevy, the officers riding quietly in the front seat exchanged looks.

Jim listened to the tape twice before he finally muttered, "It certainly doesn't look too good for that gal, does it?"

Jennifer just sat quietly and stared at the silent recorder lying in her lap as they drew nearer to the city of Phoenix, in the Valley of the Sun.

Chapter 10

Jim was going to drop Jennifer off at the police department on the way back from Carefree, but she got him to stop at a discount department store first. When she came out, she was carrying a small plastic shopping bag. She quickly tied a handkerchief around his head and let him look into the mirror and asked if he thought he'd be recognized. It felt very strange on him, and when he looked into the mirror, he remembered his mother wearing one in the same manner as she worked around the house. It was also the same way many of the younger male population were going around now. When he put on the sunglasses she bought for him, he was forced to shake his head. Those items clearly changed his appearance a great deal, and with this different car under him, he was sure he could drive through the police parking lot without being recognized. But he wasn't about to try to enter the building itself because he knew he'd be recognized by somebody before long.

He pulled to a stop in front of the building, and Jennifer got out with instructions that she was to try to find out as much as she could about the hit-and-run death of Harris. He released a deep sigh as he watched her thick waist and trim bottom going up the steps before he reached down and shifted the gearshift lever into low gear. Once more, he mentally kicked himself for the blunders he'd allowed to happen in their relationship.

Jim followed up on several leads he'd wanted to check out more thoroughly, but all of them proved to be nothing more than time-consuming dead ends because he was unable to add anything new to the case he was working on. It was beginning to appear that there were plenty of corrupt high officials around or officials who had found themselves under the man's thumb. This arrangement meant that the men working for Williams were having no trouble finding someone to hide behind as well as being able to get all kinds of information that they needed to remain one step ahead of the law.

He had the urge to contact Jennifer to see if she'd found anything out, but he didn't want to lead them to her in case her phone line was tapped or someone happened to overhear her side of the conversation. Right at this moment, she had the potential of being a very useful set of eyes and ears in that office, and he didn't want to destroy that small advantage.

Just a little after midnight, Jim slipped on a dark turtleneck sweater and a black pair of jeans. It didn't take him long to cover the distance to the address he wanted because the traffic was light; he was also quite familiar with the route he wanted to use. He left his car two blocks away from the captain's house and began jogging down the dark alley that would take him to the rear of the house.

Jim crouched behind a row of plastic garbage tubs and watched the men in the parked car as they maintained surveillance on the dead captain's house. It was clear to him that Williams suspected that Jim would try to get into the house and had instructed his crew to do all they could to prevent it. From the amount of men who were surrounding the house, it appeared that they intended to do just that. As soon as Jim saw the car parked in the alley, he knew immediately that it had nothing to do with the police. He was positive that neither of the two men inside that car had anything to do with law enforcement as well because he recognized the man he saw sitting on the passenger side. The driver appeared to be sleeping, and both men had long hair. But Jim recognized Wales immediately because of the man's long and crooked nose.

He remembered it well because he was the one who had changed the angle of that nose. Wales had vowed to kill him for breaking his nose and sending him to the hospital, but so far, it had only been hot air. Jim didn't intend to give the man any chance to fulfill that vow.

He reached under his shirt, eased his Special out of the holster, and then began to use his military training to get him closer to the car. As he worked his way closer to the car, Jim began hearing the snores of the man behind the steering wheel. He hoped he wouldn't have to use his gun because the loud report would wake everyone within blocks, and it wouldn't be long before the police would show up. He needed someone to break the silence that Williams had wrapped his activities in, but he didn't want to do it with his gun. It wasn't the lives of Wales and his partner he was concerned with; instead, it was his own ability to move about undetected that he didn't want to jeopardize. If he made too much noise here or left any bodies lying around, he knew he'd have the police out looking for him in force. He had to make every move with concentrated care and silence.

The first indication Wales gave that he knew Jim was around was when he stiffened as the muzzle of the revolver pressed into his neck. The man opened his mouth in surprise, but Jim's hand quickly covered it.

Before the man had a chance to recover from his shock, he heard Jim hissing in his ear for silence. The man didn't move as Jim reached through the window and felt for the man's gun. His fingers encountered an empty holster, but when he leaned in closer, he saw the faint outline of the gun on the seat beside the man's leg. He had taken it out of his holster because with the silencer on it, it didn't fit in its customary place. The Special pressed hard into the man's neck as Jim reached across and lifted it off the seat. Just as he wrapped his fingers around the silenced gun, he found he was touching the second man's gun with the back of his hand.

Seconds later, the Special was back in his holster, and Wales was feeling the weight of the heavy silencer as Jim placed it against his temple. The man was trying to remain as silent as he could because he was sure he knew what Jim was capable of. He was fairly confident of the cop's scruples that he didn't have to worry about getting shot in cold blood, but he also knew any suspicious movement would quickly end it all for him. There was no doubt in his mind that he wouldn't hear any "stop or I'll shoot" commands coming from Jim at this point because the look of death in the officer's eyes was shining strong and steady.

Jim whispered, "Wake your partner, but don't try to pull anything. I've got two silenced guns, and there are only two of you. I think you know me well enough to know that I won't hesitate to pull the trigger if either of you try anything."

Wales didn't move his head as he reached over to tug on his partner's sleeve. Apparently, the man had awakened a short time earlier and was now playing possum because the man suddenly reached under his jacket as if to pull a gun. Jim waited long enough to make sure a gun was being pulled, and then he pulled the trigger on the gun in his right hand. The noise it produced was minor, but the damage it inflicted was anything but.

The back of the man's head disappeared, and the door post behind his head was showered with bone fragments as well as releasing a pink-and-gray mist. The man slumped against the door and shuddered several times before all movement stopped.

There was no mistaking the smell that quickly began to permeate throughout the interior of the car as the dead man lost all control of his body functions nor was there any mistaking the sweat that was rolling down the face of Wales.

With one silencer pressing firmly against the man's temple, Jim reached across Wales and smashed the dome light with the second silencer. The interior of the car remained dark when Jim slowly opened the door and began to pull Wales out.

As the door latch released, Wales suddenly threw his shoulder against the door. That abrupt movement knocked the gun out of Jim's left hand before it threw him back against the fence, which caused several more stars to appear in his vision. His abrupt stop against the fence caused several of the neighborhood dogs to begin barking.

Wales made a desperate dive for the dropped gun. The modern-day bandit moved fast, but before he could scoop up the fallen gun and bring it to bear on Gray, he ceased to exist, other than as a body. When Wales made his move the silenced gun in Jim's right hand softly coughed a second time. A small hole suddenly appeared in Wales's forehead, and the back of the man's head exploded in a colored mist, just like his partner's had. The rear window in the black automobile shattered when the bullet hit it, but after encountering the thick bone in the man's skull, the bullet didn't have enough energy left to power its way through the thick glass.

Jim pushed himself to his feet and waited several minutes as he eyed the buildings nearby and listened for any sign the scuffle had been heard. Finally, satisfied that not even a dog had heard the muffled shots, he reached into the car and pulled the keys from the ignition. It only took a couple of minutes of heavy-duty straining before he had both bodies lying in the trunk, and then he spent several minutes cleaning up most of the blood off the rear passenger window and doorpost so it wasn't so obvious. Jim climbed onto the rear deck of the big car and brought down his foot hard next to the hole in the rear window. It took several blows with his foot and then a quick strong push with his hand before the rear window dropped onto the rear seat. The removal of the rear window had only gotten the attention of several dogs again several houses farther down the block, but he didn't see any lights coming on in any windows. He pushed several pieces of glass down to the gravel of the alley before he stepped back and saw that the car had lost all exterior sign that anything had happened or that there were two bodies lying in the trunk.

Jim slipped into the space between the houses and then cautiously looked up and down the quiet street. It didn't take him long before he was able to pick out another pair of gunmen stationed down the street. The car was parked where the occupants wouldn't be highlighted by the street light. But they had parked close enough so they could watch the Harris home. It was clear Williams didn't know what other evidence Harris had been able to dig up before he'd been taken care of, but the man and his cadre of killers intended to prevent anyone else from finding out about it before they were ready to start digging for it themselves. They obviously felt forced to hold off on their own investigation for the present because they couldn't be sure there wasn't police surveillance on the house. Considering the way the man had died, they had to know that if they bothered Harris's wife in any way, it would bring an awful lot of pressure down on them even though they appeared to have the control of several higher officials who were paving the way. They apparently were quite sure that if any attention was brought to the case now, there could be terrible consequences. They'd been fortunate enough to have the commander assign an incompetent officer to investigate the case of Harris's death, as he'd done when Sanchez had been killed in that "accident." But sooner or later, someone was going to stumble in the right direction, and they needed to be ready on all fronts to keep their little kingdom from crumbling around them.

Jim was tempted to subdue the hoods in the second car but he knew if one of the men raised a fuss and it caused one of the people in the neighborhood to bring the police into this little foray, he'd have a tough time getting this far again the next time. He turned around and headed for the window he knew was next to the new widow's bed. He looked around for a moment, and then he pulled a pen out of his pocket and gave three quick taps in the lower right corner of the window. He waited several seconds before he added another tap. He repeated the series of three taps and then one.

After his fourth set of taps, he heard movement inside, and he quickly retreated to the rear door. Her face showed surprise at seeing him this way, but her eyes appeared dull as she opened the screen door and stepped aside to let him enter.

The woman didn't say hi or ask him why he was here. Her first words were, "It wasn't an accident, was it?"

Jim slowly shook his head and said, "No, ma'am, I don't think it was an accidental hit-and-run. I'm sorry to be so blunt, but I don't have much time, so I'll get right to the point. I think he was getting close to something big. Did Captain Harris leave any papers around that he didn't want anyone to know about? It's very important."

She looked at him in the thin light coming into the kitchen from the streetlights and slowly said, "If I wasn't so sure he trusted you, I wouldn't even consider giving you any information. But I was awake when you tapped on the window the last time you came over in the middle of the night. I overheard the two of you talking so I know that he'd want you to have the papers he'd hidden." She sighed and then added, "Just wait in here. I'll have to switch the light on in the living room. I'll be back in a minute."

The widow came to a quick halt when Jim whispered a loud "No!" He moved closer to the woman and said, "You've got to do it without any lights."

Her form straightened as she regarded him. Finally, she said, "They're watching the house, aren't they?" When Jim finally nodded his head, she moved past him and looked out the back door. He could see the dullness had left her eyes as she said, "That car out back. Is that one of theirs too?"

Jim slowly nodded his head. "Yes, it is, but they won't be bothering anyone from now on."

She quickly exclaimed, "Good!" The harshness of the word as it escaped her lips surprised her more than it did Jim. She stood and stared at him for a long moment before she said, "I'll get the papers for you. My husband thinks he...well...anyway, he thought he had some important information that would put some of the bad guys out of commission for a long time as soon as it could be confirmed." She turned and headed through the doorway without another word.

He watched the widow as she took a picture of herself off the wall and then took the hard backing off. Between the backing and behind the picture, he saw her drawing several sheets of paper out. She laid them on the seat of the davenport, and then she repeated the process with the picture of her late husband. After she removed the papers, she stood and stared at his picture for a long moment.

There were tears in her eyes when she handed the papers and a computer disc to him. She didn't try to hide the quiver in her voice as she said, "As far as I know that is everything. I hope there's enough to get those..." Her voice cracked, and her shoulders shook with the violence of her sobs.

Jim tried to console her, but she turned and ran from the room. He slowly folded the papers and slipped the papers and the CD into his pants pocket before he headed for the rear door. As he stood in the darkness behind the house, he tried to decide if he should go after the second pair of men or if he should just leave well enough alone. It rankled him to think that Williams was so sure of himself that he would be so blatant about watching the place, but on the other hand, he didn't want to overextend his reach and end up losing everything he'd gained so far.

He flipped a mental coin, and then, with a deep breath, he turned in the direction of the street. As he worked his way down the street, he watched the movements of the men in the second car for twenty minutes so he could come in from the rear—before he saw the opening he'd been hoping for. The passenger got the driver's attention away from the house and onto himself when he twisted in the seat in an attempt to reach for something in the rear of the car, and that's when Jim made his move. When the man straightened out in his seat again, Jim was already kneeling beside the rear tire of the car on the passenger side. He forced himself to breath through his mouth for several minutes until he was breathing normally and was mentally ready for action once more. The man looked over at the driver as he made a comment about this surveillance being such a waste of time. When the man started to look back in the direction of the house, he found himself staring into the huge hole in the end of the silencer.

The man behind the wheel saw Jim standing beside the car at the same time, but when he saw the gun was being held on his partner, he thought he had time to make his move. It was too late for him when he saw that the man was holding two guns. He heard a soft chug, and then he made a grab at his chest where a deep pain suddenly gripped him. The pain in his chest felt terrible, but slowly, it didn't seem to make any difference anymore because after a few seconds everything started to go numb. For a long time, the man sat and stared at the spreading stain that his blood was causing on his shirt before he slowly tried to raise his hand in an attempt to put his finger where the source of the bleeding was. He tried several times to stem the flow of blood from his chest, but his arm was just too heavy to hold it up there. He looked up at Jim for a moment with a questioning look on his face before his eyes returned to his chest. It took him several more seconds before it finally dawned on him that he had just taken a bullet in the chest. He tried to get his mind working, but it was getting so hard to think, and then it slowly ceased to make any difference to him. His head slumped to his chest, and his glasses dropped to the tip of his nose where they hung precariously.

The man who was sitting in the passenger seat was instantly sweating and pleading for his life as he waited for the second shot. Jim gruffly ordered the man to muscle his partner into the back seat and to make sure he didn't make a sound when he did it.

Another dome light was smashed with the muzzle of the heavy gun after the second man slid over until he was behind the steering wheel. It was clear he was not very happy about being the lone man in the car with this ruthless man as well has having to be the driver. Although he knew how to drive a car, the man had no driver's license and had never liked being behind the wheel. Knowing that voicing any kind of objection would probably get him killed, he quietly put his hands in clear view on the steering wheel and waited.

Jim quietly closed the door and then he said, "All right, cowboy, let's ride. Let's do it nice and quiet. I want you to do everything legal so you don't attract anyone's attention. If you do anything to get us stopped or tailed, you're going to end up as dead as your partner. You'll live a lot longer if you follow orders. Got that?"

Sweat flew from the man's face as he quickly nodded his head. The man started the car's big engine and then sat a few moments while he took a number of deep breaths before he pulled the gearshift lever down with the urging of the big silencer against his temple.

The man came close to making some serious mistakes as he drove away because of all the distractions within his range of vision. He gulped hard when Jim tapped the heavy silencer against his forehead when he almost ran a stop light because he was watching his passenger so intently. After the second close call, Jim made it clear what was going to happen if it happened once more. From then on, the scared man kept his concentration on his driving even though he was constantly trying to find a way to get the upper hand on this renegade cop. He reached up and felt the knots on his forehead after his third screw up and finally figured out that he was going to live a lot longer if he simply followed orders. One of the taps, the last one Jim had been forced to administer on his forehead, had been hard enough to break the skin, and a thin line of blood angled down across the bridge of his nose.

Jim dug into the glove box to make sure another gun wasn't tucked in there, but what he found caused a smile to stretch his lips. He flipped it open and then punched in the numbers on the small cell phone and waited for an answer. He listened to the sleepy sound of her voice, and then he growled, "Back door, sweetheart. Five quick ones." Without waiting for a reply from his pretty partner, he cut the connection and leaned back in the seat. He watched the driver with his peripheral vision while he continued to search for any signs of a tail or for any police who might find the car interesting for some reason or other.

He directed the man to the rear of Jennifer's apartment building, and then they sat in the darkness and waited until the rear door finally opened. He quietly watched the rich form of Jennifer moving away from the apartment door in her tight jeans and form fitting blouse. It didn't take long before he found his heart was beating just a little faster. He still had troubles when he saw her moving so gracefully without all the padding around her waist that she had used to neutralize her attention-getting form. She sent his temperature climbing as she trotted in his direction when she finally saw him waving.

When she saw the strange man sitting under the steering wheel and then got a view of the gun Jim was holding on that man, she hesitated for several seconds before she moved closer and stopped just out of arm's reach near the driver's window. Her brow furrowed in puzzlement when she heard her partner telling her that she'd have to share the rear seat with the garbage. She opened the rear door and stared at the body for several seconds before she reached in and pushed the dead man's arm off the seat so she could sit down.

She lifted her eyes from the dead man as Jim said, "We had a little problem at the captain's house. I need someone to drive my car."

Jennifer's eyes grew wider as she looked at Jim. "Is that where you got this pair? Did they do anything to Mrs. Harris?"

Jim quickly shook his head. "No. This is one of four men who were staking out the captain's house. The other three thought they were fast enough to beat me. This one is the only one who used his head for something other than a target. We're going to take him back home. He said the four of them were living in a house just south of Broadway. If he isn't telling me the truth, then I guess we're all going to be in a lot of trouble." Jim threw a menacing look in the driver's direction before he continued in a soft voice. "The only thing is, he won't be alive to see it, and he knows it. Right now, I think he's telling the truth, but we're not going to take any chances." He looked at the driver, and in a harsh tone of voice, he said, "After seeing the way the captain's widow is taking her husband's death, I'm almost hoping this character tries something." Jim picked up the second gun, and after he made sure the safety was on, he handed it back to Jennifer. "I'd like you to get used to the feel of this gun. The weight of the silencer is going to cause you to shoot low if you don't pay attention. Just handle it a little and get used to it. With any luck you won't have to use it."

Jennifer gave the weapon a quick inspection, and after she slipped the clip back into the handle, she said, "I've done a little shooting with one of these. They had a couple of them at the academy, and we were allowed to fire quite a few rounds through them." She leaned forward in the seat and touched the silencer to the back of the driver's head and added, "Just remember what I said, butthead. Guys like you have had your way much too long, but that's about to change. If you so much as twitch your nose wrong, I just might take it as a signal for some of your friends." She was grinning as she hammed it up for Jim's benefit as he watched her. She put a force in her voice that even surprised her when she said, "Jim, I just want you to know that if this thug tries anything at all, you'd better be ready to grab the steering wheel because I'm going to blow his spine in half right through the seat."

Jim was trying to keep from laughing as he watched Jennifer pantomiming in the rear seat. He thought her little act was hilarious, but he didn't have any problem seeing the way the driver had taken her threat.

The driver gripped the steering wheel harder so his hands wouldn't tremble so violently, but it didn't work. He was really regretting leaving the soft work of pushing drugs around the schools near his neighborhood, but the money had just sounded so good and so easy. He didn't get any satisfaction from knowing the man who had talked him into being an enforcer for Williams was now sprawled out on the floorboards behind him. It really didn't make him feel one tiny bit better.

Jim directed the driver to the location where he had parked the Neon, and once more he watched the smooth movements of Jennifer as she walked to his car and unlocked it. He took a deep breath and motioned with his gun for the driver to take off when she waved an okay.

The driver surprised him when he said, "Man, you got some doll there. I knew a couple of gals like that a few years ago. They were real lookers, but after they got into drugs a couple of times, they couldn't let it go. The hard stuff they got into really took them down in a hurry." He looked over at Jim when he finished his little remark, and the cold look in the man's eye stopped any further remarks on the spot. Little did this man know that years ago, Jim had lost his wife when she was unable to handle the loneliness that came with being the wife of a young rookie cop. She had taken up doing drugs. In the end, she knew there was no return trip, so she had purposely overdosed. That was the main reason Jim was completely single-minded when it came to drug pushers. He had never known any emotion as sharply as the one called hate after he lost his little Ming.

The man pulled up to a large rambling house on the north side of the street, but before he reached up to the visor to punch the door opener, he made sure Jim knew what he was going to do first. He'd always had the opinion that he was a real tough character, but he was finding out he wasn't nearly as tough as his passenger and that broad of his were. It didn't take long after he'd gotten behind the steering wheel to realize how close he was to dying. Over the years, he'd gotten used to living, and he intended to do everything he could to keep things that way. He pulled into the garage, waited for the Neon to stop beside him, and then punched the door button once more. While the smaller car pulled into the garage, he decided he didn't really owe Williams that much at all.

Chapter 11

Jim had to squeeze through the open door of the car because Jennifer had gotten just a little too close when she parked the Neon; her chagrined grimace showed she realized her mistake. She stood in front of the hoodlum's car and made it clear that she'd book no funny business. It was obvious to Jim that she knew how to handle that heavy gun because of the easy way she was handling it. She also made it crystal clear to the man, as he stepped out of the car, that she wasn't going hesitate to pull the trigger if she decided the time had come to use it. He made it crystal clear that he believed every word she had uttered.

They entered the kitchen, but before they switched on the lights, Jim let her know that he wanted to search the house. Jennifer used her cuffs and secured him to the refrigerator door and then stood guard in the kitchen while Jim did his searching. Jim dodged from room to room with his gun ready in his hand as he searched for any guests he hadn't been told about. Jennifer stood next to the kitchen table with her gun covering the doorway leaving the kitchen as well as the unhappy man handcuffed to the door handle. She knew the handle could easily be broken or ripped off the door, but she also knew it was secure enough to give her the time she needed to move the gun in his direction and pull the trigger to eliminate any threat he might pose.

Jim stepped into the kitchen several minutes later, and then quickly began pulling shades and closing curtains before he switched the lights on. All three of them were forced to squint until their eyes became used to the light, and then Jim left the room once more. The way he left showed he had something particular in mind.

Jennifer heard some beeping sounds, and then there was a flickering light coming from a dark room. She stepped past the handcuffed man and into the living room doorway, but she stayed where she could keep an eye on the man. She saw Jim was sitting in front of a cluttered desk and was obviously perturbed with his inability to make the computer do what he wanted it to do.

Jim looked over his shoulder. "Are you any good with these blasted things? I never could get these stupid things to do anything right."

Jennifer quickly nodded her head, but she looked over at her prisoner for a moment. "What about this one? Do you want to leave him in here alone?"

Leaving that man alone was one of the last things he wanted to do, and minutes later, the man found himself shackled to a weight-lifting apparatus that was equipped with a weight-lifting bar on it that looked like it already had over three hundred pounds connected to it. The man could sit on the bench, but he needed to remain bent over or he had the choice of sitting on the floor. The man quickly chose the floor, and he sat cross legged as he watched Jennifer's fingers flying across the keyboard of the computer.

Jim watched her playing the keyboard like an experienced piano player. He waited until she was successful at bringing up a portion of the information that Harris had stored on the disc before he nodded his head and said, "All right, sweetheart, I just wanted to make sure there was something on that disc to justify coming back here and working with the computer after we move the other car."

Jennifer quickly eyed the handcuffed man. "What about butt-head here? We can't leave him like this. If he gets loose somehow and gets away or even gets to a phone, then we're going to have a lot of trouble coming in our direction, or even waiting for us, when we get back here."

Jim agreed as he looked at the man for a moment, but then a smile crossed his face. "Okay, cowboy. I want you to slide under that bench until just your head and shoulders are sticking out right under the bar that's holding the weights." When the man was positioned where he was told to, Jim took his own cuffs and secured the man's right hand to the second leg of the weight-lifting frame.

Jennifer was watching him with a puzzled look on her face, but when she saw Jim placing a barbell across the throat of the prisoner, she began to grin. While Jim began putting the weights back on the barbell, she was on the other side and was grunting to add more weights to balance out the ones Jim was placing on it. When they finished, there was almost five hundred pounds of steel imprisoning his head even though the bar was barely denting the man's throat. With his hands cuffed to the legs of the bench, there would be no way he would be able to eliminate any of the weights from the bar in order to make an escape effort.

Just before Jennifer headed for the door behind Jim, she looked down at the cuffed man and said sweetly, "You know, since we've become such good friends, I think it's about time you tell us your name. I'm getting tired of trying to think of names for you, even though you really are a butthead."

The secured man took a deep breath, and then he said, "My name is Sampson. Todd Sampson."

Jennifer looked down at the man and moved the silenced gun over his frame. "Well, Sampson, meet Delilah. I just want you to know that if you try anything at all, you're going to loose more than your hair."

The man's knees involuntarily pulled closer together as the muzzle of the silenced gun crossed the general area of his genitals, and sweat once more broke out on his brow.

Jennifer smiled sweetly as she added, "Now you be sure you don't go anywhere without me, Sammy boy. I'll be back in a little while to tuck you in. Sleep tight."

The sights of the gun once more crossed over Todd's family jewels, and he felt sweat beginning to cause his shirt to stick to him. He'd been having some erotic thoughts about himself and this beautiful broad while he'd been watching her moving about the room. The kind of thoughts he'd been having was beginning to arouse him. When he saw where the gun was being aimed, it quickly dismissed all thoughts of intimacy, and he quickly began to shrink to a size that was even much smaller than normal. He cowered on the floor and felt like a whipped pup when Jennifer walked out of the room. Even when watching that shapely bottom moving away from his position, there were no erotic thoughts floating about in his mind any longer.

On the way back to the Harris home, Jennifer told Jim about the obvious amorous condition Sampson had been in and how she had rectified the situation. They were still laughing and joking about the man's predicament when they got near the alley that held the car with the bodies in it.

Jim explained where the car was located in the alley. When he got out, he said he was going to take a quick look around before he jumped in the car for the return trip to Williams' house. Before he left, his last instructions to her were very emphatic and specific: "Wait in the car until I come back."

Gray slipped away from the Neon and disappeared in the darkness as he moved into the shadows of the alley. Jennifer sat and frowned as she stared across the hood of the small car. Her fingers caressed the heavy silencer absently as she fought against the resentment of being left behind. It was clear in her mind that she was being left behind in this situation simply because she was a female and therefore didn't know how to take care of herself. She began to fume as her mind refused to leave the subject alone.

Jim knelt beside the same trash barrel he'd used earlier as he eyed the car once more. It appeared quiet in the neighborhood, and he prepared to move in so he could get the car out of there before some well-meaning citizen saw the parked car in the alley and called the police. He was just coming off his knees when he saw a movement. He quickly checked the alley behind him as he settled back down behind the trash container.

The shadowy shape slipped out of the Harris backyard gate and became more distinct in the open drive of the alley before it disappeared behind the black shape of a large bush. The bush was only feet away from the car holding the remains of the two unlucky watchers. After several minutes, Jim saw the shape floating closer to the car. Finally, the shape straightened as the cautious man moved alongside the vehicle. Presently, the shape bent once more as the man tried to see into the car. The shape slowly straightened once more when he was unable to find the men who were supposed to be there.

Jim heard the perplexed man releasing a soft but irritated sigh as he looked up and down the alley while he searched for his partners. He was positive this man had nothing to do with the police force, and once more, he was thankful for the silenced guns he'd had dropped into his possession by the timely deaths of the first gunmen he'd encountered. Jim remained poised for action as he watched the man quietly moving around the alley while he tried to determine where his partners in crime had disappeared to.

There wasn't a sound in the alley, but suddenly, Jim knew he wasn't alone. Besides the man standing next to the car, he knew someone else was near. He slowly turned his head, and his heart skipped a number of beats when he saw a large man down on one knee in the center of the alley. There was no mistaking the stance the man had taken nor was there any mistaking the gun that was being aimed in his direction. The light from a distant streetlight reflected from the smooth metal of the gun and its steady shine showed that this man wasn't a novice with that instrument because there wasn't even a hint of a waver

Jim slowly reached down and placed the confiscated pistol on the ground before he raised his hands high in the air in an obvious show of surrender. There was a soft murmuring as the man said something soft. Seconds later, he heard the static-filled reply as the man beside the car spoke into his own two-way radio.

Without moving from his shooter's stance, the man motioned for Jim to stand and then to move in the direction of the car.

The second man braced his left elbow against the top of the car and was clearly prepared for any kind of trick at all as he watched the figure moving in his direction through the darkness. The gun never wavered from the target he'd mentally pinned over the heart of the man approaching him in the alley. When Jim drew near the car, the criminal motioned for Jim to stop and kneel on the ground. As Jim complied, his hands still high in the air, the man raised his radio to his head and told the second man to advance but to keep his eyes open for any sign of a trick because he absolutely didn't trust this man.

It was almost instantaneous as the second man came up behind him that Jim felt the barrel of an unsilenced gun pressing against his neck. He knew he'd been in some pretty deep stuff before in his career as a police detective, but it had never gotten anywhere this deep. He was finding himself in quite an uncomfortable situation because he was on his knees, pressing his hands against the trunk of the car, and had two guns aimed at his head. He knew any sudden movement from him would quickly be met with lead from those guns near his head. He also knew it wasn't going to make any difference to him how loud the guns were when the hoodlums pulled the triggers because he'd be past hearing at that point.

When Jim looked up, he saw the first man he'd encountered had taken over the task of covering him while the second man moved back a step. Seconds later, the man behind Jim jerked him to his feet and began to frisk him. It only took a moment before his Special was in the man's possession, and Jim suddenly felt even more naked than he had earlier.

Hoping to find some kind of an opening where he could get the upper hand, he waited until the man was frisking close to his crotch before he remarked, "Hey there, I think you're having just a little too much fun down there, aren't you?"

Before he had a chance to say anything more, he felt an explosion right behind his right ear as the man swung his gun in retaliation to the remark. Jim blinked his eyes to clear his vision, and then he realized he was once more on his knees. The officer slowly shook his head as he tried to shake the bobbing lights and spinning stars out of his own little solar system. Slowly, the pain from the blow really began to make itself felt, and the pressure of his hands against his head didn't do a thing about stopping the pain. The wet warmth he felt dripping from his gripping hands told him he'd be extremely lucky if he got out of this predicament in one piece.

The men each grabbed an arm and slammed him up against the car so hard it caused a number of dogs to begin barking nearby. The man who had come up behind Jim leaned close to his face and whispered, "Who are you, and where are my partners?"

Jim shook his head once more to stop the double vision he was experiencing at the moment and immediately regretted that movement. He took a deep breath before he said, "We got a call about a car being parked here in the alley, and I was told to come out here to investigate. Sergeant Kantz said I was to give him a call back at the station as soon as I found out what was going on down here."

Before Jim realized what was happening, he felt the man's fist pushing deep into his lower abdomen. Jim doubled over from the blow and tried to catch his breath as well as keep from emptying his stomach. He was finally able to suck in some air, but he failed miserably in trying to keep from retching. Although the sounds were faint in his mind, he heard the man talking in a soft but harsh voice.

After the man pushed Jim against the car once more, he said, "The next time I ask you a question, I better not hear another lie. You were carrying a gun with a silencer, and a plainclothes cop on a routine check wouldn't be doing that. Now, one more time. Who are you, and what are you doing here?"

Jim held up his hand for a moment and then slowly reached into his back pocket. The faint light from the distant street lights glittered off the badge Jim held up in the air. The man in front quickly grabbed the metal shield from Jim's fingers and held it up to the light.

There was astonishment in the man's voice as he said, "Hey, this guy really is a cop." It was silent for a moment, and when the man started talking again, there was a completely different tone to his voice. Now it carried a very menacing tone as he said, "You know what? This is the guy that's been giving the boss all the headaches. This is that Detective Gray he's been hollering about. This is the guy we're supposed to looking for. Well, looks like we don't have to do any more searching for this guy."

The man who had delivered the blow to Jim's stomach said, "Well, you know, man, this will put us in a pretty good light when we deliver this guy's body to the boss. Wales told me the other night there'd be a good reward for the man who brings this troublemaker in. And as far as I know, the offer is for either dead or alive."

The man took a couple of steps away from Jim so he'd have a better line of fire. Before he could deliver the killing shot, the first man said, "Whoa, wait a minute. You know how bad the boss wants this guy, so wouldn't you think there would be more of a tendency to make him really break loose with the cash if we bring him in alive?" The first man saw his partner's hesitation, and then he added, "I'd sooner take him in and let the boss do the trigger-pulling. Not only do we get the cash, but if he does the deed himself, then it's just another thing we've got that we can hold over him if we happen to get caught or something like that. He won't let us sit in prison if we got information like cop-killing on him. Man, this guy is money in the bank for us."

Jim slowly allowed himself to take a deep breath as the man behind him stopped to think. The man stood for almost a minute before Jim heard the scuffling of his shoe in the darkness.

His voice was soft, and it gave evidence that he was not completely convinced as the second man as he uttered a slow "Yeah, well, okay." The man pushed Jim against the car once more, placed the muzzle of his gun against the side of Jim's throat, and growled, "But before we leave here, I want to know where my friends are." He looked around for a moment before he added, "I ain't sold on taking you back alive, so don't think you're gonna hold out on us, cop. Now," he growled in Jim's ear, "where are those men who were in this car?"

Jim had his hand on the trunk of the car to keep from being bent over the fender. "I'm sure they're close by here somewhere."

The man released a growl from deep in his throat as he raised his hand to deliver another blow to the back of Jim's head. Just as the man started to bring the heavy gun down toward his head, Jim felt a sharp pain in his shoulder. In that same instant, the man's partner suddenly dropped his gun and grabbed his chest.

The other man stared wide-eyed in shock at the actions of his partner, and Jim knew he didn't have much time before the man recovered from his shock. He quickly brought his arm back and shoved his elbow into the man's soft beer gut as hard and as deeply as he could.

Even while the man was doubling over from the blow, he didn't take his eyes off his partner as the man slowly folded to the ground with a slowly spreading stain on his right shirt pocket. The only sounds that came out of the second man's mouth were grunts of pain as he tried to catch his own breath from the blow to the stomach. Slowly the man dropped to his knees as he gasped for air. When he was finally able to speak again, he said, "I knew we shoulda killed ya. Right from the start, I knew we shoulda put a gun to your head and killed ya."

Jim watched the gasping hoodlum for the space of several heartbeats before he glanced down the alley. He saw the silenced gun was in Jennifer's outstretched hands as she slowly and cautiously advanced in his direction. He easily saw the whites of her eyes because they were wide and unblinking as she methodically and laboriously placed one foot in front of the other and approached with extreme caution.

She almost appeared to be in shock as she stepped closer to the car. Jim quickly asked, "Are you all right, Jennifer?"

She slowly looked down and stared at the dead man lying on the ground beside the car. Jim had to ask the question a second time before she finally looked up at him. It took a moment before she gathered her senses enough to be able to speak. The young woman still appeared to be in shock as she stuttered, "D...d... did...I...do...do that?"

Jim looked down at the corpse, and in an effort to minimize the effect on her, he said lightheartedly, "You sure did, sweetheart. You saved my life by pulling the trigger when you did." She appeared to be unable to function on her own at the moment, so he opened the car door and got her to sit on the seat. He returned to the rear of the car and held a gun on the living, but gasping, gangster while the man muscled his partner into the trunk to join the other bodies.

When the man saw the remains of his working buddies already lying in the trunk, he almost fell over with his burden. The man eased the third body into the trunk and quickly arranged all the arms and legs so the lid could be closed. It took a little time and some effort to finish his job, and his face appeared to be a little on the green side when he finally managed to close the trunk lid.

Jim was going to tie the man's hands behind him with a piece of electric cord he'd found in the alley, but just when he got the man standing against the car with his hands behind him, they heard someone calling out from a back porch. The woman was demanding to know what was going on, and her voice was so high pitched that he knew the entire neighborhood was going to be awake in a matter of minutes if someone didn't quiet her down. He quickly called out, "Police, ma'am." He turned to Jennifer and said, "Go and talk to that woman before she wakes the dead. Let her know we're police so she doesn't make a call and give us more headaches. Ah…tell her we just got a break in an ongoing investigation and that she should be quiet about anything she heard because we don't want to alert the rest of the gang or something like that. You got that, sweetheart?"

Jennifer slowly pushed her way out of the car and through the backyard gate, but she was lacking in enthusiasm as she did Jim's bidding. By the time the door to the house closed and Jennifer returned, she appeared to be more herself again. She helped Jim as he worked to get his man tied up to his satisfaction before she finally noticed his bloody arm.

Jennifer suddenly looked at his blood-soaked shirt and pointed. "You're bleeding! How did that happen?"

Jim stopped what he was doing and just looked at her while she pulled his sleeve up so she could check out the wound.

As soon as she had the wound exposed, she stopped what she was doing and stared at it for a long moment. Suddenly she looked up and said, "Oh no! Did I…?" She took another deep breath and softly added, "Oh my!"

Despite the painful graze on his arm, he was forced to laugh at the look on her face. He gave her a gentle push down the alley in the direction of the Neon. "Don't worry about it. We'll take a run down to the firing range after this is over, and you can do some practicing."

She looked over her shoulder as she headed for the car. "Butthead." There wasn't much force behind her words.

Jim was still feeling plenty of pain in his abdomen from the blow he'd gotten, but he was nevertheless grinning as he pulled out of the alley in the car that belonged to Williams and his men. It only took a minute before he saw the headlights of the Neon pulling in behind him.

There were a few people heading for work already, but there wasn't really much traffic yet as they headed for the south part of town. Less than a half hour later, they were parked near the house. Jim was tempted to go in alone and check to make sure no changes had occurred while they were gone, but then he decided against it because he didn't want to leave the thug alone, and he wasn't too sure about Jennifer's condition after what had happened.

Finally, he shook his head and decided to take that chance. He was confident that the weights had been too heavy for the man to get off and the man would still be lying on his back in the living room. With just another second of hesitation, he took his foot off the brake pedal, pulled up to the garage door, and hit the door opener button. He looked at the interior of the garage for several seconds and then decided to go for it. Jennifer parked the Neon a little way down the street from the house. As soon as she stepped inside the garage, Jim hit the button to close the big door.

With the complaining gorilla belonging to Williams walking ahead of him, Jim stepped into the kitchen. Everything still appeared to be as he had left it, and when he moved into the living room, he saw the man they had left behind was still keeping company with the weight-lifting equipment.

The look of anticipation fell from the man's face when he saw who was coming through the doorway. Before the man on the floor had a chance to speak, the unhappy and chagrined man standing in front of Jim said, "She got Mel. She got him with one shot. He didn't have a chance." The words came out as though he was resigned to his fate. It was clear he didn't expect to get out of this predicament alive, and Jim didn't do or say anything to alter his thoughts.

After Jim made another thorough inspection of the house, he stopped in the doorway of the living room where Jennifer was holding a gun on the thug. He stopped beside the young woman, and when he looked at Jennifer, he said, "Why don't you take the Neon and head back home? I'll find a way to pick it up later. I don't know yet what I'm going to do with those two jokers in the living room, but I intend to spend the day trying to decipher that code that Harris used." He looked at the clock on the wall and said, "You can still get a couple of hours' worth of sleep before you have to show up at work. I think you'd better take the opportunity and get some sleep while you can."

She turned to face him, and she was laughing as she said, "Butthead. Today is Saturday. I don't have to be at work again until Monday morning. And don't forget, I've seen how you handle the computer. I think if we want to get something done on this case, I'm going to have to be the one sitting in front of the computer until we find out what we've got on that CD." She started to turn away when a thought hit her. "What are you going to do about that third car that's parked back there near the captain's home? You know it won't take long before someone in the neighborhood calls in about the abandoned car sitting in front of their house." She hesitated for a moment before she added, "These guys probably have their cars parked somewhere in the street out front."

Jim shrugged his shoulders. "Let them call. To begin with, it shouldn't cause any problems for us because there aren't any bodies in that car's trunk and nor does it have any of our prints on it, so I don't really care what happens to either one. If the police impound those vehicles, it could also give us the benefit of getting Williams all confused and concerned about his missing men. Maybe he'll get worked up enough and make some mistake that will help us hang his backside on the barn doors." He looked at his partner and laughed. "We'll let some of the other detectives worry about the parking problems in this town. I think we'll just forget about those cars and work on the problem at hand."

Jennifer looked into his eyes for a long moment before she finally nodded and acknowledged his line of thinking. She slowly released a small smile as she turned away from him. After two steps, she stopped and looked over her shoulder. "Just be a good little girl and stay in the car, huh? I expect to hear something from you on that subject before we're done with this. You betcha!"

As Jennifer walked to the computer desk, she was very aware that Jim was watching her every move. *Maybe he had spent the night with that other broad,* she was thinking, *but I don't think that's something I'm going to have to contend with again.* She flipped the switch on the computer. As she reached for the switch on the monitor, she paused long enough to look over she shoulder. She had been right because Jim was watching her every move, and there was desire in his eyes and on his face. For some time, she'd had her doubts about her own ability to attract this man, but now she decided that maybe she did have what it took to turn him on. Just as she surrounded herself with that thought, another thought crept in and hit her that maybe it had been the violence of the night that had stirred up his juices. She didn't really believe that he had become so twisted that the killing had made him look at her in such a desirable way. Whatever the reason was, she was sure of one thing. If it turned out that it was killing that turned him on, there was no doubt in her mind that she was quickly going to be a part of his past, not his future.

Chapter 12

Jim could hear the computer keys clacking as Jennifer continued in her efforts. Painstakingly, she tried to find some clue that would provide the means for breaking the code that Harris must have concocted during his last days alive. Jim's mind had become a blur from staring at the screen for such a long time. To bring things back into focus, he went into the living room for a change of scenery.

The men were still lying side by side, and Jim had to put in a strong effort to keep from laughing at the human pretzel he saw on the floor. When he had tied up the two men, he had used both pairs of handcuffs as well as a length of heavy wire from the garage. When Jim left them, he knew the men weren't going to go anywhere without permission because he had them positioned in such a way that they would be unable to combine their strength to lift that heavy weight off their necks.

The two men glared at Jim when he entered the room, but they wisely kept their silence. They had quickly learned that the loudest complainer was going to be the one who ended up in the most twisted position. Because they had learned so slowly, each of them had found themselves rearranged to the extent that they had finally learned it was better to be silent than to be uncomfortable.

The two police officers had spent the remainder of the day as well as much of the night working on the computer, but nothing so far had shown them they were gaining on the problem. Jim's eyes were burning as he dropped into the recliner that was set in the corner. He played with the remote for several minutes until he stopped at a talk show where they were beating up the pros and cons of approving contraceptive use in the nation's schools. It slowly slipped from his fingers and found a resting place on his stomach. The TV continued to drone on with its senseless chatter, and in the background, the clacking of the computer keys were like a sedative as he dropped into a deep sleep.

Captain Harris was in the middle of another tirade in which Jim was once more the center of attention when suddenly a door slammed. The sudden sound startled Jim out of his sleep, and he jerked in the chair.

Jim remained in the easy chair, but by the time he heard the stranger's voice, he already had his Special in his hand.

The man's voice sounded angry as Jim heard him say, "Where the hell you guys at? You're supposed to be watching the captain's house. The boss is gonna be mad as…"

The man stopped talking and came to a sudden stop when he saw the pair of men handcuffed together on the floor. He stood without moving, and with his mouth hanging open for a long moment, he took in the odd scene. The newcomer was a well-dressed man in a suit, and it matched his complexion and hair. The man clearly considered himself a class or two above the average working man. It was very clear this was an impression he was proud of and wanted everyone to be aware of. It was also clear he wasn't ready for this kind of reception. When he finally came to his senses and began to reach for his gun, he quickly learned he was much too late.

Jim waited for a long moment as the well-dressed man gaped in the direction of the two prisoners before the man finally came to life. It only took the cocking sound of the .38 Special to bring the man's actions to a halt. Jim would have sworn the man quickly lost several shades of color when he saw the gun aimed in his direction. Jim was hoping the man wouldn't make him pull the trigger because if he did, he was sure the police would quickly be there to investigate the loud gunshot. He'd never had much use for automatics, but this was one time he was really wishing he'd kept the silenced gun with him. It wasn't really doing him much good lying beside the computer.

His thoughts were interrupted when he heard Jennifer saying, "If he makes a move, I want him. I don't like loud noises when I'm tired." He saw she was holding the silenced gun with both hands at full arms' reach, and it appeared she was ready to use it.

The man's eyes shifted between the man with the revolver who was leaning back in the recliner and the pretty blonde in the doorway who was struggling to hold the heavy gun steady. It was clear that he realized how unprepared he was to meet this situation when he took a deep breath. As he slowly expelled the air from his lungs, his hands eased away from the weapon under his suit coat.

The men under the weights were quick to push the blame of being caught away from them. "They caught us by surprise, Henderson. They killed Mason, Wales, and Moralas. We didn't have a chance."

Jim motioned with his gun, and the newcomer immediately understood the silent command and raised his hands higher. "Keep him covered while I'll pull this dog's teeth," he told Jennifer as he brought his chair to the upright position. He began frisking the man and then he said, "So you're Henderson, huh? You're a hard guy to get a picture of. You're one of the men I've already linked to Williams and all the killing and drug dealing that's been going on here. It's nice to make your acquaintance, but judging from the look on your face, I don't think the feeling is mutual, is it?" Jim smiled at the cold glare he got from Henderson.

The man didn't move as Jim frisked him after removing the .45 Auto from his holster. Jim gave him a shove and told him to sit in the corner while he went through the garage door in search of something to use as a restraint.

When he returned with a handful of plastic ties from the Neon, which were a good substitute for handcuffs, he saw a deep look of concentration on Jennifer's face. He didn't bother asking about it because his first chore was to make sure this newcomer in the fancy suit wasn't going to cause a problem.

Jim straightened from where Henderson was sitting all trussed up in the corner and walked over to where Jennifer was still standing. "You know, sweetheart, that character's suit and shirt probably cost him more than I make in six months."

When Jennifer neglected to offer a comment on his remark, Jim looked over and saw the look of concentration and puzzlement was still clearly visible on her face. He looked back at the object of her attention. "What's wrong? What do you find so interesting?"

She was silent for a long moment before she slowly turned toward Jim and softly said, "You know that first day I was with you on that shooting incident? Well, think about some of the descriptions we got when we interviewed several of the witnesses after the shooting." Jennifer looked back at Jim for a long moment before she turned and stared at the new man. "Who does he remind you of?"

Jim slowly turned and faced Henderson, and it only took several seconds before he began to nod his head. He didn't say a word to Jennifer as he headed for the front door of the house. He stood and looked at the car that was parked in the driveway for a long moment before he returned to where Jennifer was standing.

He stood and faced Henderson for another long moment before he whispered to Jennifer, "You're right. This joker drove up in a nice silver Lincoln. I think we've got the guy who was doing the chasing the other night."

Jim stood thoughtfully as he stared at Henderson before he turned and went back into the garage. When he returned, he was holding a board that was one inch thick, four inches wide, and three feet long.

Henderson gazed at Jim in a very unconcerned manner until the crack of the blow to the bottom of his foot caused at first surprise and then pain. His mouth dropped open, and he squirmed about on the floor as he tried to stop the pain coming from the bottom of his foot.

Jim smiled at the man. "Now that I have your attention, I think you and I need to have a little talk. I think we'll start our little conversation by having you tell us where a certain tan Chevrolet Suburban is at this time."

The man began to laugh at Jim's suggestion, but the look on his face quickly changed, and a cold look of hatred took the place of the humor that had been there. "What you already did will be classified as police brutality. Anything you get out of me will be thrown out of court. Didn't you already learn that? There's nothing you can do to make me talk that's going to stand up in a court of law. Just let us go, and we'll forget about what happened. I'll even see about getting the bodies taken care of." The self-assured grin returned. "There's nothing you can do, so just make it easy on yourself and let us go."

Jim changed the attitude of the man when he lifted the man off the floor. The young officer pulled the man forward with the lapels of his jacket and then made his head bounce off the wall when he pushed Henderson back. "I want some answers out of you. What happened to that person you were chasing the other night? What happened to that yellow bug you caused to wreck? What happened to that driver?" Jim found he was almost hollering, and he forced himself to take a deep breath to calm himself down.

Henderson let his back slide down the wall until he was once more in a sitting position. The man gave his head a quick shake. Then he quietly sat and glared at Jim while the officer took a number of deep breaths as he tried to calm himself down. There was a moment of silence before he propelled a globule of saliva in the direction of Jim's face.

Jim ducked back but not in time, and it struck him on his right cheek. He quickly reached for the man's throat and pinned him against the wall while he casually used the man's own jacket to wipe his face clean. Jim's face appeared calm as he pushed himself to his feet. He looked down at the satisfied look on Henderson's face for several minutes before he turned.

He walked up to Jennifer and reached out to her slender arm. He gently began to guide her back into the bedroom that held the computer. "Sweetheart," he said, "up to now, you've just seen me trying to get this bloodsucker's attention. I want you go back in there and start on the computer again. I also want you to turn either the radio or the television on loud enough that it'll block out any sounds from out here." He saw she was going to object, but he quickly added, "Right now, there isn't anything that can be done to discipline you because of this case. So far, everything you've done has been legal. I plan on getting some answers, and right now, I'm not worried about legalities." He hesitated for several seconds before he added, "I don't plan on being the reason for you not getting the promotions you want. Just go in there and close the door. We still need the code to the information on that disc, so I want you to concentrate on that. I'll take care of everything out here. All right?"

Jennifer slowly looked at Henderson before her eyes strayed back to Jim's face. She saw an anger deeply etched on his face. She also knew he was asking her to leave to protect her from any legal ramifications. There was no doubt he intended to get those answers whether she was in that room or not. It was very clear that Jim took Henderson's action of spitting on him as a complete rebuke of the law that Jim was dedicated to. Jennifer was well aware that there were some angles to the law that he didn't agree with, but that a little cutting of some corners was agreeable as far as he saw it. It was clearly written on Jim's face that he absolutely didn't agree with the total disregard of the law as it was demonstrated by this character.

Jennifer opened her mouth to ask him to think twice before he got in over his head, but as soon as she looked over at him, she slowly closed her mouth. She looked at Henderson for a long time before she slowly nodded her head. She held the silenced gun against her thigh as she slowly backed up several steps before she turned, went into the bedroom, and gently closed the door.

He could hear her tuning the radio station, and seconds later, he heard the volume being adjusted to a higher level as she complied with his wishes. He turned his head and looked at Henderson for several seconds before he picked up the remote control and turned the volume up on the television. The sound had been set very low earlier, but now he wasn't interested in taking a nap. He had other things on his mind.

As he reached for Henderson's coat once more, he saw the man preparing to spit once more. Before the man could complete the action, Jim quickly backhanded the man and snarled. "If you try to spit on me again, you're going to spend the next few minutes spitting out a lot of teeth or swallowing them because I'm going to take my fist and shove them to the back of your throat. Am I making myself clear?"

Jim grabbed the lapels of the expensive jacket and lifted the man to his feet again. He stood nose to nose with Henderson for several seconds before he gave the man a shove into the kitchen. Jim placed Henderson in a kitchen chair so hard the chair almost went over backwards. "All right now, just so you understand what you're up against, I'll tell you a thing or two."

Another quick backhand caught the man unawares, and before the blood began to drip from his split lip, Jim continued. "Number one, I'm not acting as a police office here. Number two, the chances of you getting out of here alive, if you don't talk to me, are actually pretty slim." Jim looked at the angry but surprised face for a long time before he said, "So far you've been running loose because we couldn't get the goods on you legally, so now I'm going to start working like you do." The man's eyes grew wider as Jim added, "Don't expect me to take you downtown where Williams' fast talking lawyers can get at you. Our talks are going to take place right here. And like I said earlier, I want you to keep in mind that I'm not working as a police officer, so any charges of police brutality just won't work in this matter. It's just you and me. I've got the questions, and you'd better have the answers. The sooner you answer those questions, the better you're going to feel when we're done.

"Now, let's get started. Do you deny chasing after the yellow VW that we talked about earlier?" He saw the hesitation forming on the man's face as he tried to think of a plausible excuse, but a quick stiff-fingered jab to the man's stomach made him change his mind in a hurry, and he shook his head as he gasped for air.

Jim smiled like a pleased teacher when his efforts of teaching were rewarded by positive results from a kindergarten child. "Good, good. Now I want you to tell me what happened after the driver lost control of that small car in the intersection."

Henderson was slow in responding, and it quickly earned him another resounding backhand to the side of his face. He shook his head as he tried to clear his head while the blood dripped from his chin and ruined the fancy suit and shirt. He saw Jim was ready to deliver another one to his face, and he quickly said, "Yeah, I was chasing him. He owed the boss a pile of cash, and then on top of that, he tried to run with the merchandise. It's my job to stop that from happening, and that's just what I did."

Henderson stopped talking, and immediately, it was obvious to Jim that the man was stalling for time. It was very clear the man was trying to think of a good enough story that wouldn't incriminate him. He wasn't ready for the second stiff-fingered jab into his stomach that almost touched his spine.

A small amount of liquid, which was mostly digested food, mixed with the blood that was dribbling from the man's chin. He tried hard to keep his food from coming up, and he tried to suck air back into his lungs.

Jim waited until he was breathing a little better before he growled, "When I ask you a question, I want an answer right away. I don't want to see you stalling for time while you make up some wild story. Do I make myself clear on that point?"

Henderson quickly nodded his head, and when Jim told him to continue with his story, he didn't hesitate. "I was after the man because he owed the boss for the last shipment, but he said he had to deliver this supply before he got the money. The boss didn't like what the man told him, and he sent me after the con artist with orders that I was to stop that scam from happening again. He knew what the deal was. What happened was his own fault."

Jim nodded his head. "I'd like you to tell me what was in that delivery he was supposed to pay for."

The man looked down at his shoes and mumbled something soft and incoherent. When Jim brought his hand back for another persuading blow, Henderson quickly jerked his head back and blurted out, "Cocaine. He was carrying cocaine for the boss."

Jim shook his head. "And you think that garbage is worth a man's life?" He watched as Henderson gave him a look that said "What kind of silly question is that?" Jim slowly shook his head as he took a deep breath and said, "I guess I know where you're coming from, don't I?" Jim parked his thigh on the edge of the table before he motioned for the man to continue.

Henderson ran his tongue over his split lip several times before he said, "I chased him all the way across town before I caught up with him. He tried to jump me, and I fired. That's all there is to it."

Jim let a derisive bark leave his lips. "Right, the guy is unarmed while you're armed. He runs away from his car in fright, but he jumps you when you get close." Jim shook his head. "Am I going to have to persuade you again? I told you before that I only want the truth. Nothing but."

Henderson was just starting to talk when a movement from the doorway caught Jim's eye. Before he could react, he felt a man's weight slamming against him. He went down under the handcuffed man, and he started to wrestle with the man who had burst through the doorway. It didn't take long to realize there wasn't any resistance coming from the man who was on top of him.

Jim quickly disengaged himself from the prone body on the floor, and then he heard Jennifer talking. He quickly got his own gun positioned and was covering Henderson when he moved closer to the doorway. When he looked into the living room, he saw the second prisoner sitting beside the weights, and all he had around his wrists were the set of handcuffs Jennifer had placed there herself.

"Go on, fella. Make one more move to get up and see what happens to you as well." She looked over and saw Jim was standing in the doorway with his gun ready and she added, "Are you all right?"

Jim nodded his head. "What happened? How'd you see what was going on?"

Jennifer said, "I didn't see anything. Something just didn't feel right. I eased the door open just as the other one started for you. I had this gun in my hand when I went to the door so I was ready." She hesitated for a moment, and then she asked, "Did I hit him?"

Jim was a little shook by the closeness of the attack, but he managed to grin as he said, "I guess we won't have to spend as much time at the shooting range as I thought. That was a good shot. You saved my life once more, sweetheart."

He moved back to Henderson after he told Jennifer to keep a watch on the man in the living room. "All right, cowboy. It's time to take the garbage out." He nodded in the direction of the dead man, and then he said, "Like they said in an old western TV series, Pick 'em up and head 'em out."

Jim opened the door to the garage, and then he opened the trunk on the second car. For several seconds, he thought

Henderson was going to get sick when the man looked into the trunk and saw the bodies of several of his partners in crime.

Henderson looked up at the man holding the gun on him. "The boss is gonna get you for this. He's gonna send his whole force out after you. You won't make it a day once word gets out on what you did."

Jim reached into his pocket for the keys to the second car. "Just dump that carcass on top of the others and then close the trunk lid." He watched as his orders were followed. As soon as Henderson closed the trunk, he tossed the second set of keys to the man. "Now open the other trunk. Don't worry, I'm not going to put you in there. Unless you give me reason to, of course."

The tough gunman wasn't as tough as he thought because when he saw the bodies in the second car, his knees grew weak and he was forced to put his hands on the fender to hold himself up. He tried not to look into the trunk as he gently closed the lid. He took several deep breaths before he turned and faced the police officer. "You can't go killing men like that." He caught himself before he blurted out that things like that were against the law. He felt the bile rising in his stomach as the man standing between the cars motioned for him to head for the kitchen once more. All he had to say on the way to the kitchen was "The boss is gonna flip out when he finds out about what you did."

Gray was not too perturbed at Henderson's observations because his own mind was working on the opposite end of the problem at figuring out a way for Williams' demise.

Jim was at a loss at determining the method the man had used to free himself and his partner, but when he finished securing the prisoner once more, he was sure the man would not be able to use his hands or fingers to touch any of the ropes, plastic ties, or handcuffs on his body. He looked down at the man tied at his feet and said, "Looks like all we need now is a branding iron." Jim chuckled for a moment, and then his humor slowly disappeared as he slowly knelt beside the man. He looked into the defiant face for several seconds before he said, "I just want you to know that you're only one step away from getting a slug in the head. When the two of you broke loose and decided to come after us, you used your last get-out-of-jail-free card. Your next bad move will get you into the rear trunk of one of those cars. You'd better keep your nose clean unless you want to keep your buddies company." He saw that the defiant look on the man's face never changed as Jim warned him, but the man's eyes told a different story.

Jim finished his task in the living room, and when he entered the kitchen, he nodded to his partner to let her know that she was free to head back to the computer once more. Jennifer had been guarding Henderson in the kitchen while Gray had been making sure the other bloodsucker wasn't going to find himself free for quite some time. She had not missed the cut lip or the blood on the fancy suit. She knew that what Jim was doing at this stage of the game wasn't exactly legal, but now she was starting to look at it in the same light as Jim had been doing. And right at this frame of time, she considered it to be a necessary stretch of the law. It was Jennifer's contention that if Jim didn't get any answers before the law intervened, there was no question in her mind that the lawyers would quickly finagle a release for these men. If that happened, there was also no doubt in her mind that she and Jim would end up in someone's trunk themselves or maybe become victims of a hit-and-run.

Jim had been quick to handcuff Henderson to the kitchen table when they returned to the kitchen. When he once more began questioning Henderson, he found the man's bravado was gone. The man's cocky attitude and tough-guy appearance that had needled Jim earlier was now completely gone. Jim was no longer relegated to having to threaten to use force to get some of his questions answered.

He hooked his leg across a corner of the table and said, "Before you got here, I had a little talk with your buddy Sampson in there. He gave me quite a few facts to chew on, and all I want to say is that both of you better have the same story in your memory banks. If I find out that one of you characters is lying to me… well, that individual could very easily end up joining his buddies in the trunk of one of the cars. I hope that's crystal clear to you because your life depends on it." He had been leaning forward with his elbow resting on his knee while talking, and now he straightened his back and tossed a pad of paper onto the table in front of Henderson. "I want you to start writing the names of all the people you know who are involved in this mess. I want to know how they are involved and how deep they are into this whole setup of yours." Jim leaned forward once more, and his face grew hard as he added with force, "I want to know where every dirty penny goes. I want to know everything there is to know about everything Williams is into. I want you to start writing, and if you can remember so much that you run out of paper, just let me know and I'll get you another tablet." He looked down at Henderson for a long moment before he added, "If you don't give me what I want, then I promise you that you won't like the persuasion methods I'll be forced to use. So far we've only been playing some kids' games. We're about to get serious here."

The look on Henderson's face never changed, and he never took his eyes off his shoes while the detective gave the warning. But Jim could almost feel the hatred the man felt toward him.

Jim checked the shackles on the man once more before he went into the living room and checked on Sampson. When he was completely satisfied with the bonds of both men, he walked into the bedroom where the computer was set up. He found Jennifer sitting in front of the computer, but her head was cradled in her arms as she leaned forward over the keyboard. She was breathing softly as she slept in the chair. Jim would have considered himself blind if he hadn't seen how her breasts were pressing softly against the keys, and for a long time he was unable to take his eyes off that part of her body.

Finally, Jim reached out and touched her shoulder. Jennifer jumped as soon as his fingers touched her skin and then she stared at him with wide but uncomprehending eyes until she finally realized where she was. She leaned back in the chair and stretched while Jim suddenly turned and faced the door as though he were checking on Sampson.

As soon as Jennifer was slumped in the chair in front of the computer, she quickly saw that Jim's attention had returned to her. It was then that she realized he had turned away because of the effect her body was having on him. It was clear in more ways than one.

Jim broke the silence. "Have you been able to figure anything out with that disc?" He looked at her tired eyes, and then he said, "Maybe you should lie down and get some rest first. It looks like you could use a little."

She smiled at him. "I'll be all right. I think I found something that refers to Hamilton, but right now that's about all I've got."

"Well, if you get tired I want you to lie down on the bed and get some rest." Jim said. He looked at her for several more seconds before he added, "I'm going to head back to the kitchen. I've got Henderson doing some writing in there, and while he's doing that, I'm going to go over some of the papers I got from Mrs. Harris."

She saw him beginning to reach forward to brush her hair away from her face, but suddenly, he stopped and looked down at her. He shook his head so slowly it was hard to see the movement before he abruptly turned and walked out of the room. Her eyes lingered on the closed door for several minutes before she released a soft sigh. She turned her attention back to the computer and the maddening code that she hoped the computer disc also contained the key to.

Chapter 13

For over an hour, Jim had been going over the sheets of information Henderson had furnished. He was trying to get the events and dates in some form of order in his mind. He figured there was enough information there to clog a computer, and he was seriously wondering about the ability of Henderson to keep all the facts straight as he flipped through the pages. He was sure Henderson had included a lot of fluff in the information he had given Jim, but until he went through and analyzed it, he would have to accept all of it as fact.

Henderson was staring at the cuffs on his wrist as Jim pored over the facts he had listed on the sheets of paper. He thought he had a solution to the restraint that had him shackled to that table, but he knew it would take some time before he'd be able to actively tackle that problem. He was wishing Gray would take his papers and leave the room for a while so he could make a try at picking that lock on the handcuffs. The time was passing maddeningly slow as he watched the officer picking through the material he'd provided. Most of it was factual, but he'd tried to throw enough bad material in with it so that it would take the pair of police officers quite a bit of time to weed through the material. He saw movement out of the corner of his eye, and when he paid more attention, he saw he was getting his wish. Gray was in the process of gathering up the papers he'd spread over the table, and now he was heading for the door. Henderson didn't even glance up when Jim reached down and rattled the cuffs before he walked out of the room.

Gray was just checking Sampson's restraints when he heard a groan from the bedroom. He quickly rushed in and found Jennifer sitting up on the bed. She was shaking, her hair was disheveled, her face was wet with tears, and for a few seconds, she appeared to be confused as to her whereabouts.

When he loomed over her, she quickly wrapped her arms around him and pulled him to her as she said, "It seems like every time I close my eyes, I see the faces of those two men I killed coming at me." She buried her wet cheeks against his neck, and her trembling continued as Jim smoothed her hair and slid his fingers along her jawbone.

He placed his cheek against the top of her head. "Hey, babe. You were protecting us when you pulled the trigger. Just think of all the lives you saved by eliminating that scum. They were nothing but killers and drug pushers. You did the only thing you could in that situation." He pulled her tighter against him and continued smoothing her hair with his hand. Gradually, her trembling eased.

Her eyes were red-rimmed and wet as she looked up at him. He kissed her forehead and then gazed into her eyes. Slowly he began to lower his head, and her chin began to rise as they moved closer. His lips moved across her eyes and then down her cheek. Her lips were moist with her tears when they began to press against his lips.

The sound of squealing tires brought him out of his cloud-nine lethargy in a hurry. Jim quickly rolled out of the bed and grabbed for his clothes. Jennifer looked up in surprise when he moved so fast and quickly pulled the covers up. By the time he got his clothes on and got to the door, all he was able to see of the silver Lincoln was the tire marks on the street where Henderson punched it. He saw the handcuffs dangling from the table brace, and he also saw the bent paper clip lying on the floor. He slammed his palm down on the table top so hard the legs bounced up off the floor.

"Jennifer," he hollered, "we've got to get out of here now. Henderson got loose, and he freed Sampson. They're probably going after their buddies right now. We might have as much as ten minutes before they pull their entire crew down on us."

He didn't think it was possible for the small engine to create that much power, but he even made the tires squeak when he floored the Neon. When he hit the corner, Jennifer had to make a wild grab to keep the computer's monitor from sliding off the back seat and hitting the floor. He didn't know where they were heading or if a computer would be available when they got there, so he had decided to confiscate the one out of the bedroom.

Jennifer looked out the back window of the Neon as they sped away from the house. "How could he open those cuffs with a paper clip? It isn't supposed to be possible." She dropped back into her seat and added, "Where are we going to go now?" She started to look forward, but then a thought hit her and her head snapped around. "I can't even go back to work now, can I? They know who I am now, so they're going to be looking for me as well as you, right?"

"I'm afraid you hit that old nail right on the head, sweetheart. They're going to be coming after both of us now." He slowly shook his head and frowned. "It's entirely my fault. I shouldn't have allowed you to stay." He tossed a quick glance in her direction. Her eyes were wide as she listened to him telling her, "It's a good thing we had all the guns in the bedroom, or we wouldn't be alive now. Knowing how they work, there won't be a safe place anywhere around here for either one of us. They're going to be doing a lot of checking on you, and then they'll be watching all your old haunts, your friends, your favorite shopping places, and anywhere else they can think you might show up at. To put it simply, I could just say that anywhere you've already been they're going to be there and waiting for you to show up again." He wasn't satisfied that he was free of any kind of tail until after he made a number of lane changes as well as doing enough cornering and backtracking. He knew beyond any shadow of doubt they'd already seen this car, so there was no getting around the fact that he had to ditch it. He was hoping the new paint job on the Ford was going to be dry when he got to the body shop.

After the pressure of getting away from the house and finding freedom, Jennifer's relief turned to dismay, and it showed very clearly on her face. When she spoke, she was unable to make eye contact with her partner, and her voice was soft as she said, "I'm sorry, Jim. If it hadn't been for me, those men wouldn't have gotten away, and we wouldn't be in this mess now."

Jim was wearing a very surprised look on his face as he took his eyes off the road and regarded the pretty blonde sitting beside him. "Sweetheart, if you want to talk about someone taking the blame, well, it was just as much my fault. Maybe more so. It's something that just happened, that's all." In a softer voice, he said, "I'm not sorry about what happened." He looked back at the road for a long moment before he reached over and put his hand over hers. He gave her a soft smile as he added, "I'm not sorry for anything. As a matter of fact, you're the first woman I've been able to talk to or feel comfortable with for quite a few years. When you come right down to it, you're the first one in quite a few years I've wanted to have around me. I enjoy talking to you, and believe it or not, I like listening to you as well."

Jennifer was silent for a long moment. Then she took a deep breath and said, "That day the captain pointed you out and told me that we were going to work together, well, I took it on myself to do a little checking on you. I asked Sgt. Roundtree about you, and he said you were hard to get along with, and a number of others agreed with that statement. He said he was told something happened long before he got to know you personally, but he wouldn't tell me anything more. He just said that when it came to drugs, you started going to extremes and that you were capable of almost anything. Sgt. Roundtree told me that if something happened that involved drugs that I needed to watch out for myself." She looked over at Gray and saw a tight look on his face as he stared at the road. "I don't mean to pry, but after what happened in that bedroom, I would like to be able to understand you a little better." She took a deep breath before she added, "I'm afraid I'm getting some pretty deep feelings toward you. I just want to know a little more about you and what makes you tick. If I'm going to be a part of your life, I want to be there in every way."

Jim's hands were white-knuckled because of the way he was clutching the steering wheel. A strong look of pain crossed his face. He didn't look over at Jennifer nor did he utter a word for such a long time. She began assuming there wasn't going to be an answer. When he began to speak, it was so soft she almost didn't hear him over the road and engine noise.

"I started working as a police officer right out of college, and I was teamed up with a guy named Melvin Scott. He was a real good officer who was the kind of guy who was dedicated to law and order and the legal way to do things and all that. We patrolled the streets together for almost two years, and one night we got a call to investigate a drug OD. When we got there, the ambulance attendants were just loading the body. Mel lifted the sheet and saw his own daughter. The guy lost it right then and there. He took off in the police car and left me standing beside the ambulance. They said he got the pusher's name from a couple of her friends, and they also said he wasn't very gentle when he asked the questions.

"Well, he went into the dealer's house with his gun drawn. There were six guys in there having a good old time counting their money. He took ten slugs before he went down, but he accomplished his mission. He killed the pusher and three of his men, but it cost him his life. He left a wife and three young children behind."

Jennifer said, "Oh, Jim, I'm so sorry to hear that." She reached over and gave his arm a firm squeeze even though his explanation didn't really answer her question of why he had been driven against the drug traders with such fury. Jim resumed talking as though she hadn't uttered a word or made a move.

"About six months after Mel was killed by that trash, I got married to Ming. She was so pretty, so small, and so…dependent, I guess you could say. She never complained about anything. She didn't even complain about all the times she was forced to sleep alone because I had to do a double shift so we could make ends meet." Jim took a deep breath before he continued, but Jennifer didn't miss the trembling of his lower lip. "I guess I wasn't very observant in those days because I never realized she was taking drugs to combat the loneliness she was feeling until it was too late. We had a couple of fights, and she swore she'd never use that crap again. But one morning when I got off work, I found her lying in the bathroom. There was a sheet of paper lying on the kitchen table, and all Ming said on it was 'I'm sorry.' The medical report said she died from an overdose of cocaine, just like Mel's daughter had."

The look of pain and raw hatred covered his face, and Jennifer was almost afraid to speak because she wasn't too sure what he was capable of doing right at that moment.

When Jim continued, he droned on in a monotone, and it almost sounded like it was coming from a machine instead of from a human being. "I did a lot of footwork, and when I learned the pusher's name, I went after him. I didn't do like Mel did though. I didn't barge into a gang meeting like he did. Instead, I waited until things worked out in my favor. I stopped him in an alley just off Van Buren. When I walked away from him, all the drugs that he'd had on him were inside him. He had the choice of taking the drugs on his own or having me force-feed him." He turned his head and looked at Jennifer as he added, "The only thing I regret about the whole thing is that he died with a smile on his lips."

Tears were gliding down Jennifer's face as she put her cheek against Jim's shoulder and said, "I'm so sorry, Jim. I didn't mean to make you go through that again. Please forgive me."

Jim took a deep, shuddering breath before he made an obvious effort to shake off the feelings he'd allowed to overcome him. Finally, he reached over and gave her thigh a firm squeeze. "It's hard to talk about, but now that it's over, I'm glad you asked. You're the first person I've talked to about her since her death. That's been over seven years ago. I've been told many times that you'll feel better once you have it off your chest, but up until now, I've been very skeptical. It doesn't feel good to go through those kinds of memories again, but I do think they were right when they say it feels better after you share it with someone who cares and understands."

He took a deep breath and, desperately wanting to change the subject, said, "All right, that's over with now. Let's get on with the problem at hand. First of all, we have to get rid of this car and get into something that won't stand out like a neon light." He knew it was a feeble attempt at humor, but he didn't expect to hear her laughing after he said it. When he looked in her direction, the tears were still showing on her cheek. As his arm encircled her shoulders, she snuggled tight against him and then released a deep sigh of her own.

* * *

"I didn't think you wanted me to paint it white because of all the white cars on the street, but I wanted to give it a light color so it would reflect the heat," Frank said as he stood in the shade of the shop while Jim and Jennifer walked around the newly painted light tan Ford.

Jim nodded his head and said, "Well, at least now I can move around without having to look over my shoulder every two seconds. I really owe you on this. If the police come around, just tell them you were told this was my personal car, and you painted it because you were told to. I'm in this thing pretty deep now, or maybe I should say that my partner and I are in a little over our heads right now." He saw the look of concern on Frank's face, and he added, "We've uncovered a pretty big rotten apple in the upper ranks of the police organization. So not only am I going to be having Williams after me, but the man they have in the police department is going to be using the police to try to stop me as well." He looked at Jennifer and then he amended the statement. "I believe I should say they'll be after us because now she's in just as deep as I am.

Frank stepped into the burning sunlight and shook his head. "Jim boy, I sure wish I could give you some names or places or something like that, but when you gave me that second chance, I stepped away from that element and haven't been near any of them since." He was quiet for a moment and then he added, "Tell you what, I've got a couple of names I could contact and see what they know."

Jim immediately shook his head. "No! They're going to be looking for us, and they won't leave any stone unturned. If you contact anyone, you'd better believe that person will contact someone else, and that person will be around to talk to you. I don't have to tell you how they'll do the questioning." Jim turned and looked at Frank for a moment before he added, "When I brought the car in here, do you remember how you talked about your family? Well, just keep that in mind whenever you're tempted to make that phone call you were talking about. They've got a lot of money laid on the line with this drug business, and a simple thing like a family won't mean much to them. As a matter of fact, if you won't give them the information they think you have, they won't hesitate to use your family as leverage to make you talk. The best thing you can do for all of us is simply forget that I was ever in here or that you ever saw this car." Jim started to turn away, but then he turned back and said, "You'd better hide this car for a while. One of the men saw it, but I don't know if they linked the Neon to us. I'd rather not take that chance."

It didn't take long to transfer everything back into the Ford, and just as Jennifer was getting into the car, Jim said, "I'll see to it that you get paid for painting this car, but right now I'm in a little bit of a bind."

Before he could continue, Frank interrupted him. "Jim boy, I told you before that I owe you so much more than I can ever repay. You offer me money one more time, and I'm gonna call the cops on you for loitering. Now get out of here, you hear! The only thing I want you to do is take care of yourself. When this is all over, I want you and your lady friend to come over to the house. I still want you to meet my family. Now beat it out of here before someone sees you standing there with your mouth hanging open like that and calls the cops themselves."

Jim pulled into the motel parking lot and quickly had them registered as John and Debra Manning from Las Vegas. The clerk didn't bother checking his ID or even the license number on the car he'd parked out of sight of the office. Jim was quite sure that this man had rented rooms to many couples without checking on anything as inconsequential as marriage certificates or driver's licenses as long as he got the money up front. It didn't take them long to carry their "luggage" up the outside steps to their room.

Jim was staring out the window at the questionable "scenic view" he was getting just off the main downtown street of Van Buren. In less than twenty seconds, he had picked out six hookers plying their trade along the street as well as three teenagers appropriating a car for a joyride. Jim slowly shook his head at what he was seeing and pulled the curtain shut.

Jim turned the TV on and then dropped into the ratty easy chair. He looked at Jennifer for a long moment before he said, "I just wish I had gotten some information about the driver of the Chevy Suburban before Henderson got away. As far as that episode is concerned, I'm still standing on the starting line and waiting for the green light."

Jennifer interrupted his line of thinking when she slid her beautifully shaped backside onto his lap. It was clear she wasn't thinking about the problems they were having as she pressed her face into his neck and then began to nuzzle his ear.

Jim sighed contentedly because it was obvious to him that he wasn't going to be doing much crime-solving for the next hour or so.

Chapter 14

Jennifer was visibly upset with Jim as he stood next to the door with his hand resting on the knob. She exclaimed, "You can't do this." She tried to take his hand in order to pull him away from the door, but he remained standing firmly. Tears of frustration and fear were brimming in her eyes, and it was hard for her to understand his reasoning. However, it was very clear to her that Jim had his mind made up and wasn't going to be swayed by any emotional demonstrations from her.

His face softened as he reached out for her hand. "Listen to me, sweetheart. You know I have to do this. I simply don't have any choice. I have to get Williams and his crew in such an uproar, and keep them there, until someone makes a mistake. For that to happen it means that I have to hit them where it hurts. I have to make them bleed until their suppliers begin wondering if Williams can pay for the stuff he's getting." He pulled Jennifer closer and whispered into her ear, "I promise I'll be careful. All right, babe?" He stood and faced her for a long moment before he added, "I'd rather be doing this with your approval."

She knew she'd struck out with her appeal for him to stay, so she tried to show her acceptance of his decision by giving a little humor as well as showing her desire for him to be careful. "Well, all right. But I warn you that if you get killed, I'm never going to speak to you ever again." Her breasts flattened as she pressed herself tightly against him.

The streetlights slowly passed as he searched the street in hopes of finding the quarry that so far had eluded him. He'd already been stopped twice by hookers, but what they had to offer didn't interest him. He was after bigger, and deadlier, game.

He was parked near the entrance to an alley as he debated his next move after yet another strikeout. He heard a soft hiss, and when he looked in the direction of the sound, he saw a black man standing in the shadow deeper in the alley. He slowly got out of his car. When he stepped closer to the black man, he saw a white man standing behind a telephone pole a little deeper in the alley. He wasn't worried about a mugging as long as he kept a little distance between himself and them, but he still kept his eyes open for the one member of their crew who could be hidden elsewhere.

The black man stepped closer to Jim and said, "Hey, man. We got some good candy here if you be lookin'.

Jim quickly set the scene. "I'm not looking for any candy. I'm looking for that good white stuff that dreams are made of. I'm looking for a steady supply."

The two men conferred in the middle of the alley before the black man said, "Hey, man. We can get all the stuff you need. How much you got?"

"I've got a lot more cash here than you've got powder. But there's a little problem. I only intend to work with Williams men because I know he can supply me on a steady basis with what I need. My demand isn't big enough to enable me to deal with the big man himself, but I can make it profitable for a couple of guys like you two." He hesitated for a second before he added, "If you work for Williams, that is."

The two pushers stared at each other for several seconds before the black man nodded his head. He turned to Jim. "Okay, yeah, we work for the man, but we gotta see the green before we go any farther. How much do you want?"

Jim had emptied his checking account earlier, and when they saw the stack of bills he pulled out of his pants pocket, their jaws dropped. They had no trouble seeing a number of fifties on the top and bottom of the stack, but they were unable to see the two hundred ones between them. "Like I said, I've got more cash than you've got powder. You call Williams or one of his men and tell him that you've got a buyer for ten thousand. Tell him I need that much right now. I could start making my money back tonight if he could deliver it right away. You can see I've already got the money with me. If the stuff checks out to be the good stuff and if things go right when we discuss the price, we'll talk again in a week or so for some more. How does that sound?"

It was hard for the men to tear their eyes away from the handful of bills in this sucker's hand. They casually tried to move around so the man would be between them, which would enable one of them to jump him from behind, but they weren't ready for the blur that Jim became when he jumped to the side and landed in a crouch. The men were no longer staring at the money because the big bore of the .45 caliber silenced gun had their entire attention now.

The black man tried to grin as he said, "All right, my man. We was just checking you out. If you was a cop you'd have come out with one o' them guns the cops have to carry." He pushed out a laugh that sounded more like a door closing on the morgue then anything humorous. "Okay, man. I gonna make the call. Should have the merchandise here in a hurry. That all right, man?"

Jim slowly nodded. "The first thing you're going to have to do is prove to me that you know Williams. It would be a simple matter to say you know him and then call some buddies and have them show up with guns. If you can give me a few names of the higher echelon, then you can make the call."

The black man thought for a moment and then he nodded his head. "That sounds fair enough. I give you five names, and you make payment as soon as the car arrives. That right?" He watched Jim's head nodding in agreement and then he said,

"There's Henderson, Gonzalas, Wales, Moralas, and Sampson." He looked at Jim for several seconds. "Those names suit you?"

Jim once more nodded his head. "They sure do. As soon as the stuff gets here, you can count the money while I make sure I'm getting my money's worth. Now why don't all of us go and find a phone. I'd just like to keep this between the three of us, so if you don't have any objections I plan on listening to your call."

The black man casually reached into his pants pocket and pulled out a small cell phone. "You see, my man, my supply is only a fingertip away." He chuckled as he punched the numbers, but he didn't realize that Jim was not only watching him while he dialed the number but was also memorizing the phone number, just in case.

It only took two minutes to make the arrangements for the shipment to be dropped off. The black man slipped the phone back into his pocket and started to leave. He nodded at his white partner as he said, "I'll be back in about thirty. You be takin' good care of our new customer now, you hear?"

Jim quickly stopped the man in his tracks when he produced the silenced gun once more and said, "Whoa, cowboy. No one's leaving here until the stuff is delivered. I'm sorry to have to tell you this, but I don't trust you yet. All of us are just going to hang out here until the delivery had been made. You can leave as soon as I'm satisfied. With the amount of money I have here, I can't afford to take any chances." He looked at the pair of men standing in the alley and added, "Any objections."

The black man quickly said, "Hey man. Was just gonna see about selling some of the candy I got with me. No sense in letting all these customers go right on by us when I got stuff to sell that'll make them happy."

Jim shook his head, and then after a moment of hesitation, he said, "I'll tell you what I'll do. When I get that big delivery taken care of, I'll make you an offer for that stuff you got on you that you just can't refuse. That sound fair?"

The gold tooth in the man's mouth glittered as he flashed a big smile and nodded his head. "That sounds cool, man, but why don't you be puttin' that rod away before somebody gets hurt?"

Jim slowly shook his head. "This is out to prevent someone from getting hurt. Mostly it's to keep me from being hurt." He stood quietly in the shadow of the building as the black man released a deep belly laugh and then sat down with his back against the building. The white man stood near the black man and fidgeted with the buttons on his shirt, but he never took his eyes off their customer with the gun for the entire time they waited.

The driver rolled the big black Olds smoothly into the alley and quickly doused the headlights but remained sitting behind the wheel while he looked at the two men who were dealing the drugs for Williams. He looked around but didn't see the man who had ordered the powder. He was impatient to get back to the office where the booze and broads were waiting, so instead of following the procedure of remaining in the bulletproof car until he was satisfied, he opened the car door and began to exit. When the dome light came on, it clearly illuminated the driver as he reached across the seat and pulled the briefcase in his direction.

The man stopped ten feet before he reached the pair of men, and his hand was inside his jacket just in case. He wasn't ready for the encounter that was ready to fall on him.

Jim remained standing in the shadows as he said, "Hello, Sampson. I see you haven't had your hair cut yet. I think Delilah would like to clip a few of those locks just for a souvenir."

Sampson's oath sounded unusually loud in the alley as he finished pulling his gun and turned to confront this new menace. The cough of Jim's silenced gun wasn't even heard when the man's own gun went off and sent dirt and brick chips flying from the wall behind Jim. Sampson never felt the projectile that tore through his brain and ended a life of crime. The hood of the car was given a liberal sprinkling of blood, brains, and shattered bone.

Seconds after Sampson's gun shattered the silence, Jim forced the two men to dump the body into the trunk. A siren was screaming, but it was several blocks off yet when Jim got in the back seat and told the black man to start driving. He made sure both men in the front seat knew it would be the end for them if they were stopped by the police. Ten minutes later, Jim had the man stop the car beside an empty lot. He stood behind the men as they searched Sampson's body. When they handed Jim the dead man's wallet, he released a soft whistle of surprise at the sight of all the cash the man had been carrying. With the money he now had in his possession, he knew he had just solved one of his biggest problems of being able to remain out of sight.

Jim slipped the cash into his pocket and tossed the wallet back into the trunk on top of the body. He moved the muzzle of the gun so it was trained on the chest of the black man, and then he said, "Here's the offer you can't refuse. Just hand me all of money you've got on you, and then I want you to dump the garbage out on the ground.

Before the black man could reach into his pocket, he watched as his partner made a desperate reach for the gun that was hidden under the loose folds of his shirt. The black man became aware of a soft coughing sound as his partner suddenly jackknifed and was flung back several steps.

The man slowly dropped to his knees and stared in disbelief at the spreading crimson stain on his chest. The pain suddenly eased, and the man fell forward. He didn't feel a thing when his face struck the pavement.

Jim moved the gun back so it covered the remaining man. "Are you going to be as foolish as your partner?" When the black man quickly shook his head, Jim added, "I was going to dump the body here, but I changed my mind. Now I want you to pick your partner up and dump him into the trunk with Sampson. I don't think I have to tell you what will happen if you try for the gun that's lying there."

The action had made the black man a believer, and when he finished with his partner's body, Jim had a little talk with the man. When the black Olds began moving once more, the black man had a series of destinations and he wasn't too happy about it. But he rationalized that at least he was still alive.

The black man knocked on the door and waited several seconds before he repeated the coded knock. A small eye-level door moved, and then Jim heard someone behind the door saying, "It's Turk out there." The voice was louder when the man stationed behind the door said to the black man, "Turk, what are you doing here?"

Jim was standing out of the speaker's point of view, and when he motioned with the gun, the black man quickly said, "Sampson got sick, and he wanted me to make the pickup for Williams." Jim had expected some kind of an argument or at least some questions, but the slide silently closed, and seconds later the door was open.

Jim caught the three men inside the small room completely off guard when he stepped into the room right behind the black man. Everyone froze for a second as they stared at the intruder, but then all three men began reaching for their guns. Jim gave Turk a shove with his left hand as the silencer on the gun in his right hand worked to do its job. The gun bucked repeatedly in his hand. The first man stopped in the progress of jerking his gun out when the silenced shell tore its way through the man's forehead and destroyed his brain. The second man had his gun out but still had a long way to bring it into alignment when the gun chugged another time. The man hesitated as his chest seemed to cave in, but somehow the man managed to start raising the gun once more.

As soon as Jim saw the third man throwing his hands into the air in wild surrender, he brought the gun back to bear on the second man, and once more the gun coughed.

Jim slowly straightened and said, "All right, Turk. If you continue to do as I tell you, then you'll continue to live. First of all, I want you to tie this clown up, and you'd better pray he doesn't get loose for quite a while. We've got some more stops, and if we get some kind of welcoming committee waiting for us, then you can rest assured that you're going to be the first one to go. Got that?"

Turk quickly got the sole survivor secured and then located several bags for the money, the drugs, and the guns. He watched as Jim stood over the tied man and said, "I want you to know several things. First of all, my name is Jim Gray. Secondly, the man who's helping me doesn't have any choice about the matter. Thirdly, I want you to let Williams know that I'm after him. Make sure you tell him that I'm not going to bother with search warrants from now on and that he can expect to see me behind him at any time or any place." He started to turn, but he looked down at the man again and said, "I think it would be a great benefit to your own health if you were to find a more legal profession. I think the life expectancy for guys like you in this field is rapidly dropping."

When Turk dropped the bags containing the drugs and money behind the front seat, Jim said, "Onward and upward. Hi-O Silver. Let's see about the next stop you've got written down on the list of Williams's places of business."

The next three stops were quiet and simple because Turk did a good job of bluffing the men. None of men in those locations suspected a thing until it was too late. However, the fourth stop presented a huge problem for Jim when Turk knocked at the door.

Jim cringed inwardly when a woman answered Turk's knock because for Jim the matter of holding a gun on a woman or, worse yet, shooting at a woman was not something he would be able to do easily. This woman obviously wasn't a trusting person, and she certainly didn't seem to care for the explanation Turk offered. As soon as Jim heard the woman ordering someone to call about the last minute switch of pickup men, he knew he had to move fast.

The silencer coughed twice, and slivers of wood flew away from the lock. When Jim tried the door, he found he had to throw one more slug into the door. It was still resisting when he tried it again, and he was forced to hit the door with his shoulder before the door began to move on the hinges. Jim pushed Turk in ahead of him, and the man quickly made a dive for the safety of the floor. Jim quickly tapped off several rounds into the chest of the nearest man before he scrambled out of the doorway. He looked around the corner of the hallway, and immediately, plaster erupted from the wall near his head. He hastily dropped to his knees and made another attempt to find the enemy shooter. A fraction of a second after he saw the man, kneeling beside the sofa, his gun spit two rounds in that direction. One round would have been enough because the first slug caught him right between the eyes and then sprayed the wall behind him while the second shot hit him in the neck and took out his jugular, which added greatly to the grotesque painting on the wall.

When he turned and looked for the woman, he found himself looking down the barrel of the largest gun he was sure he'd ever seen from that perspective. The woman had taken on the hardest look of any woman he'd ever encountered. She didn't say a word as the barrel followed his every move as he gently placed his gun on top of the small television. He continued moving slowly as he straightened and finished turning. He knew he was only a second away from the end if that was the way she decided to play it. And the simple truth was, there was absolutely nothing he could do about it.

Jim took a deep breath as he watched the woman's smile widen and her finger tighten on the trigger. He knew there was no way he could jump her and wrestle the gun away from her because she was standing too far away from him. Jim was aware that the best he could do was do a lot of dodging back and forth as he tried to rush her, but it would only prolong the inevitable. He didn't put much faith in attaining very much success in attempting that, but right at that point, it was the only choice he had.

Jim was in the process of gathering his muscles for an attempt to leap to the side just as it appeared she was about to pull the trigger. He took a deep breath, and just as he was about to launch himself forward and to the right, something happened that made him freeze.

Turk surprised both of them when he rolled against her legs just as she was pulling the trigger. He rammed her legs hard enough that it threw her off balance for several seconds, so when the gun went off, it punched a hole in the wall three feet above Jim's head. By the time she had regained her balance, Jim had already grabbed his gun and had thrown a slug in the direction of her gun.

Jim's heart jumped into his throat because he saw he'd not only missed hitting her gun, but after he pulled the trigger, his gun locked in the open position. He was out of shells.

Jim knew he would be dead instantly if he made any attempt to dive for any of the guns lying on the floor, so he decided to attempt a bluff as he mentally crossed his fingers and aimed the silenced gun at the bridge of her nose.

The look on her face told him that she had no idea that the gun was locked open, but it appeared that she wasn't going to let that change her way of thinking because her own gun didn't waver as she aimed for his chest.

Jim had one hope now and that was to talk her into dropping the gun. He nervously took a deep breath and said, "You know, lady, neither one of us has to die here. All I intend to do is put Williams out of business and behind bars if I can. Just lay your gun down, and both of us will walk out of here alive. If you pull the trigger, it will be just like committing suicide because my reflex action will take you out as well. Like I said, it doesn't have to be this way. Just put the gun down, and the only thing that I'm going to do to you is simply tie you up. When your friends come for the money, you'll find yourself free and alive." He saw hesitation and indecision on her face, and while the gun wavered a little, it still wasn't enough to take the chance of going after it.

Jim's blood froze when he heard the sound of a gun being cocked, and for the eternity of a second, he waited for the killing shot. When his eyes shifted to the source of the sound, he was stunned to see Turk kneeling on the floor and that now he was holding one of the guns that had belonged to one of the dead men. He realized he was not the only one having trouble taking his eyes off the black man because the woman was having the same problem as she stared into the muzzle of the black man's confiscated gun. They both were very aware that his gun wasn't wavering either.

Turk appeared unaffected by the violence in the room, but his voice was hard when he said, "Lady, when I was in Nam they called me a killer of babies and women. I didn't do neither of them things, but that doesn't mean I can't pull the trigger on a woman now. Put the gun down now, and you'll live. We don't have much time because the shots will be pulling the cops in here before long, and I don't have another twenty years to give them in prison. Put the gun down. Now!"

The indecision on her face quickly melted away and was replaced with a look of resignation as the gun began pointing lower and the woman lowered her arms. It clattered when she dropped the automatic pistol to the linoleum-covered floor. Jim remained standing in the shooter's stance as he waited to see what Turk's next move was going to be. If the man turned on him, Jim knew he was dead unless the man was blind and couldn't see that the slide was locked open, which was a chance Jim wouldn't have bet much on. The only choice he had available was wait to see what Turk was going to do.

Turk faced the woman long enough to slide her gun away from her with his foot, and then he made a half-turn and looked at Jim. The gun was still aimed waist-high, but now it was aimed at the space between Jim and the woman. The man's dark face showed the fight that was going on inside him because he went from indecision to resolve and then back to indecision. Suddenly the man simply lowered the hammer on the gun and tossed the revolver in Jim's direction.

The black man laughed out loud when the woman started throwing obscenities in his direction. He walked over to Jim and easily slipped the empty gun out of the man's hand and then turned and faced the woman. "Lady, for such a big mouth, you do got a mighty little brain." He held the gun up so she could see it, and then he added, "You just got took by a gun with an empty clip." His laugh almost shook the room as he faced the white-faced angry woman. His laugh lasted only a moment before he looked at the surprised officer and said, "Well, boss. Now what?"

The question galvanized Jim's reflexes, and he immediately began thinking again. "First of all, get this broad…ah…female tied securely, and then we'll make a quick check of the place. Like we did in the other places, we'll grab anything that will make Williams squirm and then beat it out of here. I don't want to get caught in here any more than you do."

The black man quickly had the woman lying face down with her hands behind her back, and then it only took a matter of seconds before he finished with that chore. He stood and saw Jim was standing in the doorway to the second room. He quietly approached the man's back, and for several seconds, he once more fought with indecision. The temptation was there to put this guy out of commission and to simply run off with the money and drugs that had been already confiscated from the previous business locations that had been hit. He shook his head and took a deep breath as he pushed in beside Jim in the doorway. His eyes widened, and for a long moment, he held his breath as though he was afraid that any breathing was going to make the scene disappear.

Along one entire wall, there was a shelving unit that ran almost to the ceiling. It was filled with bags of every size, and each one contained a white powder. Neither man had to guess what was in those bags, but the biggest attraction for the eyes was the shelving unit on the far wall. The entire fifteen-foot unit was almost full of stacked bills. It took them several minutes to overcome the shock of finding this kind of stock in the back of a small business that was supposedly used as a pawn shop.

Jim finally roused himself and began thinking. He pointed to the rear door and told Turk to check it out. Seconds later, he began to fill all available bags, boxes, and suitcases with the stacked bills. The voice from the back door told him that it led into the alley and that the alley was empty. The black man moved quickly as he hastened to follow Jim's directions of bringing the car around to the back where it wouldn't be so easily seen.

By the time the man had parked the car by the rear door, Jim already had all the available bags full of money and lying near the door. It only took several minutes to remove the bodies, and then they began loading the bags, it was immediately clear they weren't going to get very much of the money into the interior of the Ford. Jim stood by the door for a long moment, and then he said, "I'm going to need a pickup truck or a van if I hope to do the damage to Williams that I want to do." He looked over at Turk and asked, "Do you think that's possible?"

The black man searched the white man's face for a moment, and then he said, "It's much too late to find a rental. How bad do you want one?"

Jim didn't hesitate as he answered, "If you can find one close by, just go and do it. We'll leave a payment with the vehicle when we return it, so don't worry about a little glass damage or something like that." He knew he didn't have much choice when it came to trusting this man. He had reached a point where he needed help. Although if he'd had a choice, he wouldn't have chosen this individual.

While he waited for the new set of wheels, Jim tried to give the front of the business the appearance that nothing had ever happened. As he returned to the drug part of the building, he heard a vehicle stopping close to the back door. Jim had his gun ready for any shift change or for any intruders who would try to spoil his plans when the grinning face belonging to Turk showed up in the doorway. Jim took a deep breath and quickly looked to see what the man had obtained. He almost grinned when he saw a compact pickup that came complete with a topper shell.

The mid-eighties blue-and-white S-10 gleamed dully in the dim light as they tossed bag after bag of drugs into the rear. It only took a matter of minutes before the shelving unit containing drugs was empty. The only evidence that drugs had occupied that space was the coating of white dust on the shelves.

Because of the lack of any kind of containers, they were forced to simply toss the money into the rear of the small truck. That took a little longer than Jim really cared for, but so far, not a hint of a siren had been heard, with the exception of a passing ambulance that had almost stopped his heart earlier. While Turk carried the last armload of money out to the pickup, Jim rushed into the pawnshop and seized the tarp he'd seen lying on the floor. It only took a matter of seconds to get the load covered well enough so it couldn't be seen from the outside. When they closed the camper shell door on the last of the cash, Jim realized he had another problem that needed his immediate attention. Could he trust Turk to drive either of the vehicles? In his estimation, the back of the pickup contained somewhere in the range of ten to fifteen million dollars in cash and possibly more than double that in drugs. If he gave Turk the opportunity to drive either vehicle, he knew he would have to face a very big question. Would the man try to escape with the goods and set up his own business, or would he honor Jim's trust?

Turk broke into Jim's quandary of thoughts and grinned. "Now you got to decide if you can trust me or not. Well, all I can say is that I know you could've done me in quite a few times already if that had been your intent. You didn't do any more harm to anyone than you were forced to, and I really don't think you are doing this out of greed." He looked at Jim for several more seconds before he added, "All I can do is give you my word that I'll meet you where and when you say."

Jim looked into the man's eyes, and then he said, "I guess I don't have any choice, do I? I know you saved my life twice in there, but that was before we knew about all this cash and garbage in here." He took a deep breath and then scribbled on a piece of paper. "All right. Here's the address of the place where I'm staying. I'll meet you there, and we'll figure out where to go from there."

Jim ignored the bound woman's hostile glare as he headed for the rear door to where his car was parked. He was still having trouble understanding why the police hadn't made an appearance, because although the business was mainly in a commercial area, it wasn't really that far from a large apartment complex. He settled back in the seat as he motored out of the parking lot and headed for the motel. His glances around the neighborhoods and up as well as down the street failed to show any evidence of the Chevrolet pickup that should have been following him. As he pulled away from the pawnshop, he briefly wondered if any payoffs had been the reason for the lack of police presence. He shook his head and hoped he was wrong.

There was only a dim light coming from behind the curtains in his motel room. Jennifer appeared to be walking in her sleep when she answered the door. Her eyes were red-rimmed, but when she saw Jim, she became more animated. It didn't take long for her to tell Jim of the discoveries she'd made in deciphering the coded disc.

Her newly resurrected excitement began to diminish when she saw Jim was almost ignoring her while he stood by the window and peeked around the curtain. He appeared to be watching for someone. Just as she heard a crunching of gravel, she also saw her partner releasing a huge sigh and showing a wide smile. He turned that wide smile in her direction, and then he moved to the door.

Turk was grinning when he stepped through the doorway, but as soon as he saw Jennifer, he stopped. He stared at the woman for several seconds before he looked at Jim and said, "Hey, man. You don't do nothing halfways, do you? What a doll." He pulled off the baseball cap he'd been wearing, and then he stepped forward and said, "How do you do? My name is Theodore J. Montgomery. Most folks just call me Turk. But, lady, you can call me anything you want to."

Jim stepped beside the man. "You're going to have to do a little more searching because I'm claiming this cupie doll. Now what took you so long? I was starting to have second thoughts about leaving all that stuff with you."

Turk's teeth sparkled as the light from the television flickered in the room. He flashed another grin. He turned his attention away from the beautiful blonde. "I just had to make a quick stop. There were a bunch of boxes beside a dumpster, and I took the time to break them down and threw them on top of the load. You know how everything is lying loose in the back of that truck. It's going to make it pretty difficult to move anything out of that thing when it's light enough for people to see what you're doing."

Jim grinned as he nodded, but suddenly he stopped and looked at Turk. "Whatever happened to that slang talk you've been throwing around all night? Right now you almost sound like an English professor."

Turk showed his wide grin once more. "When they finished with me in Nam, I spent a couple of years in England. I got to know some real nice people there." He glanced up at Jim. "Might be a good time for me to head over there and look them up again. Things could get a little sticky for a while around here."

He looked down at his feet for a moment before he grinned. "Trouble is I'm just a little short on cash right now."

Jim laughed as he pulled Jennifer against him and looked over the top of her head. "I think we can figure something out there. My only concern is that Williams doesn't get it back. The money we don't end up using to bring Williams down is going to be a present to the police widows and orphans fund, as well as buying a lot of equipment for the department." He looked at Turk and said in a serious tone, "You saved my life tonight, Turk. I think you've got every right to have some of the cash."

Jennifer stared at the two of them, and there was no question in either man's mind that she had no idea what they were talking about. Her eyes began to widen as Jim told her what had happened during the night and what was in the rear of the pickup that was sitting in front of the motel door. She sat, speechless, and stared when Jim picked up one of the bags he'd dropped by the door on his return. She remained speechless when he let her take a look at the cash lying inside.

Jim and Turk watched her amazement. When they looked at each other, they burst out laughing so loud it didn't take long before the next-door motel resident pounded on the wall in a demand for silence.

Chapter 15

Because Jim didn't know anyone who had a garage and who he could also trust, they were forced to make a drive out of town. Jim and Jennifer rode in the car while Turk followed in the S-10, which also now carried a different set of plates. Jim cruised north past the Lake Pleasant turnoff and finally got out of the long line of cars and pickups that were pulling boats. He followed the road until it turned into gravel before he began looking for a place where they could transfer the load in the pickup into boxes. He wanted to get a long way away from any kind of traffic because they didn't need a nosy passerby finding them working along the road and taking an interest in what they were doing.

The bottom of the Ford scraped its way across several rocks as he worked his way up a dry wash and away from the primitive, but occasionally traveled, dirt road. Jim was aware he was going to have to do quite a bit of backing up to get out of this location, but he was satisfied with the amount of privacy he was going to have when he stopped the car. They were setting at such a secluded location he was sure the only way anyone could see them working, at the rear of the truck, was if a plane flew almost directly over them.

Turk was in a jovial mood this morning as he worked between the vehicles. The man was continually laughing and making jokes as he carefully transferred cash from the bed of the truck into boxes. Jim grinned at the man's jokes, but he made certain of two things when he was working near the man. First of all, he made sure the guns were out of Turk's reach; and secondly, he made sure he didn't get into the situation where he had to turn his back on the man. Jim was quite confident about the man's intention to honor his word, but then again, there was a lot of ready cash lying in the back of the small truck. Seeing all the money in the truck lying right next to all those full bags of powder would be a great temptation for a lot of men. Jim was very aware that having all this kind of material, and in this amount, lying within reach would be more than enough to tempt many people to go back on their word.

It took several hours to box the money neatly, and then it took another hour to place the bags of powder into more boxes. Because they didn't have respirators available, it took longer to box the deadly powder than he really wanted to spend with that stuff. But as far as he was concerned, the matter of safety came first. They'd been able to get some rubber gloves, but all they could get in the way of dust masks were the white fiber ones that sort of caught the larger chunks of dust when they inhaled. It was painstakingly slow work, but they finally got the last of the powder into the last box they had available. All three of them stepped back away from the truck with a sigh of relief.

As they began stripping off the dust masks and rubber gloves, Jim said, "We've got the easy part done, so now all we have to do is drive back to town and find a good place to hide this outfit while we try to stay out of the reach of Williams and his crew of bozos." He took a deep breath of fresh air, and then he added for the benefit of the others, "From here on, they're going to be watching anyone who had anything at all to do with me. They're also going to be watching anyone coming or going from any bus station, train yard, or airport. They're going to be using their inside contacts to let them know if someone suddenly has a large deposit or needs a huge safety deposit box. We're all going to be under the gun if anyone slips up. If they get their hands on any one of us, you can rest assured that there won't be any last-minute reprieve from the warden or the governor."

Turk's joking around had slowed down, but the grim thoughts Jim was expressing had little effect on the grin on his face. When Jim stopped for breath once more, Turk said, "All a man would have to do…ah, no offense Jennifer, all a person would have to do is go and buy a car from a private party. There are plenty of people who have cars advertised to sell in the paper." He glanced sideways at Jim, and then he added, "I mean it could be a factor if a guy happened to have enough cash on hand that he needed a quick way out of town. It would be the easiest way out of here because there are so many cars running over the road that there's no way they can even get a look at all of them, let alone getting a good look at the driver and determining if that person had anything to do with that heist from their warehouse." Turk pushed several small rocks around with his foot. "Course, like I said, it would sort of depend on if the guy had enough cash to make it worthwhile."

It was Jim's turn to laugh now as he moved to the side of the pickup and picked up a box.

Turks eyes bulged when Jim set the box on the tailgate and said, "This box is for you. I hope it shows how much Jennifer and I appreciate all the help you've provided." His smile disappeared, but the glint in his eyes didn't as he added, "I know it isn't full, but I think it will be when you pick up all that money you've been putting by that big rock you've been visiting on those 'nature runs' you've complained about having to make.

For all of ten seconds, Turk's face carried the insulted look of injured pride, but slowly that look faded and in its place the grin began to reappear. Without a word, Turk turned and walked to the rock in question. When he returned, he was carrying an armful of small, bound bundles of cash. It was very clear that he hadn't been just grabbing bundles at random because there weren't any bundles that contained bills that were smaller than fifty dollars.

Jennifer watched with wide eyes as Turk reappeared with the cash, and then as she tried to keep the grin from showing, she said in a loud voice, "I don't believe this. It looks like there's a crook amongst us."

Turk's grin widened as he countered with, "Yeah, there is. Trouble is I'm just not as good at doin' this kind of thing as you all are."

The sun was beating down on them as they drove away from the self-storage units where they had hidden the pickup. It was safely stored in a tight-fitting garage. They had encountered an elderly and suspicious clerk, but he quickly became mollified when Jennifer told him that she was going to move into Jim's apartment and that they just didn't have room for all of her teddy bears and knickknacks. When Jennifer left the room, Jim didn't miss the old man's sigh of yearning. He wasn't sure if the sigh was for the form that was walking toward the front door, or if it was for the opportunities he'd had in years past and wouldn't be involved with again. Jim held any remarks in check and simply signed the card that had been placed beside the cash the man needed for the first month's rent.

They drove to a local convenience store where Turk bought a paper. The man was reading through the columns that advertised cars and trucks when he suddenly looked up and asked, "I was going to ask earlier. but I forgot about it at the time. How come you were so determined to store that truck over here in Glendale instead of one that was closer to downtown or even one that was nearer your own office?'

Jim used the rearview mirror as he looked at the man in back. "I choose this one because I wanted to make sure Hamilton wouldn't have any chance of covering this up or helping Williams to reclaim some of his lost possessions. I figure the best way of keeping Williams from getting any of this back will be by calling the police, the newspaper, and all the TV stations. I'm going to tell them about the drugs, but I'm also playing with the idea of saying there might be a bomb hidden somewhere on the truck. I figure that will create a little more interest by the news media, and it will also make sure that someone doesn't dive in and help themselves to some of the boxes before the police get there.

"I figure that if someone is tempted to grab a box and run, they'll be forced to wonder if they just might have the box with the bomb in it." Jim released a short laugh as he added, "Can you picture the guy running down the street with a box under his arm and all the while wondering if he had that special box, and if he did, when was it going to blow? Isn't that what you'd call pressure and stress?"

All three of them began laughing as they pictured the man running and wondering. Jim was still grinning at the thought when he pulled back into the street and headed for the location of the first car Turk wanted to look at.

Jim and Turk were looking at the plain white Chevrolet sedan the latter had purchased when Jennifer said, "You probably have somewhere around a half of a million dollars in that box, and you still spent almost a half hour dickering with that woman for a lower price." She shook her head. "Can you tell me why you spent that much time just so you could save three hundred dollars? It doesn't make any sense."

Turk grinned again as he held up a finger. "If I had shown that woman that I was real anxious to have this car and then showed her I had the cash to pay for it, what do you think her first reaction would have been? To begin with, she'd have probably called the police as soon as I drove down the street. But because I talked her down to the amount of cash I let her know I was willing to spend to begin with, for her it would be just a matter of not losing face by accepting less money without a fight. It's just a matter of dickering, that's all." He winked at Jim. "This way she's happy because she got pretty close to the amount of money she wanted for this set of wheels, and because she had to work for it, she won't even give a thought to giving the police a call."

The next few minutes were spent transferring the purchases Turk had made from the back seat of the Ford into the white Chevy. Turk was standing by the door as he prepared to leave, but he was obviously stalling for time as he threw out a few more jokes that his heart wasn't into.

Jim watched the man's actions, and finally he said, "All right, there's something bugging you. That much is very obvious. What is it?"

The grin slowly faded from the black man's face, and then he stared into Jim's eyes for a long moment. "I've got some information that I know you could use, but it's also something that could kill you. I've been fighting with the decision of whether or not to tell you ever since the first door we knocked on when we were out getting all that money."

He looked down at his new shoes for a long moment before he started talking once more. "If I told you what I heard a couple of days ago, it could be sending you to your death. I like you, man, but I guess all I can do is give you the information and then hope for the best." Turk pulled his wallet out of his back pocket and then slipped a couple of business cards out. He held the cards between his first two fingers as he held them out for Jim to take. "What you'll find on the back of each card is a location of one of Williams's strongholds. I was able to overhear a couple of his goons talking the other night, and as soon as they left, I wrote the locations down. I was thinking about going on my own and seeing about the chances of ripping him off." He appeared to be having second thoughts at what he was doing, but after he took a deep breath and shook his head, he continued. "Williams usually stays at one of these houses where he figures it's safe. From what those men were saying, there could be anywhere from ten to thirty gunmen roaming the house and grounds of each location at any given time." Jim saw Turk was fighting for the right words, but before he could say anything, Turk shook his head and held his hand up to stall off anything Jim had to say. So Jim leaned back against the white car and waited.

Turk appeared uncomfortable for a long silent moment before he said, "I can't afford to get into this kind of shoot-out. I ain't no gunman, that's for sure. I spent a lot of time shooting at men in Nam, but things were different there. All my life I've been trying to get enough money so I can get a start somewhere else. And now that I got it, I can't go and do something foolish like getting involved in something like this. I just can't." He looked at Jennifer for a long moment. "Now you make sure this character does some real thinking before he goes off and gets himself shot up. Make sure you remind him that he's got a real good lookin' doll to take care of. You got that?"

The man suddenly turned and got into the white Chevrolet, but before he could get the keys into the ignition, he saw Jim reaching through the window and gripping his shoulder. When he looked up, he saw a soft smile on the officer's face.

Jim gave the man's shoulder one more squeeze before he stepped back and said, "You're right. This doesn't have anything to do with you, so you just get on out of here. I hope you're able to get all that money over to England without any problem, but most of all, I just want to thank you for all the help you've given us." He grinned for a moment. "When we were first getting started on our little collection, I had quite a bit of reservations about you, but you have really proven that I was right to trust you. All I can do is to tell you to go in peace."

Jim raised his hand in farewell as he stepped back from the white car. Jennifer moved up beside him and wrapped her arms around his waist. She rested her head against his chest as they looked at the somber face staring back at them from behind the steering wheel.

The Chevrolet sedan started to move away, but it came to a sudden stop after traveling only several yards. Turk was still staring straight ahead as he said, "You ain't gonna let this lay, are you?"

Jim looked at the rear window of the car for several seconds. "No, I can't let this information go without trying to do something about it. I think you already knew what my reaction was going to be even before you gave that information to me."

Turk's aggravation was obvious as he stepped out of the car and faced Jim and said, "But why, man? You got all that money now. Just take it and buy yourself some island. You and that gorgeous doll could spend the rest of your lives just sippin' rum while a dozen servants take care of all your needs. Just picture it, man, the two of you lying on the beach. The sun is going down, and one of your servants brings down another drink or two while the chef throws together a meal of prime rib or shrimp or something like that." He stopped trying to describe the good life when he saw Jim slowly shaking his head. Turk was almost pleading when he said, "But why, man?"

Jim's answer was short and his voice was cold as he simply said, "Because it was men like Williams who killed my wife. These are men who make their living by feeding on unsuspecting and trusting people. They get rich on the pain they're inflicting, and then they use some of that money to buy protection from the police so they can get richer and cause more pain." He stopped talking and took a deep breath when he felt Jennifer's hand on his face. The fury inside him was making him tremble, and when he looked down at his partner, he could see the concern in her eyes and on her face.

Jennifer tried to smile as she looked at Turk. "Everything will be all right. Jim just needs to cool down a little right now, but you can be sure he won't go rushing into any house with guns drawn." She grinned as she poked Jim's ribs with her elbow. "I'll take good care of Butthead here. You make sure that you take care of yourself and make sure you drop us a line after a while to let us know how you're doing. Don't you dare forget to let me know what England is like this time of the year. Now scoot on out of here." She waved her hand at him, and then she tried to muscle Jim in the direction of the Ford.

She had a small problem getting him to move at first because Jim balked for the first several steps. With her calm and gentle but constant urging, he finally began moving on his own. Jennifer got him to slide past the steering wheel and got behind the wheel herself. She looked over at Jim's face. "Jim, a couple of times now I've seen how you react when the subject of drugs and your former wife is brought up. You've got to learn to control the anger you feel when that happens."

She saw he was going to argue, but she quickly waved him off. "I'm not saying you should forget what happened. I'm just saying that when it comes to that anger, you should use it against them. Right now, the way things are, you're letting it dictate how you're going to live your life. You can't do that if you go after the men in those houses, and I know that's what you're going to do. I don't want you to go that route, but I know you will anyhow. I just don't want you to let that anger take you down. Use it against them. Yes, I know that after what happened to your wife it's easier said than done. But it can be done. It needs to be done."

Jennifer checked the road for traffic before she pulled away from the curb. She didn't tell Jim that Turk was still sitting in his car and staring in their direction as the transmission shifted into a higher gear and took them away from the scene.

The slim remainder of the afternoon was spent inside the air-conditioned comfort of one of the valley's many discount department stores as Jennifer helped Jim in his attempt to create the perfect wardrobe for the job he had in mind. Her attempt at getting a working set for herself was very quickly and very emphatically vetoed by Jim.

The sun was just touching the horizon when they got back to the motel and began carrying the bags into the room. Jim was trying to be cheerful, but in Jennifer's eyes, it was a clear attempt to camouflage his own feelings of anger and nervousness as well as the apprehension of what was in store.

Regardless of what she said, Jennifer knew by the look on his face that Jim was going to do what he thought the situation required. She knew he was still haunted by the death of his wife, and whether he admitted it or not, she was sure that he felt a continuous guilt over her death. From the way he had spoken about the death of his wife, Jennifer was sure that he felt guilty. She was beginning to know how his mind was running in this state of affairs, and while she knew it wasn't right, she also couldn't deny that those feelings could easily be there.

Jim tossed a handful of shopping bags on the bed and watched as Jennifer went back out to the car for the remainder. He looked down at his hands. No matter how hard he tried, he just couldn't stop the trembling.

Chapter 16

The hard motel bed moved gently as Jim threw the covers aside and dropped his feet over the side. He sat on the edge while he attempted to shake the sleep from his mind before he looked over at the sleeping form of Jennifer. He wanted to take her into his arms again and hold her until this entire mess went away, but he knew that wasn't going to work. For the first time since he'd met, and then lost, Ming, he was having misgivings about taking the chances he'd never given any thought to before. For a long moment, he watched Jennifer's sleeping form moving as she breathed softly under the single sheet they'd covered up with before he shook off the yearning he was feeling. He moved quietly through the darkness until he was in the bathroom where he softly closed the door and flipped the light switch. He took a long look at his face in the mirror before he began slipping into the camouflaged outfit.

When he was fully dressed, he looked into the mirror once more and regarded the stranger who was looking back at him. With the exception of the black ski mask and the black soft-soled, slip-proof sneakers, he thought he appeared quite military-looking. He amended that thought when he looked at the two guns equipped with silencers protruding from his belt and the way his pockets were bulging with spare clips for the silenced guns.

He stared into the mirror for several minutes as he tried to think of something he might have missed that could come to his advantage, but he drew a blank. He pulled the ski mask off and pushed it into his back pocket before he put the guns and clips into a small carryall that wouldn't draw any attention. He looked into the mirror once more and then ran his fingers through his hair before he took a deep breath and snapped the light off.

Jennifer was still lying as she had been, and once more, Jim stood as though he was in a trance. He watched her breasts rising and falling as she breathed softly in her sleep. Once more, he began having second thoughts about what he intended to do because it was appearing that he had found something very special. He was reluctant about doing anything that could cause him to lose what he'd found. Before he allowed those feelings get very far in his mind, he shook his head and turned away from the bed. He closed the door to the room so softly there wasn't even a soft click as the lock engaged. Moments later, the car was easing into the street as he forced his mind to dwell on the oncoming project.

Jennifer felt the bed moving as Jim moved to get up, and it took all the power she had to refrain from doing what she so desperately wanted to do. She didn't want him to leave her, but she knew it was something he felt he had no choice about. She wanted to throw her arms around him and show him that she could make him forget all about the drugs, but she knew she could never make him forget about what had happened to Ming as well as all the innocent DOAs he'd encountered. She sensed rather than heard the motel door closing, and then she opened her eyes. Jennifer was completely unaware of her nudity as she stood by the window and held the curtain aside so she could watch Jim as he drove out of the parking lot.

She let the curtain fall back into place and then slowly went back to the bed. She gently sat down and stared at the light patterns flashing across the wall as cars passed by. She pressed her hands against her hips in an attempt to stop the shaking that had started several minutes earlier. A tear slowly trickled down her cheek as she prayed for his safety.

* * *

Jim slowly passed the first house, and he was impressed at the
security that was being displayed there. Several of the large homes
on this block had fences, gates, and large circular driveways;
the one he was looking at was one of that elite style. Several
large stretch limos were parked in the driveway of the mansion
he was interested in. It wasn't difficult to see the large number
of men moving about and trying to act busy as they worked to
appear inconspicuous while moving about the front yard. Several
of the men were leaning against the cars and were giving the
appearance of bored drivers who were waiting for their boss to
get tired of the party. The others were slowly moving around in
front of the house like they were also bored and were waiting for
something to happen. Jim had no doubts that these men were the
outer ring of security and that it would take a superhuman effort
to get past these men by the use of force. They may look bored,
he thought, but there was a studied alertness in their movements
as this bunch kept the front and both sides of the house under
surveillance at all times. He didn't even consider checking the
back because there was no doubt in his mind that there would be
plenty of eyes, and guns, hidden in the shadows of the backyard.

The twenty-minute drive brought him to the second house
that Jim was interested in. It was almost fifteen miles farther
south, but it was also set in an exclusive community that catered
to the rich. The main difference between these two houses
that belonged to Williams was that this house appeared dark
and deserted. He didn't see any movement from the front yard
although he was sure men had been assigned places from which
to keep intruders from wandering about.

Jim didn't take a chance on having the car seen a second time
and putting them on alert, so he only made one pass before he
parked the car a block away and around the corner. As he looked
up and down the street, all the windows he could see from the
street were dark, but he knew it would only take one insomniac

to be walking by a window when he made a move to bring either police or their own men on the run.

As soon as the car was parked where he wanted it, he quickly moved to the front and opened the hood. He spent a moment under the hood as he tried to create the illusion of having car trouble before he eased the hood halfway down and then walked away. The carryall was swinging easily from his grip as he moved away from the car. The new sneakers allowed him to move lightly but quietly as he began sprinting as soon as he was in the sheltering darkness of the alley.

He had to stop for a long moment before he was certain which house he was planning on visiting; from the back, to him, they all appeared to look alike. It was the soft sneeze coming from the shadows that confirmed his choice of houses.

Jim was lying in the deep shadow along the back fence as he watched. The alley fence was a regular wood fence, but a steel wire mesh fence had been installed right next to it on the inside. Several boards had wide cracks in it, and that enabled Jim to observe without stepping up to the gate where he could easily be observed. He remained motionless for several minutes as he searched for some evidence of guards when he heard the man sneeze once more. There was a slight movement from the heavy bushes lining the walkway to the house, but seconds later, everything was silent and unmoving as though nothing had ever happened. Jim realized that luck was riding with him so far because if he had gotten to this location twenty seconds later he would have missed where the man was posted.

There was only a soft click as the latch released, but he was sure the guard had heard it. He didn't latch the gate as he quickly moved off the brick pathway and eased under heavily flowered branches next to the fence. He wasn't yet in place when he heard several soft clicks coming from the same area he'd heard the sneeze earlier, and then there was silence as the man waited with his gun on full cock.

It was quiet for several minutes, and then the gate suddenly moved. When the wooden gate moved, it revealed a large man's silhouette against the sky. Jim held his breath and grimaced when the armed man almost stepped on his arm as he checked the alley. Jim did all he could do to remain motionless when the man had moved into sight. The man remained standing quietly as he closed and latched the gate Jim had just gone through when he entered the yard. This man had not come from the direction that the sneeze had been heard coming from. He was watching the legs of a second man who once more came close to stepping on his leg. He moved several feet away from the gate and then quietly stood in the darkness and waited.

The man held his gun at waist level as he moved past Jim's location and searched the darkness nearer the house for any sign of an intruder. It took Jim almost five minutes of waiting and sweating before the two men decided that the latch just hadn't been set right and that simple gravity had made the gate open. One of the men murmured something to the second man, and then he turned and padded across the lawn to take up his former position.

Sweat had already soaked the material of the mask, and now it was starting to trickle over Jim's eyebrows and into his eyes. He pressed his face into the fabric of his shirt at his elbow until much of the moisture had been soaked up before he made his move. He was wishing for even a breath of a breeze as he waited for the man to get out of sight.

Jim slowly slid out from under the branches and began to gather his feet under him. There hadn't been a sound from the sneezing guard since the second one had gone. Jim wanted to keep his movements just as quiet as he knelt with his gun pointed in the direction of the guard. He stood quietly for a long moment, but then he slowly bent over and felt around under the bush until he found a small stone.

When he tossed the stone in the direction of the gate, he immediately got the reaction he wanted. As soon as the small stone clattered softly against the brick walk, the bushes quickly moved aside as the guard stepped into view. Jim didn't give the man a chance to say anything as the silencer quickly descended upon the man's head. There was a dull thud as the man dropped his own silenced gun to the walk before he followed it down in an unconscious sprawl. Jim released a soft sigh and frowned as he checked the man's pulse and respiration. The silencer on the gun had just been too heavy and had caused more of a crushing force than he had anticipated. He had intended to take at least one man alive out of this place so he could get some more answers, but it was clear this man wouldn't fill the bill.

Jim stood quietly and listened carefully for a long moment until he felt certain the soft sounds weren't going to be investigated by another member of the guards. He rolled the man under the bush and secured the man's gun under his own belt before he started for the rear door of the mansion. He stood by the door and slowly turned the doorknob until he heard a soft click. As the door opened, he quickly pressed tightly against the wall in an effort to keep from presenting a target in the doorway in the form of a silhouette.

The room he entered was bathed in total blackness when the door closed. There wasn't even a light coming from under a door to show him the right direction to move in. He kept the pistol ready as he slipped a small penlight from his shirt pocket. He held the lens of the light deep in his fist to keep too much light from showing, and then he hit the button for a couple of seconds. Once more, in the deep darkness of this small room, he moved in the direction of the door he'd seen. He was very conscious of every sound he made, and he was even sure the enemy could hear his heart beating as he cracked open the second door. He took several steps into the room, and then he stopped. His eyes drifted upwards when he heard the muted sounds of music coming from an upstairs room.

Jim had the illumination from a distant streetlight to show him the general layout of the big room, but he was unable to pick out individual objects as he moved deeper into the room. One of the objects he wasn't able to pick out was a piece of pottery set along the wall. When his foot touched the ancient bowl, it rocked on the hardwood floor and created a hollow moaning sound. That sound drew an immediate response as a man suddenly rose up from a recliner that had been setting along the darkened wall near the window.

Jim stood without moving as the shape crouched near the window and looked around the room. He watched as the shadow moved nearer to the center of the room and then produced something that appeared to have the shape of a flashlight. Jim ducked as low as he could just as the blinding light flashed in the direction of the still-rocking pot. From low on the floor, he squeezed the trigger and felt the recoil of the handgun. The man jerked back as though suddenly yanked by a cable when the shell hit him in the chest. The items in his hands flew across the room. The flashlight bounced off the thick glass of the window and clattered to the floor while the man's gun hit a painting of a Spanish village and sent the entire picture and frame crashing to the floor where the glass shattered.

Jim sprinted in the direction of the stairs, and he no longer tried to do anything in silence because he was sure everyone inside the entire house had heard the noise. He was also sure that anyone he met would be holding a gun and looking for any sign of an intruder. With that thought foremost in his mind, he started up the elaborately curved stairway's carpeted steps and was holding his own gun out in front of him. His feet didn't make a sound on the thick carpet that was covering the steps as he quickly climbed to the second floor.

The stairs ended in an elaborate alcove where an archway showed the way to a hallway that would take you to various rooms on the second floor. A portico that was adorned in rich tapestries overlooked the lower lever.

He had just attained the upper level when he saw a rectangle of light invading the darkness as someone opened a door almost directly below him. Jim crouched by the railing and watched as a man slowly moved into his line of sight. He had foolishly left the door open as well as the light on, and now he was allowing his shadow to lead the way across the room.

The man was hunched over as he moved in the direction of the shattered glass. By the way he held his gun, it was very clear that he was ready to pull the trigger at the first sight of an intruder. Jim reached into his pocket and then flipped a coin ahead of the man.

The coin clattered to the floor after ricocheting from the glass top of a huge coffee table. As the coin raced across the floor, it was followed by a series of soft pops as the nervous man fired his silenced gun in the direction of the sounds he'd heard. The man never heard the single pop that put him to his knees and then slowly caused him to fall forward on his face while the blood flowed freely from the large exit wound in the side of his head.

Jim stopped in front of the door where the music was coming from and slowly opened the door. As the door opened wider, he found himself facing a man who was just as shocked as he was. The man quickly grabbed for his shoulder holster, but he didn't get any further than the snap over the hammer of the gun before his fingers grew too numb to do any more. A dark stain slowly spread out from the hole in his white shirt as the man looked down at his chest in disbelief. The man slowly lost all strength in his legs and dropped to his knees. Seconds later, his neck received a severe twisting because the way he fell caused him to hit his head against the wall at an angle. His head was forced back, and

Jim was sure that even if the bullet hadn't killed him, the broken neck would have finished the job.

Jim rapidly moved from room to room, and when he was sure the upstairs was secure, he began his search once more on the lower floor. He stopped searching only long enough to relieve the bodies of any clips that would fit his gun. He was very thankful Williams had insisted that all his men use not only the same caliber gun but also the same make gun. Jim knew that if his personal hunt continued, as he hoped it would, there would not be any shortage of shells for his confiscated gun.

Jim stood by the front door after he was sure the entire house was clean and free of what he considered garbage. He opened the door several inches and watched for any movement or sound in the darkness, but it remained silent. With only a distant streetlight to give illumination on the huge expanse of the front yard, he knew he had to do something different to rid the yard of any vermin.

The mask quickly found a secure place in his back pocket, and Jim breathed a sigh of relief as he felt a cooling breeze drift through the narrow opening in the door. He pushed his damp hair back with his left hand before he took a deep breath and pushed the door open. He gave a quick look around before he called out softly, "We've got an intruder upstairs in the house. One of you guys move over here, but I want the rest of you to cover the back in case they try to escape that way."

There was a soft rustling as a man moved out of the bushes near the door. The man had so much confidence in himself and his partners that he never questioned the strange voice. He was so sure of the defenses they had set up, it never dawned on him that the enemy could have gotten through and might be standing behind the lines. When Jim ordered the man to spread the word, the man silently obeyed and quickly moved into the darkness to convey his orders. He returned in less than a minute, and he quickly told the man standing in the doorway that he had been unable to find Ralph, but Tony was covering the rear door. He made several remarks about what Williams would do to Ralph. The gun slick said he knew the big man would ream Ralph for not being in the place he'd been ordered to guard, but Jim didn't think any threats from their big boss would make any difference to the dead man.

When the man stepped through the door, Jim pushed him gently in the direction of the stairs. The man balked when he saw the crumpled form in the center of the room. The light was still shining from the room the man had come from, and Jim had no trouble seeing the man kneeling beside the dead man. He also didn't have any trouble seeing the man's head slowly rising as it finally dawned on him that he had been following the orders of a complete stranger. Although he was aware that the man behind him was holding a gun, he tried to spin and bring that man down. But he was much too slow.

As soon as Jim saw the man bending over the dead man, he knew an attempt would be made. And when it happened, he was ready for it. The man had only made a quarter turn when Jim's gun gave another soft cough. The bullet took a small amount of skin from the bottom of the man's elbow before it continued on past the arm and began shattering ribs, lungs, and a large portion of his heart. The man didn't have a chance to groan before even that action was beyond his ability.

Three more clips went into Jim's pocket before he moved to the rear door. Williams's goon didn't hesitate to come to the door when he heard Jim's rasping whisper. "Come here, Tony. Ralph thinks he's got the intruder cornered upstairs."

Tony moved by Jim without any idea that the man wasn't one of them, but he also stopped short when he saw the bodies in the center of the room. Like his partner, he realized his mistake too late, and he was much too slow to elude the bullet that awaited him as he tried to kill the man who had tricked him.

Jim took the time to search for any incriminating evidence, but he came out of the house with absolutely nothing he could use on Williams other than a few small bags of coke as well as several guns and clips. He headed for the back gate, but just as he approached the bushes that were hiding the first dead man, a sudden thought hit him between the ears and he stopped. A slight grin passed over his face as he turned around and went back into the house.

Jim argued with his alter ego for several minutes before he finally picked up the phone to place a call to the motel. He decided that she should at least know where he was as well as what location he was aiming at. He knew she would be upset with him because she hadn't even wanted him to go forward with this first phase of his battle.

He wasn't surprised when the call was answered on the first ring. Jennifer sounded quite upset and his announcement, of what he'd done and what he intended to do, didn't help her disposition.

He tried to calm her down, but she continued to interrupt to demand that he stop his foolishness and get some kind of backup. She soon found that Jim was adamant. He heard a reluctant wish for good luck, and seconds later, she added a soft "butthead" just before the phone receiver settled on the cradle.

* * *

Jim stepped out of the quick cold shower, and minutes later, he was wearing a suit that he had no doubt would have cost him many months' pay. He was sure the man who had been upstairs had been the crew chief, so Jim decided to take the man's place and see what happened. He made a quick check of the man's wallet before he slipped it into his pocket and recognized the name as one that had been on his personal list of wanted men.

Jim wasn't whistling as he came back down the steps, but he was feeling better than he had been although he wasn't too sure how the next leg of his journey was going to fare.

The garage wasn't locked, and when he stepped inside, it didn't take him long to decide to use the Jag XKE for his mode of transportation. He felt the cool air of the after-market air conditioner cooling his face as he pulled out of the yard. The automatic gate was already closing as he pushed his foot down on the throttle and left the not-so-safe-house behind.

A deep breath left his lungs as he opened the window. The suited thug who was in charge of the gate was checking out the driver, and from the look on his face, it was clear he was familiar with this car.

Before the man could demand any identification or explanation, Jim took a firmer grip on the silenced gun he was holding against his leg, and he said, "Where's Tom? I've got to talk to him right now."

The man immediately became uncertain with the situation because of Jim's tone of voice and his cocky attitude. He glanced around before he said, "Cory is gonna be real pissed off when he sees you driving his car. And besides, Williams is throwing a party for a lot of important guests. He ain't gonna be too happy about gettin' visitors."

Jim wedged the gun between his leg and the car seat before he moved with lightning speed. He grabbed the man's suit lapel and pulled him down and forward until his face was close to his own. "Get this clear, and you better listen good and get it right the first time because I'm not going to say it a second time. Cory isn't in any position to tell me what car to drive because the men I represent own him lock, stock, and barrel, just like they own Williams. You better remember this. I don't work for Williams. He works for me. You got that? He's really dropped the ball here in the past couple of weeks, and the big boys sent me out here to check on what the nature of the problem is." Jim looked into the wide eyes of the guard, and then he added, "If you know what's good for your career, you'll be very discreet about anything you say and about who you say it to. I want to see for myself how he's handling this problem, and I don't want him to have the time to make up any alibis. I'm going to drive up there and have a quiet talk with Williams. I want you to go back to your station and act like nothing ever happened." He looked into the thug's eyes for a moment before he allowed his to soften. "There might even a position available for a good man who can follow orders at a time like this."

Jim slowly released the man's suit and then made a show of gently smoothing the material. He tried to make it sound casual as he asked the man's name. He was sweating as he leaned back in the seat and put the car in gear. As he moved up the circular drive, he saw the guard pulling a radio out of his pocket. But after several seconds of indecision, he put it back and resumed his position near the gate. The man was still watching the tail of the XKE as it made the loop and disappeared from sight.

Jim watched a large group of drunken revelers moving about the lawn, but he was more concerned with the roving security that seemed to be everywhere. He knew he was in the lion's den now, and the only thing he had going for him was bluff. He stopped the car right in front of the steps to the house where several of the security men were talking and motioned one of the men over.

With an air of unquestionable authority, Jim said, "My name is Jim Masters. I'm here to talk to Williams. Park this junker where it'll be readily available. I don't have much time, so I'll be leaving right after I have a little talk with Tom." He threw a quick haughty look of superiority at the man. "If you've got any questions, you can check with Craig at the gate. He'll fill you in with everything you need to know."

Jim turned walked up the steps and past a group of drinkers who were congregating near the door. The coolness of the interior made itself felt as he approached the door, but he realized that it wasn't just the heat that was causing his sweat to run down his back and chest. He lifted a drink off the tray of a passing waiter, and the change of weight or balance on the tray didn't faze the man or even cause him to slow down as he rushed to satisfy the needs of other drinkers.

The party was going strong in most areas of the house, but he quickly noticed one door that appeared out of sync with the rest of the house. While the crowd was moving around freely and all other rooms were open, the door to this room was closed, and a man was standing guard in front of it. Jim maneuvered himself into a position where he wouldn't be easily observed but where he could keep the door in sight. It didn't take long before the door opened, and he watched his commander making an exit. The guard beside the door quickly motioned to several lovely females standing by the window, and the commander immediately found himself in the presence of both ladies. Jim watched the scene from the corner and released a small grin. The women were both streetwalkers he'd seen before, only now their apparel was elegant and a far cry from their normal working clothing. They had gone from hot pants and tube tops to flowing gowns. He was sure Williams had spent a small fortune insuring that his guests would be taken care of in any way they needed. The man needed to make sure his goals weren't disturbed by anyone; therefore, payments were being made in cash, and in flesh, to insure those goals.

Jim took an involuntary deep breath when the man he sought stepped out of the room and began to mingle with the crowd. Jim started to move forward to confront Williams, but he suddenly saw Henderson moving into his line of vision. Jim quickly reached up with his hand and covered his face as though his temple had begun throbbing in pain. He finally began breathing again when the man walked right by him and stopped in front of his boss. Henderson said something to Williams that produced a laugh from both men as they began to wander among the guests. Henderson was laughing at something Williams had said when he turned and stepped into the office of the big man. Jim spent several minutes checking out the throng before he turned his attention to the guard and saw how quickly the man became distracted when a pretty female passed him by. It was obvious the man was enjoying his post, but he also demonstrated he was there for the sole purpose of guarding the room.

He had intended to confront Williams in an effort to scare the man enough to make him say a few things that would open a few more doors, but now Jim was having second thoughts. There were always at least two men shadowing him while the other guards in the room were always keeping an eye on the boss. He looked in the direction of the closed door and decided that his best bet on getting any more information would be Henderson once more. The fate of the female who had been driving that Chevrolet Suburban still nagged at him, and he knew he should be able to get that answer from Henderson. The man had managed to keep Jim from getting that information once, but Jim was determined to make sure it wasn't going to happen a second time.

Jim stood quietly until Williams wandered out to the swimming pool where a group of shapely female bathers were frolicking in the nude. Using the air of superiority as a shield, Jim approached the guard and bluntly told the startled guard he was going inside to talk to Henderson, and he didn't want any interruptions. Without waiting for an answer from the man, Jim simply opened the door and entered the room.

As Jim entered the room, he saw Henderson standing with his back to the door and laughing into the phone receiver. The man quickly threw an annoyed look over his shoulder at the intrusion, but other than that, Henderson tried to ignore Jim.

That action didn't bother Jim because it was giving him time to check out the room. He wasn't sure if he liked the idea of having a door leading out onto a patio, because while it could offer him an avenue for a quick departure, it could also provide an easy entrance for some of the guards.

Jim had his suit coat open and had his hand on the pistol just in case, but he wasn't at all prepared for what happened when

Henderson put the phone down and turned around. The first thing Jim noticed was the large automatic in the man's hand, and it was immediately trained on his chest. Jim took a deep breath and slowly moved his hand away from the gun under his arm.

Henderson was grinning as he said, "The last time we got together you were in charge of the party, but this time I'm the one who's going to be having the good times and you're going to be answering the questions." He had a puzzled look on his face as he sat on the corner of the desk and looked at Jim. "Whatever possessed you to come here? You certainly didn't think that no one would recognize you, did you?" He sat and looked at Jim for a long moment in silence before he finally pushed himself away from the desk.

Henderson kept his gun trained on Jim as he slowly walked to the door. When the guard opened the door in answer to the soft knock, Henderson said, "Have someone get Williams. There's someone here he's going to want to talk to."

Jim felt hope surging through him when he saw that the door had only been opened up enough for each of them to see the other's face. The man standing outside the door had not seen the gun in Henderson's hand. There was still a chance he would be able to get the upper hand on Williams because the man was going to be walking into a situation he wasn't prepared for. It was a slim chance, but Jim clung to it because it was the only chance he had at this time. He hadn't been prepared for the quick recognition Henderson had demonstrated or the way he had kept that recognition hidden from Jim. The way things were setting right now, he knew he was going to have to jump instantly at any chance that might arise if he wanted to get out of this alive.

There was a soft sound of argument right outside the door, and then the door opened. Jim was standing between Henderson, who had resumed his seat at the corner of the desk, and the door. He took a deep breath in anticipation of his meeting with Williams. The voice that met his ears surprised him because it wasn't the gravely voice of Tom Williams, but instead it had a soft purring, although inebriated, quality of a female's voice.

The satisfied smirk on Henderson's face disappeared, and he immediately stood and demanded, "What are you doing in here? I told the guard to send somebody to get the boss. Beat it!"

The shapely form stumbled in the direction of Henderson and slurred, "But I just talked to him, and he told me to tell you that he'd be here in a minute." She moved unsteadily in the direction of Henderson again, but this time the man just watched the shapely streetwalker and almost forgot about Jim as the movement under the revealing dress captured his attention. The dress was low-cut in front and was intended to catch and hold any man's attention. It got the attention it was designed to do. She moved alongside Henderson, and that was when Jim, in shock, almost called out her name.

The woman stepped beside the seated man, and his eyes never left the generous amount of cleavage her dress allowed to be seen. It was clear that if Henderson had been able to lift his eyes away from her generous body, he would have immediately recognized Jennifer. There was a commotion outside the door, and then Tom Williams walked in. There was a big smile on his face when he faced the detective and his hired gun.

"Looks like you really did it this time." He looked at his man and gave him his orders as well. "Good work. Now just make sure to keep him sound and safe until all these people leave. I want to have a nice, long talk with him later." He gave the good-looking gal standing next to Henderson a complete visual evaluation before he walked to the door, wearing a huge grin. He was already anticipating the grilling he was going to apply to this meddlesome detective. He was still leering at the beautiful body as he closed the door.

She pressed her body tighter against Henderson's chest, and seconds later, his arm went around her waist and pulled her closer. He was still staring at her full breasts when he felt something hard touching his head. His eyes shot up to her face. Immediately recognition registered, and in seconds he lost he instantly lost several shades of color.

Jennifer recognized the indecision in his eyes, and she smiled as she said, "If you don't do anything funny, then I won't have to pull this trigger. The guard sent me after your boss, but I just made it look like I was talking to him, so don't expect him to come in and rescue you. You've got Jim covered, but I've got a gun aimed at your head. And at this range, I don't see how I can miss. I think you can understand that much, can't you? Put the gun down right now." The last part of her statement almost came out like a growl.

The indecision was clearly written on Henderson's face as he looked into her eyes. He knew if she pulled the trigger, the loud report would bring every gun-toting man in the place into this room. The problem with that was that if she pulled the trigger, it wouldn't make any difference to him if this pair was caught or not. Slowly the gun muzzle began to drift lower, and she had no trouble removing it from his grasp.

She backed away from the desk and was just starting to move in Jim's direction when the door suddenly opened and the guard stuck his head in. Once more, Jennifer's cleavage got full attention as she smiled at the man. He didn't notice that she was no longer stumbling around or slurring her words because his attention was firmly riveted on her chest. Jennifer purred, "I just took this gun away from this character. How come you allowed this stranger to come in here with a gun on him?"

That statement caused the man to break out of his trance, and he immediately came through the door and then reached for the gun Jennifer was holding. The look on the man's face went from longing to suspicion to shock and then to absolute pain as Jennifer's knee literally lifted the man off the floor with the impact. His face got extremely red right before his knees collapsed. The man didn't have a chance to call out. The pain was so severe that he couldn't draw in enough air to even release a moan before he passed out between Jim and Henderson.

Before Jim could begin asking why she ended up here, Jennifer said, "I think we'd better get out of here while we've got the chance. They're going to be checking this room out in a couple of minutes."

Gray looked at the fallen man. "I agree. But first there's got to be a safe in here that contains some good information we could use." He looked at Henderson. "I've a number of things I want to accomplish before I leave here. One of those is that I want to get you out of here alive because there are a number of things that you need to explain to me. But I'll tell you this much that if you can't give me anything I need while we're still here then I guess the risk isn't worth it. I can easily plug you and leave you in the closet. I think you know that because of this silencer no one will be any wiser until we're long gone." Jim moved closer and waved his gun around the man's genitals while he watched the uncomfortable look on his face.

Jennifer released a soft laugh as she stepped up to the desk and played with the cigarette lighter in her hand. "If he doesn't obey you, I can always shoot him with my gun." She waved the lighter in front of Henderson and then laughed at the look on his face.

His face got red as he looked at the lighter. "Are you telling me that's the gun you held against my head? You mean that you..."

Jennifer backed away from Henderson and threw her arms wide as she said, "There weren't any guns lying around here when I came into the room, and there sure isn't any place I could hide a gun on me with this dress, so what do you think I held to your head?" She tossed the lighter on the desk and then walked over to the unconscious man and pulled the gun out of the man's shoulder holster.

Jim got Henderson's full attention once more when he nudged the man's genital area with the silencer. "Get the safe open now. If someone comes in before we're ready to leave, then you can kiss your butt good-bye because I'm going to nail you, cowboy."

Henderson's knees appeared to be just a little weak as he moved a picture and revealed a combination safe hidden underneath. It took less than ten seconds before the safe was open, and Jim immediately shoved Henderson aside. He moved in front and began unloading it. Everything in the safe, including the gun Henderson had been hoping to use, went into a briefcase setting beside the desk.

When they checked the pulse and respiration of the guard, they found both were very weak, but no one in the room seemed to be very concerned. Henderson was shouldered with the responsibility of moving the big man into the large closet. Jim and Jennifer remained on guard just in case someone came into the room before they were ready to leave. They were very ready to take care of the outcry it would create. However, any gunplay occurring from within the mansion would certainly be their downfall because there were just too many guards for the two of them to handle.

Jim was very thorough when he explained how the exodus was going to be handled, and he made sure Henderson knew he was going to be the first one to go if someone tried to stop them. Henderson slowly nodded his head as he got a gentle push toward the door.

Jennifer walked out first, and quickly checked to make sure Williams was nowhere around where he could see them walking out. As soon as Henderson cleared the doorway, she wrapped her arms around his free arm while he carried the briefcase in his other arm. Jim walked behind the pale man and tried to look like he had nothing on his mind except some private party for the three of them. Jennifer weaved and stumbled as she held tightly onto his arm while they moved through the crowd. It appeared as though she was hanging on because she was afraid she was going to fall, and it was just the impression they wanted to give. Very few members at the party paid any attention to the man bringing up the rear.

Jim was especially glad of this fact when the commander himself stopped the exiting trio and gazed longingly at Jennifer and said, "You can't leave with her yet." He ran his fingers through Jennifer's hair and almost pulled her brown wig off. "I saw her earlier and I could sure make some plans for this little dolly tonight."

Jim was ready to bring his gun out and bring the commander along with force when Jennifer gave the man a sweet smile and said, "These two won't last long, honey. I'll be back in a little while, and I promise you that when we get together, I'm going to give you more than you can handle." She tweaked his cheek gently, and then she turned to Henderson and said, "Let's go, baby. I can't wait much longer."

Hamilton watched the three people leaving in the car and shook his head as he wished he could be in Henderson's boots. He didn't know how hard Henderson was wishing the same thing.

Chapter 17

Jim paid close attention to Henderson as the man drove away from the house and through the gate. It was clear that the man was in fear for his life, but for some men it was times like this that caused them to do something that they normally wouldn't do

The man at the gate stepped up to the car. His mouth dropped open when he looked in and saw Jennifer, wearing an outfit that almost revealed more than it concealed, sitting between the men. She was sitting between two men and was using the armrest for a third seat in the small two-seater. Jim didn't mind that most of her butt was resting on his left thigh. The guard at the gate didn't pay any attention at all to the men riding along in the car. He knew he'd gotten the poor assignment from the start, but there wasn't much he could do about it, being as low on the totem pole as he was, but now he fully realized how low his position really was. He took a long, last look at her long brown hair that almost covered her generous cleavage before he waved them through. He stared at the taillights of the departing sports car, with a strong longing for that good-looking doll that lasted for a long time after the car pulled onto the street and disappeared from view.

Jim wanted to begin sorting through the papers to see what he'd been able to collect out of the safe, but he recognized the fact that Henderson was going to be desperate enough to try anything until there was absolutely no doubt in his mind that there was nothing he could do about it. There wasn't anything this man wouldn't do to get out of this situation if there was a chance he could do that and still remain among the living. He knew he had to keep a very close watch on Henderson because the man had even been slick enough to pick a pair of handcuff locks that were supposed to be pick-proof.

It was clear to Jim that Henderson's eyes didn't miss anything on the way back to the first mansion, and because of that, his grip on the gun never eased off target and neither did the pressure on the trigger. He directed the unwilling driver to park the Jag behind the Ford, but when he stepped out of the car, he found a surprise waiting for him.

From the corner of his eye, he saw a shadow moving away from the bushes along the sidewalk, and he instinctively spun around, dropped to one knee, and brought his gun to bear on the moving shadow. There was only a fraction of an ounce left to add to the pull of the trigger before Jim sent its missile on its deadly mission when the shadow said, "Where you been, man? I been waitin' here for almost two hours. Was about ready to give up on you."

Jim squinted as he stared into the darkness. "Turk? Is that you?" Jim shook his head as he stared at the black man standing before him. Jim quickly lowered the gun and released a deeply held breath before he irritably said, "I hope you know that your little move right now could have gotten two men killed. You with a bullet to the chest and me by having a heart attack." He took several more deep breaths, and then in a softer tone, he said, "What are you doing here? I thought you were going to be making arrangements for your trip to London, not popping out of the bushes at three o'clock in the morning."

Turk quickly said, "Well, to start with, I think we'd better get out of here first. We can swap stories when we get out of here. I was in the house a few minutes ago, and I saw the mess you left. I was still in the house looking around for your body when one of their men stopped in. When he saw what had happened here, he left in a hurry and on the run. There's going to be a mess of

Williams's men showing up before long." Turk stopped talking when he saw Henderson sitting behind the wheel, but even that event was obliterated from his mind when Jennifer started getting out of the car.

She was still listening to his long, low whistle when she gave up on adjusting the top of her dress and simply asked Jim for his suit coat. She looked sheepishly at Jim and then at Turk and said, "When I was playing the hooker act at Williams's place, I was doing my best to put on an act so I could get some information. Even though it bothered me to go showing so much to everyone, I felt it was something I could do because it was part of my job. This is different. I'm with friends now and having this skimpy dress on in front of you two is making me very uncomfortable and absolutely and totally embarrassed."

Turk put his arms around Jennifer after she had the coat firmly settled across her shoulders. He pulled her tight for a moment, and then he said, "We understand, baby. I just want to let you know that gals like you are what dreams are made of." He released her, and then with a deep sigh, he moved back an arm's length and gazed wistfully at her face. Abruptly, Turk turned around and moved to the far side of the car. He assisted Jim in moving Henderson to the back seat of the Ford, but his eyes spent most of the time watching Jennifer as she got the last of their possessions out of the Jaguar and slipped into the front seat of the Ford.

When questioned about his Chevy, Turk replied "I moved it after I saw the results of your encounter here. I moved it a couple of blocks away to where I can get it after the heat dies down."

Jim climbed into the rear with Henderson and made sure his gun never wavered from the gangster.

Turk slid in behind the steering wheel and began driving. He wanted to talk to Jennifer, but he found she was very involved with the contents of the briefcase. After several minutes of trying to carry on a one-sided conversation, the black man grew quiet although Jim saw the man continually glancing over in Jennifer's direction with loneliness and desire written all over his face.

They drove past the motel a number of times before Jim was sure there wouldn't be any surprises waiting for them when they walked into the motel room. Henderson was quiet as they transferred him into the motel room and cuffed him to one of the two hard-backed chairs in the kitchen. He frowned as they cuffed each hand to the side of the chair and then used plastic ties to secure his arms to the chair as well. He knew there was no way he would be able to duplicate his recent escape by working the locks. He realized he only had one chance to get away and that was to make them so angry they'd make a mistake as they were securing him so he began to implement his plan by showing a big, knowing smile. It was nothing more than an attempt to make them wonder. He knew that if they finished with their work before he got them distracted, he was going to be here for a long time. He took a deep breath and then he said, "It would make things a whole lot handier if you locked me in the bedroom. It would be much easier to secure me to the bed than it will be on this chair." He hesitated for a moment, but then his grin grew larger. "Of course, that might put a little crimp on your free time. Sampson and I were thinking about breaking in on you two the other day because of all the noise you two were making, but we decided the risk wasn't worth it." Henderson's laugh was loud in the quiet room as he looked into Jim's eyes. He saw the anger on the man's face, and he decided he was close to getting the only chance he was going to get out of this man. He added, "You two made more noise than…"

Henderson felt his teeth giving as the big fist connected with his mouth, and his chair went over backwards from the blow. His head bounced twice when it hit the hard linoleum floor. Henderson blinked his eyes, and it took a long moment before he saw that Jim was still standing where he had been and that it hadn't been Gray who had nailed him. He saw an angry black man standing above him, and that man was rubbing his knuckles.

Turk waited until the man was able to understand him before he said, "You say anything else about that young lady, and I'll make sure they never find your body. Or any parts of it. You got that, white boy?" Turk's teeth were showing as he snarled his warning to the man on the floor.

Jim watched as the angry black man stormed out of the motel room, and he knew the black man had just confirmed his suspicions about why he had returned. He'd already known that the man had carried a deep appreciation for Jennifer's good looks and great body, but now he fully realized that the man's feelings had gone much deeper. He stared at the door for several minutes before he finally bent over and muscled Henderson's chair upright once more. He looked at Henderson's bloody mouth and forced a grin. "You know what? I don't think he found your remarks too funny either." Jim leaned closer to the man. "Actually, you came out of that pretty good because I wasn't going to use my fist on you. I was going to use this silencer on your teeth and let you spit teeth for the next hour or two. I really think you'd better remain silent unless you're asked a question. It could be hazardous to your health."

Jim turned around and saw that Jennifer had just seen the results of Turk's anger. But it was clearly written on her face that she had witnessed him moving away from the injured man, and he could see she was accusing him of hitting a defenseless man. Jim released a grin and hoped it didn't look forced as he said, "I guess someone took exception to something this guy said. I don't think he'll make any more smart remarks again."

Jim wasn't about to put the blame on Turk even though that was where it belonged. But as it turned out, Jim didn't have to say a word to clear himself.

Jennifer brought a wet cloth for Henderson's mouth, and as she began to clean the blood away from his face, Henderson couldn't stop using the opportunity for a lot of ranting and raving to gain some support from the woman's corner. "These two jerks had me handcuffed to the chair, and they started pushing their questions at me. Then they said I wasn't talking fast enough, and that black bas…" Henderson stopped talking, but his mouth remained open wide as he stared as the heavy silencer that was poised to deliver a teeth-shattering blow.

Jim's voice was as cold as ice as he said, "Henderson, if you know what's good for your teeth as well as your general health, you'll stop that garbage you're spewing. That man just saved you a lot of pain by putting you down on the floor before I got to you." He turned and looked at Jennifer. "This poor excuse for a human being started making remarks about some sounds coming out of the bedroom when they broke loose, and Turk sort of took exception to it." Jim was quiet for a moment then he motioned for Jennifer to step out of the room, and he followed her into the next room. "I think you're the reason Turk came back. It's been pretty easy to read the man tonight because it's been quite obvious."

Jim pulled her body close against him and rested his cheek on the top of her head. He breathed in the store-bought fragrance of her fake hair, and for several short moments, he was able to forget about the thug in the next room. He cupped her chin, tilted her head back, and gently covered her lips with his own. He had to fight down a burning desire as he forced himself to release her because time was important. He had a number of serious matters to contend with before Williams and his men found their hiding place. He looked at the beautiful woman. "I suppose we're going to be forced to confront the problem with Turk sooner or later, but right now, we have to be concerned with the information we need to get from Henderson."

He watched as Jennifer removed the long red-haired wig and shook her blond tresses into place before he added, "Sooner or later, Williams is going to get wind of where we're hiding out, and he'll come in force. Right now, from the way he's going to have to look at it, we've done way too much damage to his operations for him to allow us to simply walk away. Besides the drugs and money he's lost to us, there's the fact that his men aren't going to be as willing to step into the line of fire as they have in the past if he doesn't get the individuals who are responsible for killing his men." Jim walked to the kitchen doorway and saw Henderson was sitting quietly as the man tried to eavesdrop on their conversation. When he resumed speaking to Jennifer, his voice was much softer as he said, "Sweetheart, keep in mind that I'm only making a guess, but I think Williams will be making an all-out assault on us. He's going to be forced to use every favor and call in every marker he's ever accumulated to find us and put us out of commission." Jim had the urge to put more emphasis on certain words to show the danger they were in, but he stopped himself from doing that because there was no doubt in his mind that she understood the seriousness of their predicament. Jim bent over and gave her another light kiss on the lips. "Williams knows that he's reached the point where it's fight or fold. I cannot see the man giving up and looking to make a fresh start somewhere else when all he has to do here is to find, and remove, the burr under his saddle that's giving him fits right here."

Jennifer leaned against Jim's chest. "I didn't expect this kind of stuff to happen when I joined the force. I always saw myself writing out tickets or working at the computer and solving some big crime that way, but not this." She took a step back and looked up at his face. "Jim, I'm scared. I never figured on killing anyone or having anyone coming after me to kill me. This has gotten way out of hand. I don't know if I can go on with this." A slight tremor passed through her body as she pressed herself against Jim once again.

Jim brushed her hair away from her face as he tried to reassure her. "Sweetheart, you've got two guys here that will do everything they can do to protect you. Just remember that they've got to find us before they can do anything, and I'm going to do all I can to prevent that from happening. Besides"—he grinned—"you aren't exactly the helpless kind of female from what I've seen."

He gave her a gentle nudge in the direction of the sofa where the briefcase was lying before he turned toward the kitchen. He faked a grin. "Now why don't you occupy that gorgeous mind of yours by seeing what kind of information you can pull out of that pile of papers we've accumulated in the last few days. All right?"

Jim was almost by the door when Jennifer called his name softly. When he turned and looked at her, he saw a nervous smile just before Jennifer said, "I still think you're a butthead."

Jim showed her a wide smile as he winked in her direction. He watched her as she started to sit on the sofa, but then it was very apparent that she wasn't comfortable in those clothes as she removed Jim's coat and looked down at her apparel. When she closed the door to the bedroom, Jim turned his attention back to the handcuffed man. The split lip had continued bleeding, and now the front of the fancy suit was well marked with blood. But Jim ignored it as he perched on the edge of the table and put Henderson under such an intense glare that it didn't take long before the man was squirming.

The man had reverted to putting his full attention in the direction of the doorway, so Jim used the toe of his shoe to tap on Henderson's knee to get the full attention of the man back on himself. As soon as eye contact was made, Jim said, "The last time I had your undivided attention, we were unable to finish our little conversation due to a mistake on my part and a little skill on yours. This time, it's going to be different because you and I are going to go over everything that's happened until I have all the answers." He pushed Henderson's chair around so he was facing the table, and then Jim slipped into the only other free chair and sat across the table from him.

He pulled a pad out of his shirt pocket and placed it on the table before he looked into Henderson's eyes and said, "Now let's take it from the top. You eliminated some guy who was trying to rip Williams off, but your actions were observed by a woman in a Chevy van. We never got past that part. Now I want to know what happened after you started after that woman."

Henderson had just opened his mouth to speak when the door opened, and Turk stepped into the room. The eyes on both men hardened as they exchanged looks, but Jim quickly got Henderson's attention back where he wanted it when he tapped on the table with the silencer. He saw Turk taking up a station next to the oven, but he never took off his eyes off Henderson, and his frowns never waivered from the man. There was no mistaking the kind of treatment the black man wanted to give the white killer for the remarks the man had made.

Henderson looked back at Jim and then tried for a quick reply in hopes the police officer would accept a simple answer. "The man got away on foot after he wrecked his car, and then when I went after the woman, I couldn't catch her because she had a faster car. I have absolutely no idea who she was or where she went."

Jim quickly straightened his legs as he shot to his feet. The chair he'd been sitting on hadn't even hit the wall yet when Jim was standing over the killer. Henderson felt his head being pulled back as Jim grabbed a handful of hair. There was no gentleness in his actions. Jim pulled the man's head back until they were looking at each other eye to eye. Jim only had to deliver three sharp raps to the man's forehead with the silencer before the man decided to start giving a more believable version of what had happened that night.

The man winced from the sharp taps on his forehead before he finally blurted out, "All right, all right. The guy ripped the boss off for several thousand dollars and a load of coke. I was told to make him pay for it, one way or the other. I caught up with him and was headed back to my car so I could call in for a cleanup crew when I saw that broad watching me. I chased after that Chevy, but I must have gotten some bad gas in the last fill because I couldn't get that thing to go fast enough to catch her. I don't know where she is because she outran me. That's all I know."

Henderson's eyes widened as Jim stood once more and reached for his hair. "I'm telling you the truth. I lost her in the dust storm after we left the freeway. I drove all the way to a place called Crown King and then back to the freeway without seeing any sign of that car. I sat by the side of the road until it got light, and then I went over it again. I found her rig where she drove off the road, but she wasn't in it. We've had her house, her friends, and her workplace covered, but nobody's seen her." He looked at Jim as he added, "I didn't touch her. I didn't shoot her. I don't have any idea where she is, but I will say this much right now. The boss wants her almost as bad as he wants you, and that broad in the other room." He threw a quick look at Turk. "He already knows about you, so he'll be looking for you as well." Henderson relaxed in his chair as he said with a grin, "All three of you are going to find that the boss don't give up too easily."

Jim wiped the grin off the man's face when he replied, "I think your boss is finding out that I don't give up very easily myself." He looked down at the notepad for a moment. "What happened to that car? If it had been left where you said it was, someone would have called the police sooner or later, and I'd have heard about it."

Henderson looked at Jim for several seconds before he sighed and said, "When I found the van, I called the boss, and he sent a truck out to pick it up. He's either got the thing stashed away somewhere, or else the crusher took care of it already. The same thing was probably done with the VW as well. I just report things like that, and the crew takes care of the minor details."

Jim opened his mouth to voice another question, but before he could say a word, he heard Jennifer calling him. He stood up and handed the gun to Turk. "If he gives you any lip, just use the silencer on his head. And if he makes any attempt to get away, just use the gun on him." He gave Henderson a hard look before he left the room. He only got three steps into the next room when he heard a loud yelp. Jim quickly turned around and entered the kitchen again where he saw Henderson shaking his head.

"Nothing's wrong," Turk said with a big grin. "I just wanted to make sure I had his attention before I told him that I wasn't going to fool around with him if he started giving me any lip." He grinned as he looked at the handcuffed man and added, "I think we understand each other now, don't we, whitey?"

The men in the kitchen once more heard Jennifer calling, and when Jim looked in Turk's direction, the man said, "Don't worry about us now. I got it out of my system a while ago, and I don't think we'll have to worry about any unnecessary noise coming from this guy while you're gone."

Jim looked back and forth between the two men several times before he sighed and turned away. Jennifer gave him an impatient look when he sat down beside her on the couch. She had changed into a cool-looking light green halter top with matching shorts, and while it covered her body, it was an outfit that did nothing to hide her shape.

Jim forced his eyes to the paper she was holding on her lap as she pointed to an entry that was halfway down the sheet. "You know earlier where Captain Harris had information on some of Hamilton's deposits in the bank? Well, in the papers you got from Williams's safe, I just found a matching list of payments. It wasn't typed in. This is all handwritten, so now all we have to do is find the person who entered these figures. Between that guy and the evidence we have here on the paper, it should give us the proof we need to start washing the commander's dirty laundry. It also gives a whole list of names and dates where special amounts of money were paid out. It even gives a number of places that Williams owns and uses for his 'businesses' like those two mansions we visited tonight. I think this information was kept so he could use it to keep certain people in line." She looked up with sparkling eyes and added, "Jim, with this information we can clear ourselves and put Williams and Hamilton out of commission at the same time."

He didn't want to throw cold water on her hopes, but he wanted to make sure she knew what could still happen. He took her hand in his. "Sweetheart, that's the information we've been looking for, so now all we have to do is get it to someone that isn't under Williams thumb or in league with him. We already know we can't go to Hamilton, but how many more people are in the same dirty boat that he's on?" He saw some of the sparkle leaving her eyes, so he quickly added, "But this gives us a big opening. If we can draw enough public interest here, then there won't be any way to cover this kind of information up because there's going to be too many people sitting in front of their TVs and watching to see how many of the 'public servants' have their fingers in this pie. All we have to do is figure out how to bring it to their attention."

Jim leaned back as he stared at the sheet and attempted to devise a plan that would get them off the hook. His thoughts were interrupted when he heard Jennifer speaking excitedly.

"We've still got that pickup loaded with drugs and money. You mentioned giving the TV stations the information and letting them pass it on to the police. How about doing that but also giving them a tape to air at the same time? You can tell our side of it without appearing in public or exposing any of us to the dirty side of the criminal justice system."

Jim had been tapping the edges of the papers against his knee, but now the movement stopped, and he just stared at the papers as he started running that idea through his mind. Slowly his head began to nod, and a smile began to appear. He looked over at Jennifer and grinned. "Sweetheart, I think you just hit the nail right on the head. If we do that, and if we can get the investigation started on a strong note, then there won't be any time for Williams, or Hamilton, to think of anything other than survival.

They won't have any reason to come after us because everything we've got on them will be in the hands of the people who can dish it directly to the prosecuting attorneys and to the public."

He was grinning as he thought about the hair-pulling contortions the TV and radio stations would be able to cause if they were handed the news in the correct manner. Once the radio and TV stations found out about what was going on, their reporters would begin turning over every stone they could find in the hopes of getting their own fifteen minutes of fame as well as getting their station's broadcast ratings moved a little higher on the scale. Jim reached out and pulled Jennifer against him as he told her what a great idea she'd had. He didn't see the look on Turk's face as the man looked into the room to see what had caused all the laughter and saw Jennifer's unresisting response to Jim's embrace.

Turk wandered about in the kitchen for several minutes before he settled back into the hard chair and darkly regarded Henderson's face. Henderson wisely opted not to say a single word.

Chapter 18

After a short discussion, Turk volunteered to go out to several camera stores to get the cameras and the camcorders they were going to need for their record keeping and for releasing the information to the news stations. He had stated that he knew where a number of electronic stores were that stayed open late.

While he was gone, Jim and Jennifer talked in length about the man's continued involvement in their not-so-legal activities when he could already be out of the country with his share of the money, but they also talked about Turk's obvious feelings toward Jennifer. They hadn't come up with any solution by the time they heard him returning with the cameras and film.

Since they were using the money they'd confiscated from Williams's illegal lines of business, they had not been worried about how much the camera or the three camcorders had cost. They wanted to make several copies of the film, but they didn't want to involve outside sources because as important as this project was they didn't want to take any unnecessary chances.

Jim had decided he wanted to make two identical full-length films for the prosecutors, and he wanted them identical down to the last detail. He decided the easiest way to do that was to use a pair of camcorders on that aspect of it. He had also made a good argument for using a third one to make a shorter abbreviated film for the news media that would give the public enough information to make them demand action but not enough to give away the meat of the case to Williams and his cronies. When they finished setting up the three camcorders on the tripods around the desk which Jim intended to sit behind, he and Turk went into the living room. They spent the next hour lending a hand with Jennifer's efforts. She had taken on the responsibility and the chore of photographing the incriminating pages of the ledger he'd taken from Williams's party house.

The next six hours were spent making a documentary film on all the happenings and information that Jim had encountered while investigating Williams and the men who surrounded and supported him. He did not neglect to state all the knowledge he had in his possession about the deaths of Harris or Tony Sanchez. Although it was hard not to include his own feelings about who was responsible for the deaths, the importation of the drugs and its distribution, he felt he had been quite successful in putting his feelings behind him and simply reporting the facts as he'd found them. Jim knew the public would make their own evaluation without any pushing from him. Jennifer had argued that the public would make up their own minds, in support of their case, much quicker by allowing the decision to come from them if they saw that it wasn't just a vindictive move from Jim because he had been kicked off the force and was now wanted by the police themselves.

The neck of Jim's shirt was wet with perspiration, and it was also dripping from his nose and chin by they time they switched off the lamps they had surrounded him with to provide the needed light. He was forced to blink his eyes a number of times to help adjust his eyesight to the gloom of the room now that the glare of the lights was gone. He leaned back in the chair and closed his eyes for a long moment while Turk began shutting down the cameras.

Jim still had his eyes closed when Turk said, "You know, we're missing one element here that could get the news out to a lot more people and a lot faster." He watched Jim opening his eyes and then leaning forward in the chair until his elbows were back on the desk once more. "We're leaving the radio stations out. I think we should make some tapes and send them around. It wouldn't take long to make a tape and then to run off a bunch of copies to send around. I speak the lingo, so I could even cover the Mexican population by making several tapes for the Hispanic stations in town. You know there are a lot of people in town here that are more comfortable talking in Mexican than they are doing the Anglo bit."

Jim nodded his head and said, "That sounds like a real good idea. The harder we can hit Williams and his crew, the less they're going to be able to do anything about it. It'll also force the police to move much faster." He was silent for a moment and then he said, "But we also forgot something else. I neglected to say anything about that young woman who disappeared. When I questioned Henderson, he said he just found an empty car hung up in the arroyo. He could be lying, and she could be dead and buried out in the desert somewhere. Or on the other hand, she could have found a way out of the mountains and now she could be hiding out. If she's still alive, she'd make a very important witness for our side when the trial started. If she's alive and hiding out, she needs to know that things are in the process of getting straightened out." Jim wiped his face with his sleeve and then he sighed and said, "How much film is left in those camcorders?"

Without even looking at the cameras, Turk said, "We should have at least a couple of minutes on the ones for the prosecution lawyers, but on the one that's being made for the news stations, there's a lot of time left." On a motion from Jim, he began switching on the camcorders and lights once more. He stood back and watched over the two cameras they intended to add the information to. Jim related what he knew about the shooting and the chase that came next, and then he talked about the missing woman in the Suburban.

When Jim finished giving his report on the two tapes for the lawyers' end of it, he began once more on the third camcorder he was going to send to the television stations. When he finished telling the camcorder what he knew had happened, he made a plea to the young woman, or to anyone who knew her, to give a call to the state attorney's office or one of the television stations or to some independent party. They needed to know if she was still alive, or if they had to begin searching for her body in the part of the high desert around where her car was found. He stared at his fingertips for a long moment before he motioned for Turk to stop the camera while he made a phone call. He was wearing a small smile when he began talking into the camera once more and gave another phone number the woman could call if she was alive and willing.

Once more, the extra camera lights were doused, and Jim began moving around the motel room as he tried to relax. He saw Jennifer was watching Turk working with the cameras as she stood behind him. As he moved into the living room, he heard her telling Turk that those cameras looked just as confusing as a VCR was. Turk's chuckle drifted into the joining room, and then Jim heard bits and pieces as the man tried to explain their workings. Jim sat down on the sofa and gratefully closed his eyes. He also made a strong attempt to shut out all sounds coming from around him.

Jennifer's voice slowly seeped into his consciousness, and then as he roused himself from a deep sleep, he heard his own voice coming from the television set. He quickly sat up and watched his face telling the world about the drugs and the killings as well as the police connections to the drug world of Williams and his minicartel. He couldn't stop the grin that spread across his face when they switched to a live view of several dozen cameras covering a ministorage location. It almost appeared to be a who's who show because everyone who was anyone, from the governor's office on down, was seen crowding around the pickup. The camera swung around and got a shot of Hamilton standing beside the governor. The governor was speaking about what she expected to happen in the near future, and that brought out several remarks from Jennifer and Jim as they watched the uncomfortable look on Hamilton's face. When several members of the news media began to converge on Hamilton for his views on the subject of the alleged police corruption, it was very clear to the motel trio that the man was having trouble making himself sound like someone who intended to apprehend the guilty party and see to their prosecution.

Jim leaned back in the sofa as he listened to the news commentators having a field day with the case that had been dropped on their doorstep. He watched Turk's face break out in a big grin when Jennifer began hopping up and down on her toes as she watched the events unfolding on the nineteen-inch screen. In her happiness at seeing the Williams empire beginning to show deterioration, she didn't hesitate to give Turk a big hug in her excitement, which spread his grin even wider. Jim also watched Turk's grin cracking for a moment when Jennifer sat next to Jim and hugged him.

Jennifer's head was resting against Jim's chest as she continued watching the television when Turk moved across the room. He stood in the doorway and looked at a totally defeated Henderson for a long moment before he turned and said, "Well, I don't think I can do you all any more good from here on in, so I think I'm splittin'. I think I'd better get out of here before the police get organized enough and start watching Sky Harbor Airport. I'm quite sure that a lot of the bad element around town will be trying to get out while the gettin' is still good. Guess I'll just donate that Chevy to some charity. Don't think Williams will be too worried about little ole me any longer."

Jim saw that the man was grinning, but he also realized that much of the grin was forced. He got up from the couch and offered his hand. "Turk, you've been a real help, and I want to thank you. I hope you'll keep in touch with us." He knew what was really on the man's mind, so he quickly stepped out of the way after they shook hands.

Jennifer moved in to give the man a hug, but Turk stopped her by taking her shoulders in his big hands and saying, "Let's just shake hands and let it go at that. Saying adios is hard enough without any of those mushy hugs and things like that. All right?"

Jennifer's eyes were beginning to water, and her chin was quivering. But she tried to hide the feelings that were showing on her face by staring at her shoes while Turk tried to hide his feelings by showing bluster.

Just before he turned to head out the door, Turk jokingly admonished Jim that if he didn't do right by Jennifer, he was going to come back from England and beat him to a pulp. The room was quiet for several minutes as Jim and Jennifer remained standing behind Henderson and stared at the closed door.

The room was dark, but with the curtains pulled back, there was enough light coming into the room that Jennifer easily dialed the numbers for Salina's home. She had tried to contact the young Hispanic woman at the police station right after Turk had left, but the officer on the front desk said Salina had just left for home, so she waited about twenty minutes and tried the young officer's apartment. Jennifer finished dialing, and then she shifted the receiver to her right hand and waited. The phone rang only three times, but it seemed like an eternity to the impatient woman as she tapped the tip of her fingernail against the plastic case of the phone. She listened to the sounds of a hurried and busy woman taking some deep breaths before she answered the phone with a simple "Yes?"

Going by the sudden intake of air on the other end of the phone line, there was no doubt in Jennifer's mind that she had taken the young woman by surprise when she identified herself. There was a long silence before Jennifer decided to take the bull by the horns. "I'm sure you've seen the news already, and I've got something I would like you to do that's directly related to this whole mess."

Salina was silent for a long moment. "Jennifer, I'm sure you know that warrants have been issued for both you and Lt. Gray. The way things are right now, you're in pretty deep. I think you'd better turn yourself in as quick as possible. The longer you try to evade capture, the harder it will go for both of you. You know that, don't you? You've got to give yourself up. The word had already come down that you and Detective Gray are to be considered armed and dangerous. The best thing you could do to prove your innocence is to turn yourself in."

Jennifer felt her face going pale when the woman mentioned turning herself in, but she pushed that feeling aside and said, "Salina, I've got proof that Commander Hamilton is involved in the drug business right up to his neck. I still can't turn myself in because I know that I'll be put in a cell until this is cleared up. I think you know as well as I do that if Jim and I end up in a cell before Williams is taken down and put away, we could very well end up dead.

"Salina, this man has gotten into places you wouldn't believe. We're close to proving that Williams ordered the deaths of Sanchez and Harris." Jennifer stopped talking for a moment and pulled in several deep breaths before she continued. "Salina, I need to talk to you in person. I've got some papers that will prove Hamilton is dirty. Jim didn't want to put that information on the air for the public to see because he didn't want to give Hamilton the chance to cover any of his tracks or to run before he could be arrested. We sent a much more detailed film to the attorney general's office and one identical to that directly to the governor's home to make sure she got all the same information and that no one would try to cloud the picture or sidestep the issue. We thought she had to know exactly what was going on. They've got all the information they need to indict and convict a lot of the dirty elements. They've got what they need to get the wheels turning, but until that happens, both of us are going to be very definite targets. The effectiveness of their organization is going to deteriorate once the police get the bigger wheels behind bars, but that's going to take a little time yet. Salina, if Jim and I turn ourselves in, then we'll most likely end up in the same jail cell with some of their people because that's the way the Williams is going to order it. I'm not ready to die yet. Not that way. Not in a jail cell without any way to defend myself."

Salina had remained quiet while Jennifer had been talking, and now it was taking a long moment before she responded. The tone of her voice held a relieved note in it when she started talking once more. "Jennifer, I'm really not supposed to tell you this. I hope you realize that I'm really breaking some rules by telling what I intend to, but I'm doing it because I believe you're sincere." There was another sound of a long, drawn-in breath before she added, "Jennifer, I work for Internal Affairs. I was sent to this station to investigate Detective James Gray because of all the adverse reports we'd been getting on his behavior as well as his methods of investigation and arrest. On top of that, there had been a number of reports of criminal activities in which he was alleged to have been heavily involved. When I saw how the two of you were interacting, I began another investigation. The second one concerned you. I felt you were clean, but you know as well as I do that feelings don't enter in an investigation like this. I'm afraid the report wasn't very complimentary to either one of you. I was almost ready to send the reports in to the head office when I saw the film on the news. I'm holding on to those reports until I see what crawls out from under all those rocks you turned over. Speaking about the news, I'm curious, how'd you get that film to all the stations and then get them to air it at the same time?"

Jennifer sounded tired as she said, "We made the tape and then called all the stations and had them meet at the most centrally located one. Tur...ah...a friend of ours took the film there, and he's the one who made sure no one saw it until all the cameras were ready to roll. You were seeing the tape on television less than an hour after Jim finished talking." She looked over her shoulder when Henderson made the chair groan. It was obvious the man was straining to break the brace his arm was shackled to. She faced the man as she as she continued talking into the phone. "I just called to arrange some kind of meeting where we could hand over the information we've got on quite a number of officials, including Hamilton. I'd like to meet you at the station in about twenty minutes, if you can make it."

It was quiet for a moment as Salina contemplated the offer. Her voice carried an excited tone to it as she said, "I just got home, but for this kind of evidence, I'll go back. It'll probably take me about a half hour before I can get there, so don't get impatient and leave before I get there. I'll wait for you on the front steps. Is that all right?"

Jennifer smiled. "That will be just fine." She hung up the phone and then quickly picked it up again and punched another set of numbers. Again, she tapped her fingernail against the case as she waited. She heard the phone being picked up, and then a curt "yeah" came across the line. Jennifer quickly said, "I just talked to her. You should be able to get the papers to her pretty quick because she should be coming out of her apartment any moment. By the way, she told me that she's Internal Affairs. She's been investigating both of us."

Jim was quiet for a spell, and then he said, "Well, that's even better. She's going to know exactly where to go, what questions to ask, and who to contact. If she's half as good as I think she is, then I think Hamilton is already on his way down the tube." Suddenly the tone of his voice changed, and he said, "Gotta go. She just came out the door. I'll be back at the motel in about fifteen or twenty minutes." There was a click, and Jennifer stared at the disconnected phone until a loud crack brought her attention back to the present situation.

She watched as Henderson quickly stood up and started in her direction. He'd gotten one hand free, but the second one was still cuffed to the chair and he was forced to carry it along with him. She allowed him to take two steps toward her before she brought the silenced gun out of hiding from beside her leg. He seemed to deflate like a big balloon when he saw his chance to escape disappearing. She motioned with the gun, and in a manner that showed how disheartened he was feeling, Henderson slowly carried the chair back to the center of the kitchen. She moved carefully as she stepped around him and moved into the next room where she settled down on the sofa so she could keep an eye on him. The muzzle of the gun never left the area of his chest as she made herself comfortable. The gun resting on her knee never wavered away from his chest as his morale quickly plummeted.

Henderson glared at her, but she ignored his hostile looks as she waited for her partner to return. Her mind was elsewhere, and when the phone rang, it startled her. She once more moved past Henderson very carefully to answer the phone. After a short conversation, she replaced the phone on its hook and looked at Henderson. She now had a slight smile on her lips.

When Jim walked in, he immediately saw the broken chair rung as well as the handcuff dangling from his wrist. Before he had a chance to ask about Henderson's attempt at regaining his freedom, he heard Jennifer talking.

Her voice was light and musical as she said, "We just had a call from the answering service you hired. They wouldn't even give me any information because I didn't have the code word. Unless it's a crank call from some butthead, it's got to be from her."

Jim stared at her for a moment as he contemplated this information. It was clear he'd already forgotten all about the attempted escape of Henderson. He lifted the phone from its bracket on the wall and quickly dialed the number. He quickly began to smile after he gave the code word and got the information the operator had been given. Without giving any word of explanation to Jennifer, he began dialing once more.

His smile was still wide as he began to speak. "Hello. I was told to call this number. I'm Detective Jim Gray. I'm looking for a young lady who drives a Chevy van." As he listened to the voice on the other end, his smile spread even wider and he was nodding his head as he winked at Jennifer.

He handed Jennifer the phone and said, "Our little Chevrolet driver is safe and sound. She was picked up that night by someone who lives in Black Canyon City. She said she'll meet us, but it'll have to be inside the police station up there. She said she was already chased, shot at, and was forced to wreck her car, so she didn't have any intention to take any more chances. I want you to call that Internal Affairs officer and tell her what you know and ask her if she would like to ride along and see the facts unfolding on that sector for herself."

When Jennifer absentmindedly called the police station, she was told that the young officer had gone home a long time earlier. She was muttering to herself as she quickly called Salina's apartment again where she found the woman going over the papers Jim had handed her earlier. Jennifer explained the situation to Salina while Jim made Henderson aware that he was getting tired of the man's constant attempts to escape. When Jennifer finished talking on the phone, she saw Henderson was in the process of holding his hand against his forehead right at the hairline. She was quite sure another knot was going to show up on his head in short order.

The drive north of Phoenix didn't take long as they headed for the arranged meeting place. Jim's Ford moved through the small town and into the parking lot at a good clip. The Ford came to a rather abrupt halt near the front door of the town police station. They looked around the near-empty parking lot just in case some kind of trap had been set for them, but everything looked to be in order as they opened the car doors.

Salina flashed her badge and took it upon herself to make sure Henderson was securely locked in a holding cell before she joined the others as they waited in the front lobby.

Twenty minutes later, the door to the Black Canyon police station slowly opened, and they saw a nervous young woman who was ready to bolt at the first sight of danger. Her nervous eyes darted from side to side as she searched the entire room with her eyes before she stepped into the brightly lit room. A tall and muscular stranger followed her and stayed close behind her as she entered. He looked like an individual who would have no trouble defending himself or her. It was quite obvious that he wasn't going to waste any time in talking if it came to defending the young lady who stood in front of him. He gave the strong impression that he had come along with the woman solely for that reason and wouldn't hesitate to step into any fracas to protect her.

The people seated in the conference room in the Black Canyon police station listened to Vicki as she told how her side of the events, which she had personally witnessed, had taken place. In her nervousness, she was repeating herself many times as she explained how she had been a very unwilling participant in the happenings that night. She finished by saying, "I guess I was pretty lucky because when I came to a stop in that ditch, I was completely out of sight from that monster who tried to kill me. I was on my way back up to the road when I saw that silver car slowly going around the corner that I missed. I started running down the road in the direction I came in, and a minute later, Hal showed up." She looked at the man sitting protectively beside her and added, "I think I was pretty rough on him before I calmed down." She reached over and put her hand over his and gripped firmly.

Jim sat quietly until the nervous young woman appeared to be finished with her statement before he slowly stood up and said,

"We brought someone along with us. I'd like to see if you can identify this person, if you don't mind."

Her protector was close at her heels as Vicki nervously followed Jim out of the room. Jennifer had gone through too much in this affair to miss out on something this important now, so she wasted no time and quickly followed in their wake. Salina, the police stenographer, and the captain of the Black Canyon Police watched as the room began to empty. When Salina rose and started for the door, the remaining two people decided to follow along and see what all the excitement was about.

When the captain followed the stenographer into the room that adjoined the holding cell, they found Hal trying to comfort a very distraught Vicki. She was trembling and was close to tears as she stared at the handcuffed man sitting on the lone cot in the cell.

Henderson was the first one to speak, and from Vicki's reaction to the jailed man, Jim had already seen for himself that Vicki did know the captive. His voice was soft and unconcerned as he smiled and said, "Well, young lady, it looks like we finally meet. This isn't exactly the way I had in mind but…"

For several seconds, Vicki stared at the handcuffs that were attached to a special belt that had been placed around Henderson's waist before she hesitantly said, "I was just going home from work, and you tried to kill me." Her eyebrows slipped up a notch, and so did her voice when she asked, "Did you kill that man in that yellow VW?"

Henderson sat quietly on the bunk with his back against the wall as he watched the crowd of onlookers. Even though he'd made a sincere effort to stop the woman who was standing in front of him, he was still surprised when she confronted him in such an angry way. He looked at her without any emotion showing as he said, "I was only doing my job. No hard feelings."

Vicki pushed away from Hal and quickly was holding the bars of the cell in her small hands as she yelled into the confining space, "You killed that man, and then you tried to kill me. Now you have the audacity to tell me that you were just doing your job? No hard feelings? What kind of monster are you? Who gave you the right to take the lives of those who don't bow down to your needs?"

Jim motioned for Hal to get Vicki out of the room because the young woman was getting worked up to the point of becoming hysterical. After the room was silent once more, Jim turned to Henderson. "If you'd like to make a few statements now, it could have a positive outcome of your trial."

Henderson smiled back at Jim and softly said, "I'm looking at the death penalty no matter what I say, so why should I help you? You know as well as I do that there won't be any plea agreements made or even offered. If any plea agreements were made, you know as well as I do that the judge would simply refuse to honor them. Things have gone way too far for me to have something like that to happen. Since there isn't any chance of me getting out of this that doesn't include taking a tour of the death house, or at least going to prison for life, I really can't see any reason to rat on some of my pals and end up sending them in the same direction." Henderson shifted on the bunk and then added, "Now if you don't mind, I'd like to get a little sleep. It's been a long day."

The captain of the police for the growing town of Black Canyon City had seen and heard enough to whet his appetite, and it didn't take much encouragement to get him to call Phoenix police for information on the status of the Williams case in Phoenix. The information coming back was extremely heartening because, with the exception of Williams himself, the majority of the man's gang was already behind bars. Jim found himself chewing on his lip when he heard that Williams couldn't be found. He barely heard Jennifer's excited squeal when she heard Hamilton was behind bars as well. Jim smiled halfheartedly in Jennifer's direction when she repeated the captain's words that none of the men who had been arrested had been allowed bond. Her excitement began to diminish when she saw how distracted her partner had become.

The ride back to Phoenix was quiet even though all of them had ample reason for showing happiness and excitement. Jim's somber mood had dulled the cutting edge of the elation that had resulted from the arrests that had been made. They were just passing the Deer Valley turnoff when Jim suddenly sat straighter behind the wheel and muttered softly, "Hey, now. I just thought of something. I think I know where he's hiding."

Jennifer's surprise showed on her face as she pushed the chest belt away from between her breasts so she could turn in the seat. "You know where Williams is now? Where? Captain Frost in Black Canyon said the police had checked all the man's known business locations, all his homes, and every one of the hideouts that his men revealed during questioning. The police supposedly have every possible corner covered. What do you know that the rest of the force doesn't know?"

Jim looked at her surprised face and smiled. "Sweetheart, there's one place the majority of his men wouldn't know about because that one place is very important to his organization. Williams knew most of his men couldn't be trusted to remain silent if they were ever apprehended, so he simply didn't let them know about his ace in the hole. I know where that hole is. I'm going to drop you two ladies off, and then I'm going to visit that man."

Jennifer had trouble restraining herself until he finished talking, and then she quickly said, "Listen, butthead, you aren't going to leave me behind while you go sticking your nose into another dangerous spot. This isn't going to be another 'be a good girl and remain in the car.' Keep in mind that I already saved your life a couple of times. I'm simply going along with you."

Jim knew from the tone of her voice that she had no intention of being denied the opportunity of accompanying him. Even before he could begin to voice any objections, he heard Salina telling him that she also refused to be left behind while he followed a strong lead. She reminded him that he was still under investigation and that she had the authority to countermand any acts he intended to follow through on.

He leaned back in the seat and smiled. "All right, ladies. You win. I just want to say that when we get there, just stay out of the way." His smile turned into a grin as he added, "I won't have any time to do any babysitting."

Jennifer's response to that remark was clearly written all over her face, but she quickly heard her partner laughing when she released a very indignant "Butthead!"

Chapter 19

The building appeared dark and deserted when Jim pulled to the curb a half block before reaching the entrance to the building he was interested in. He turned the ignition off and then took out his revolver and began checking it carefully. He turned toward the back seat and said to Salina, "This is the place where a friend and I came into possession of most of the drugs and money that were found in that pickup. He's in there. I can feel it right here." He thumped his chest as he spoke. He reached under the seat and brought out two of the silenced guns he'd taken from Williams's men. "I'm going in there. I'll let you know when it's safe to come in." He reached over and handed the gun to Jennifer. "That's just in case of an emergency." He started to get out of the car when he resettled back in his seat and looked at Jennifer's face, and with a straight face, he said, "Now be a good girl and stay in the car so you don't get hurt."

He heard a firm "butthead" as well as a snort of exasperation to his orders as the women opened their doors. He was grinning inwardly as he gave them a strong look that indicated his disapproval of their actions, but he didn't say a word because he knew this was not the time or the place for an argument. As a matter of fact, he hadn't expected them to do anything else.

He knew it was only a matter of time before someone would spot them and sound the alarm. Jim was well aware of the necessity of getting in fast and quietly. Williams was running now, and any interference would be dealt with severely. Jim was going into the building with the knowledge that he could be going to his death. He also knew that he could possibly be leading the women to their deaths, and it rankled him to see how determined the women were in following him into the building. There would be no quarter given, nor one asked for. Williams was not going to hesitate to use a gun because he was already facing the death penalty for all the deaths he'd ordered. One more death, male or female, wasn't going to make any difference to this man.

Jim put his back to the building as he moved in the direction of the door. He motioned for the women to stay far enough behind him so if someone spotted him, he'd still have room to move. Surprisingly, they granted him that luxury as they stayed almost fifteen feet back.

A soft tap on the door caused a shadow to darken the glass in the door peephole. He quickly heard a soft curse as the individual on the other side recognized him, but before any alarm could be sounded, the small glass window of the peephole exploded inward when Jim used the silenced gun.

He waited several seconds for any sign of alarm, but other than the sound of a body falling to the floor, there wasn't another sound coming from within. He tried the doorknob, but he found it resisted any effort to make it turn even after sending a silenced slug into the lock. It took three more shots before the door moved, and then it was only after he applied the sudden weight of his shoulder behind it. Jim was afraid the sound of the shells hitting the metal lock was going to alert someone, but after standing in the corner for several minutes with his gun trained on the door to the adjoining room, he began to relax.

He motioned the women to locations that would give them some protection as he edged closer to the door. Both women showed an apprehension to stepping into the widening pool of blood surrounding the dead man's head, but they both appeared to be ready to use the guns they held in their hands. He looked over his shoulder as he put his hand on the doorknob. The thought suddenly hit his mind that he'd never had such a good looking backup crew behind him. Although he was feeling apprehensive about going through that door in such an open fashion, he gave the women a wink before he began to turn the knob.

As the door opened, he saw the room was obscured in darkness, but he quickly saw light showing from under a door on the opposite side of the room. With the light coming from the room behind them, they quickly made sure the main room, which still contained several empty shelving units, was clear and secured. The building appeared to be empty, but in the silence of the first floor, they heard a squeaking floorboard from above them.

Jim quietly opened the door that had shown light under it and found a dimly lit stairway showing the way upstairs. With the women crowding at his heels, Jim slowly climbed the stairs. As he slowly moved up the steps, he was very careful about putting any weight on any step that started to squeak. The females lined up behind him and watched him closely. They skipped the same steps he did as they followed him up the dimly lit stairway. Although their weight on the steps differed greatly than his, they closely followed his example.

After pointing out the places he wanted the women to watch from, Jim stood with his ear against the door. He stood there long enough to hear the clacking keys of a computer before he began to apply pressure on the doorknob to the lighted room. The knob turned easily, but he was afraid of a squeaky hinge, so as soon as he had the knob turned all the way, he drew back to a full arm's length and then put his shoulder to the door.

The door flew open, and Jim quickly saw Williams sitting behind a desk. The glow from the computer lit his face as he looked up in surprise. Jim was suddenly too busy to watch, or enjoy, the reaction on Williams's face because he was turning to confront the guard.

He came through the door with such force and speed that the shot fired at him hit the door frame well behind him and before another shot could be fired he was on the floor completing a quick roll. The shot had come in his direction much quicker than he had anticipated so Jim knew he needed to speed things up on his end. Without aiming, he threw a quick shot in the general direction of the guard who was standing next to the window. It appeared that the quick reacting man had been checking the parking lot when the door exploded in on them.

As Jim finished his roll it appeared that the man had been injured with his first snap shot although it certainly hadn't been a hard hit. As Jim stopped his roll the guard was already bringing his gun around in the general location of the intruder. Jim hit the trigger two more times and immediately saw the man being given a shove strong enough that it moved him back against the window with enough force to keep him going through the glass and into the space beyond.

Setting against the wall, directly across from Williams's desk where the man was sitting, was a short sofa for the man hired to protect him. It was located only feet from the window that had been used by the guard before Jim had caused the door to explode. Jim reached up and grabbed the couch by the armrest and pulled hard. Hoping for the best he watched the couch flipping over and he quickly scrambled to get behind it.

It was going to be a lousy place to be when bullets started flying in his direction. It was going to be something like playing the lottery. Instead of picking numbers and crossing your fingers it was going to be crossing your fingers and finding the right place to be when the bullets started flying. The problem here was that it worked both ways because Williams was out of sight behind his desk, which gave the detective no firm target as well.

Lying flat on the floor behind the couch Jim called to Williams, "Why don't you just give up and save us all this trouble? You know you won't be able to get out of here no matter how you try to shoot your way out. You sure can't expect any help because your entire gang has already been apprehended and is going to be looking at many years behind bars. The ones that were missed by the police so far will be busy digging holes to hide in so don't expect help from any of them. Last I heard was they even had our good Commander Hamilton in the slammer, so your normal easy way out of jail is going to be unavailable. For about the next twenty years anyway."

Without lifting his head to see where he was shooting Jim raised the gun over the sofa and triggered off two quick shots. Seconds later he heard a loud crash and at the same time he felt a solid vibration on the floor. Risking a quick look around the end of the sofa he saw that Williams had tipped the desk over and now he had the thickness of the desk top to protect him instead of the flimsy sides. He guessed that he had gotten close enough to the gangster with his last shots that it had rattled his cage somewhat. He was feeling anything but comfortable with his own position but hearing the desk tipping over caused a grin to appear. He knew he was getting under the man's skin and that was what he knew needed to be done. Jim was inclined to believe that his opponent was losing his composure and his confidence, which is what he'd been working for.

The overturned desk must have given the man an upsurge of confidence because within seconds of the turning over of the desk the man began punching holes in the couch. The detective tried to push his way deeper into the floor of the room but he was entertaining the thought that just maybe it was panic that was suddenly causing the increased barrage coming his way and not a surge of confidence.

Fortunately the man was shooting to maim or kill someone who would be on their hands and knees but since Jim was lying on his belly, and trying to get even lower, the shots continued to come high and were missing by almost a foot.

After taking a quick look around the end of the sofa, as took a very hurried look, an idea suddenly began jumping around in his mind. Earlier he'd been able to catch a quick bit of movement around the bottom of the desk and he'd been tempted to put a slug into the man's knees or ankles. It hadn't worked out for him at that time but now he was working on another approach. Since he couldn't see under the desk any longer that also meant that William's sight was just as restricted.

He wasn't exactly smiling now but he was feeling much more optimistic as he quietly reached behind him to begin pulling his handcuffs out of the holder. While crowding the end of the couch Jim called out to Williams, "I'm going to give you one last chance to give up. I've run out of patience so if you don't toss out your gun I'm simply going to toss a grenade to your side of the desk. That desk will keep me from getting any damage but it just may wrinkle your features just a bit. Although I will admit that the noise just might give me a bit of a headache it's nothing like you are going to go through."

The man's voice was slightly higher in pitch as he called back, "You know as well as I do that you wouldn't dare use something like that in here. It would probably kill both of us and I don't think you are about to commit suicide. We can end this real nice and easy by both of us simply tossing our guns aside and walking out of here together. I've also got a lot of money stashed away and if you allow me to walk out of here I can make you rich."

Jim allowed the man to hear him laughing before he answered, "You already tried to kill me so many times and now you want me to take your word that both of us can walk out of here just like we were friends? You should really get an agent for that kind of standup comedy show. Trouble is you won't be able to take it on the road, at least not for a long time."

Jim took a deep breath and repeated his offer, "You've hit the end of my patience. Give it up now or else I make the toss. If you don't toss the guns out then you better stick your fingers into your ears because it's going to get noisy. You've got ten seconds to toss your gun out."

With a loud voice Jim counted down from ten and when he hit one he sent his cuffs in an overhand toss and he did it with considerable force. He aimed his throw so the cuffs would hit the wall directly behind the desk and hoped that the cuffs would make a good clatter when they hit.

As soon as the cuffs rebounded off the wall and hit the floor Jim quickly jumped up from behind the soda just in time to see Williams frantically clambering out from behind the desk. It had offered him protection from the gun in Jim's hand, but now with the impending explosion it was the only thing that was going to keep from getting out alive. At least that is what his thoughts were telling him.

It had been a long time since he's seen a grown man move with such speed but now Williams was in full view. He was facing the wall where the 'grenade' had landed and suddenly he came to a complete stop. He stood and stared at the cuffs lying on the floor and knew that he'd really been suckered. He knew Jim was standing behind him with a gun aimed at his back.

All of his life he'd always managed to pull the wool over eyes of his pray but luck had really turned against him. He didn't consider it anything but luck because this so-called detective sure didn't have it in him to outthink a man who had made millions over the years. He admitted that he might be in a pickle right now but he'd gotten out of tight spots before and he had no doubts that he'd survive this one as well.

He was still holding his gun in his hand as he forced a grin in Jim's direction, commended the man by telling him, "That was quite a cute trick, using those handcuffs like that. Now what do you suggest we do?"

Jim stepped closer before he gave his 'suggestion. "Before we do anything else I want you to place your gun on the desk and then move back to the wall. I've got a couple of questions for you to answer."

It was clearly obvious that Williams was debating his chances of being able to spin and put a bullet through the detective before a bullet came in his direction but after making eye contact with the cop the look he received made him change his mind. This man appeared way too eager to pull his trigger.

With obvious reluctance he slowly placed his gun on top of one of the drawers, which was now the top of the desk. Steeling himself for the worst he took a deep breath and slowly backed up until he was against the wall. He watched with hate in his eyes as Jim reached out and picked up the gun he'd placed on the desk. It bothered him that the man law man had never taken his eyes off him during the entire time he'd been disarmed and forced back to the wall

Williams took a deep breath, and then he said, "You know you're making a big mistake, don't you? I've still got so much more pull then you can even imagine. I've got so many contacts in so many places you haven't even looked into yet that I'm going to promise you this much. I'm going to be out on the street again before you even finish with the paperwork. Save yourself a lot of headaches. Just turn around and leave. I'll never spend a day in jail, and you know that. Just let it drop." He pulled his lips to the side as he bit his cheek. "I can also make it very profitable for you. You could walk away from here a rich man. All you'd have to do is turn around and leave here. Just forget that you ever found this place. How would a hundred thousand sound to you?"

Jim shook his head before he answered, "That doesn't really sound too bad but I'd need a couple of perks to go along with that. He saw the light beginning to shine in the crime leader's eyes as he assumed he'd found the man's weak spot. "In order to complete the deal I'd need you to restore the lives of Captain Harris as well as Sanchez. Now that's only the beginning but if you can do that then we can start talking about the price of me leaving here and allowing you the freedom you desire. How does that sound?"

The light in the crime leader's eyes faded as Jim continued. "You've caused so much pain and suffering that it will be hard to pin it all down in black and white. Now you think that a measly hundred thousand dollars will buy me off when you have tried to have me killed so many times. Buddy, you haven't got a clue what it's going to take to make me happy." He hesitated for a short spell before he added, "To begin with when it comes to money I think you already know that I have most of your ready cash and anything that you might have stashed outside the country you better keep in mind that we also have your accountants and it won't be long before they are singing loud for a small reduction to their own sentences.

As Jim stood and stared at Williams the man was sure that he knew something was on the detective's mind from the look on his face. The look turned to puzzlement as Jim began checking the magazine on the gun he'd taken from the desk.

Williams watched as the detective slowly checked the gun he'd pulled from the desk. It only took a moment to see that the gun was fully loaded and ready to go. He watched as Gray placed the gun on the desk and then pulled the clip from his own silenced gun and quickly checked the number of shells remaining in that gun. His mouth slowly dropped open as the detective stood and stared at him for a long moment with a thoughtful look on his face. Slowly the man reached forward as he placed Williams's own gun near the edge of the desk. His jaw dropped even farther as he watched in surprise when Gray placed his own silenced gun near himself on the other side of the desk.

Detective Gray slowly looked up and said, "You know what? I think you're right. I really don't think you'll spend any time in jail.

"It's because of that statement you made just now that you've gotten yourself down to one choice to make." He watched Williams looking at him with a strong look of curiosity and distrust on his face. The look quickly changed when Jim added, "I guess the correct way of saying it is that you don't have a choice at all. Go for your gun. If you beat me and get out of here alive, then you'll be free from the threat of jail. If you're not fast enough, then jail won't even be an option because you'll be dead."

Jim watched Williams's back straightening as he contemplated the chance for freedom. The man remained standing against the wall until Jim said softly said, "I really do believe you won't have to spend any time in jail because of the way you've spread all that cash out in your attempt to buy everyone who had any power. Well, right now there isn't anyone left around you that have any of that power you need…so, because of the way things are setting, it gives you this one choice. Either you make a grab for that gun, or I'll simply put a bullet between your eyes. You've killed too many people because of drugs and because of the money you've been getting from the sale of drugs. Now keep your hands at your side and start walking forwards. When you think you're ready, all you have to do is reach for it. Maybe you'll get me, and maybe I'll get you. One thing is for certain. The buck stops here."

Jim was going to continue talking, but the sudden lunge from Williams made him cut his words short as he grabbed for his own gun. The room shook with the loud report of the gun in the hand of Williams while the soft "chug" from the other gun was never heard as both guns sent their lethal missiles airborne at the same instant.

Jim felt the air movement as the slug came close to his head and took a nip out of his ear, but he was too distracted to feel anything. He was ready to send another round in the direction of Williams even as the man was slammed against the wall.

The man leaned against the wall and stared at Gray in disbelief as he felt his blood draining from the big hole in his chest.

He tried to take a deep breath and to shake that deep pain in his chest, but suddenly the pain started to fade. He had thoughts of raising the gun and pulling the trigger once more, but quickly the urge to fire another round began to lose importance to him. His knees started to buckle, and darkness moved in on him.

Jim watched the man going down, but before the sound of the man falling reached him, he heard a sound at the door. He turned quickly and already had his gun pointing at the door before he saw the women coming into the room.

Salina stared at the body of Williams for a long moment before she said in a quivering voice, "I heard the last part of that. How could you do that? I think we could have talked him into giving up. How are you going to explain that without facing a murder charge or at least a manslaughter indictment?"

Jim turned to face Salina, and in doing so, Jennifer saw the blood dripping from his ear. The young woman quickly moved to his side and, using her handkerchief, began pinching the ear to stem the flow of blood. Jim allowed Jennifer to voice her concerns before he said to Salina, "Young lady, I gave him a lot more of a chance than he gave Harris or Sanchez. Do you really think there was any chance that he was ever going to spend any time in prison?" He saw Salina was going to present her side of the argument that it wasn't his choice to make, but he put up his hand to stall her until he was finished. "If he had been allowed to take his chances in court, there's no doubt in my mind that within days, I'd end up having some kind of fatal accident or maybe even a heart attack because of some drug that some of his men would force into my bloodstream. The same thing would end up happening to Jennifer, to you, to Vicki, and her new friend, as well as many others who were standing up against him." Jim hesitated for a long moment as he allowed her to do some thinking. "If you really think I'm just a killer, then there's the phone. Pick it up and call for backup." He looked at the young Hispanic officer for several seconds as she was torn between her job and the truth he was putting before her. Jim added, "I don't like killing. With men like him, it isn't as hard for me as it normally would be because he's the one who made the choice. No matter what line of thinking you use, I want you to keep in mind that they deal out death every day when they hand out those little packets of powder or those crystallized stones. Also keep in mind everything that happened was because of the organized crime ring that he was in control of. You've also got to think about all the people who died because of him as well." He took a deep breath and then in a low voice, he added, "The next time you get the chance I'd like you to read the obits and see how many young people, as well as adults, have died because of the crap this man was selling. Yes, I know someone else will take his place as soon as they know there's an opening and they figure out a way to fill it. But at least for now, we've stopped a big supply from coming in. You're going to have to make a choice now." He looked over at the young woman who was still holding his ear. "Jennifer is in this thing as deep as I am, so I'm going to ask her to go along with me. I think Michigan or Texas or South Dakota will have a more restful climate than Phoenix for the next few months. You can easily stop me from leaving by using that phone. Or we can give you a call in a month or so and find out how things are going."

With his arm around Jennifer's waist, he moved into the doorway. Jim stopped and looked back at Salina as he saw her staring at the phone for a long moment before lifting the receiver. He pulled Jennifer tight against him as he looked down at the pretty blonde and whispered, "We've still got a couple of bags with a lot of spending cash so...do you think you could handle being alone with me in South Dakota while we do a little fishing on Pickerel Lake? I spent a lot of time there in my youth, and I think I could use some quiet time trying for some of those northern pike, or maybe even bluegills. I think we just need to do something to get out of the rat race for a while." Jim gave her a soft grin. "If fishing doesn't suit you, then maybe we could even go to Hawaii for the next couple of months while they sort out the mess here?" He was quiet for a moment. "After a couple of weeks or possibly a month, maybe we could even look up a friend in London and see how he's doing by then."

Jennifer felt her eyes misting as she gripped his hand tightly and raised her lips to his. The silence of their embrace was shattered when Salina called out, "I might end up being sorry for doing this...but I'm going to suspend both of you with pay because of the danger to your lives. I want you to remain out of sight, but available. Make sure you give me a call from time to time. Now both of you get out of here before the whole police force shows up."